CLANDESTINE PASSION
BOOK 2 OF THE LOVELOCKS OF LONDON

Age and rank divide them. She will not face her weakness. He will not embrace his strength. Never have two people needed each other more.

Wealthy widow Catherine Lovelock will never love again, and even a handsome, gray-eyed souse of a rake won't be able to convince her otherwise. Besides, James Cavendish is seventeen years younger than she. He couldn't possibly be interested in bedding her. Or could he?

Heir to a duchy, James Cavendish serves his country and his future king by spinning a web of lies and destroying his own reputation. His work is the only thing that gives meaning to his life—until he meets the one woman who can unmask him.

For too long, Catherine and James have played roles. She, the good wife and mother. He, the dissolute rake.

The truth will come out when the clothes come off.

Detailed content notes available on the author's website:
www.felicityniven.com

CLANDESTINE PASSION

CLANDESTINE PASSION
THE LOVELOCKS OF LONDON
BOOK TWO

FELICITY NIVEN

BLETHERSKITE BOOKS

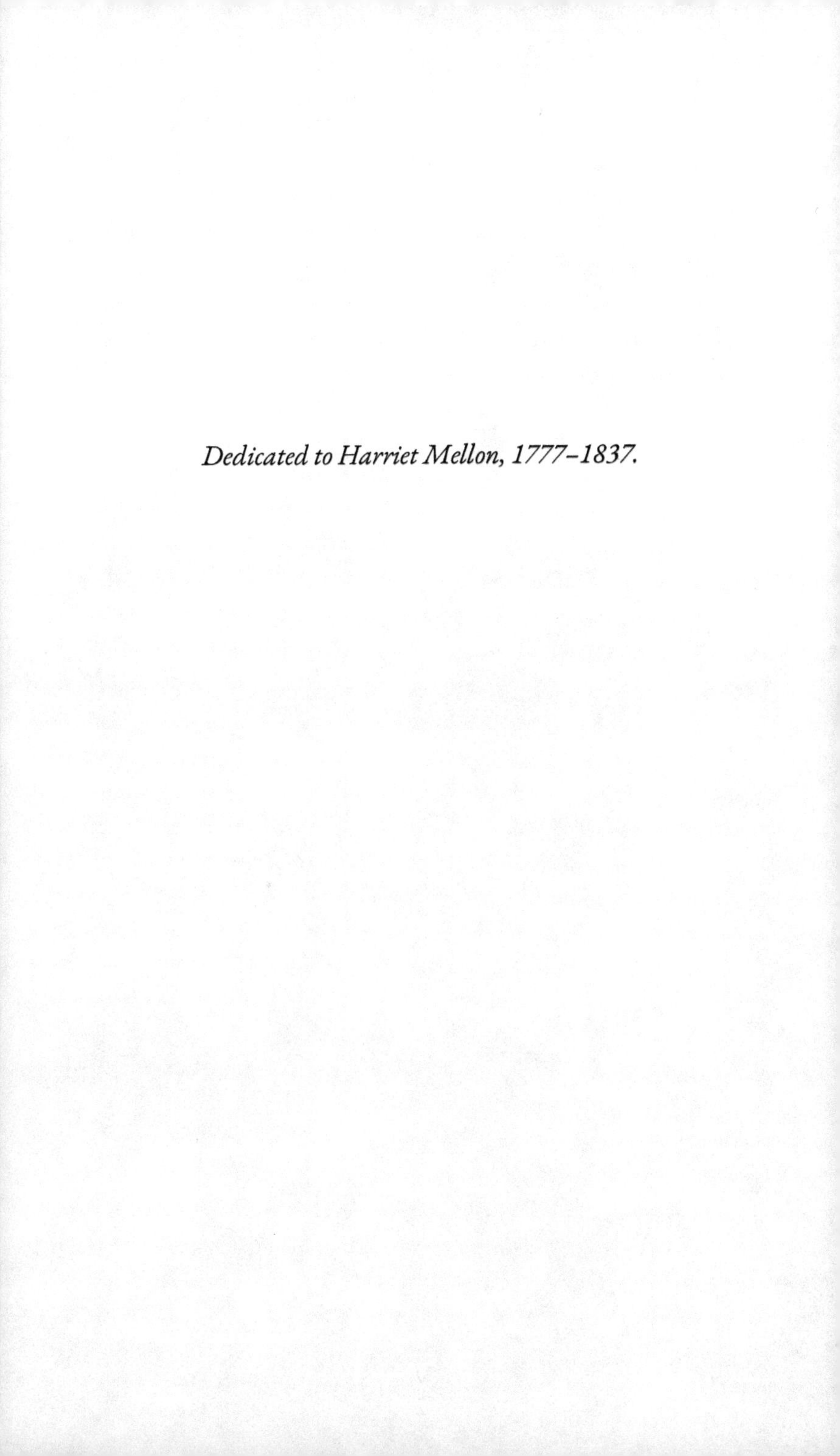

Dedicated to Harriet Mellon, 1777–1837.

Contents

Part Four

PROLOGUE

Two copies of the plans existed. One set was held at the American Consulate in London, very much out of reach. The other set was meant to be safe amongst the papers of the Navy Board at Somerset House.

However, the Somerset House plans vanished at some point during the year 1819. Their absence was only discovered in December of that year during the course of an annual inventory.

The clerks at the Navy Board were all questioned. Finally, one young man admitted he had allowed a respected gentleman to be alone in the underground archive during a fine day in April. The clerk had not meant for the visitor to stay so long unattended, but the gentleman had been most insistent. He had to find some important documents. It might take several hours.

Alas, the respected gentleman's visit happened to be coincident with the third Varnishing Day for the Exhibition at the Royal Academy of Arts, just across the courtyard of Somerset House. The young clerk—Reginald Moss was his name—had long harbored a desire to see the pictures hung and all the artists gathered in the Great Room. He went, and, indeed, it was a momentous event. Mr. J.M.W. Turner himself swept into the Great Room and magicked up a picture from a blank canvas in the matter of an hour.

By the time the imprudent Mr. Moss returned to the archive, the respected gentleman was gone.

One bureaucrat recommended prosecuting the young clerk for treason, but that idea was quickly dismissed. Ultimately, the fool was only reprimanded for carelessness and demoted, and new procedures were put in place at the Navy Board.

After all, it was difficult to argue the plans were of any value either to the British empire or to an enemy of the same. No one seemed to care the Americans had a set of plans themselves, even though the British government had commissioned and paid for the bloody thing. No one gave a fig that Mr. Fulton, the American who had dreamt up the design over ten years ago, had built—and subsequently scrapped—a similar ship for the exiled Napoleon Bonaparte, to boot.

And why should they trouble themselves? It was absurd to suppose anyone might use the plans to build a vessel that could be only twenty days at sea and held a crew of six and dipped down under the water such that it became sub-marine. Besides serving as an expensive underwater coffin, what use could such a ship have?

The Royal Navy ruled the seas. Nothing was going to change that.

Part One

ONE

Those eyes.

Catherine lost sight of the gray eyes in question as Lord Daventry bowed over her hand. He touched the very tips of her gloved fingers, and a thrill raced up her arm to the crown of her head.

James Cavendish, Marquess of Daventry. Of course, she knew his reputation. He was said to be inebriated at all times. She had even seen him stagger across a ballroom once or twice, but had they ever been introduced?

No. She would have remembered.

More than a hint of the boyish still lingered about him. Slim and tall. Thick waves of golden-brown hair begging her fingers to lace into the tousled curls. A jaw with such clean, almost translucent skin that either he could not yet sport a beard or his valet was the best barber in London.

And those soft, gorgeous, gray eyes, crinkling at the corners when he laughed. And he seemed to laugh frequently.

The thrill that had traveled from her fingers to her head was coursing downwards through her chest, joining a glow in her belly and spreading lower to her nether regions.

Stop it, Kate. You're a mother, a widow. You're no mooning girl, willing to pull up your skirts for the first set of handsome eyes you see. For a reckless, feckless, young rake. That part of your life is finished, thank goodness. No one will have that power over you, ever again. No one, not ever.

Lord Daventry straightened from his bow and looked down at her with those very seductive eyes.

"A prodigious pleasure, Mrs. Lovelock. As usual, the radiant Lady Huxley only attracts the most beautiful ladies to her ball. Like moths—nay, butterflies—to a flame, what?" His voice was a light tenor, teasing and melodious.

Lady Huxley playfully struck Daventry's shoulder with her fan and moved away to tend to her other guests. The young man swayed, tottered, and Catherine almost put a hand out to steady him, but he recovered his equilibrium on his own.

"Upsidaisy," he said and laughed.

Had James—Lord Daventry—asked Lady Huxley for the introduction? Possibly. Over the last four years, many lords and landed gentlemen had asked to meet Catherine Lovelock, and she had no illusions about why. She and her daughters were welcome at balls like this one because of the Lovelock banking fortune. Her husband's death had left her one of the richest women in England, and her daughters likewise possessed enormous dowries.

Oh.

Oh, no.

Perhaps James had asked to meet Catherine because he had designs on one of her still-unmarried daughters? How infuriating. A dissipated libertine like Daventry had no business going after her daughters. Not when she wanted him for herself.

You desire him, don't you, Kate? So much so that you're

jealous of your own daughters. You're as unbalanced as he is. Unbalanced, unhinged, and undone.

"I must agree with Lord Daventry. There is an astonishing array of beauty on display in the ballroom tonight, but you outshine all the other ladies, Mrs. Lovelock." This was from James' friend who stood next to him. "And I would be honored if you would be my partner for the next dance."

The friend's name was—Catherine searched her memory —Thomas Drake. The Right Honorable Earl Drake. Very tall, like James. But with wide shoulders and a broad chest, a head of raven black hair, and ordinary blue eyes shadowed by dark rings belying fatigue, some worry nagging at him.

"Thank you, my lord," Catherine said and curtsied. "I am very pleased to accept your invitation."

Why, why, why did it have to be Lord Drake and not the beautiful James who took her arm and led her to the center of the ballroom? And why, with an acquaintanceship lasting no more than half a minute, had she had come to think of Lord Daventry as James?

Utter foolishness.

Catherine smiled and curtsied as the music began. Her disappointment in her partner would not be apparent to any onlookers. Her years on stage at the Theatre-Royal, Drury Lane had made her a mistress of dissimulation. She appeared just as she should—a respectable widow, flattered but not overwhelmed to be dancing with a young lord.

As they began the first figure of the dance, Catherine nodded and spoke to Lord Drake about the weather, the company, the beauty of the Elgin marbles. Finally, near the end of the dance, she felt she could query the earl and not betray her very real curiosity.

"Have you and Lord Daventry been friends for a long time, my lord?" she asked as Thomas Drake took her hand to walk down the row of fellow dancers.

"Oh, yes, since we were boys. His father and my father were quite good friends."

Catherine recalled her *Debrett's*. James was heir apparent to the Duke of Middlewich. With a bevy of sisters, he was the duke's only living son.

But the earl appeared much older to her than James.

"You are of an age, then?" she asked as she passed under his arm.

Thomas thought. "Yes, I'm just thirty years of age, so Jamie is twenty-eight now."

Not James, but Jamie.

Jamie.

And twenty-eight. Older than she had thought, but still far too young.

Far too young. Far too silly. Far too drunk.

And she was far, far, far too attracted to him. She could already hear the alarums sounding in her head.

The dance was over, and Sir Francis Ffoulkes was at her side, reminding her she had promised to partner him in the quadrille. Thomas Drake bowed and thanked her for the dance as Sir Francis' arm guided Catherine to a new place on the ballroom floor.

She mustn't agonize. Having a fancy for a man was revitalizing. Even a fleeting fancy for a frivolous young man like James. She was still a woman, after all. She wasn't dead to feeling.

But—she used her most severe voice on herself—neither Fancy nor its more wicked cousin Obsession had a place in guiding her behavior. She had made that mistake in the past and never would again. She was stronger now and had a tight grip on the leash of her lust demon.

An unassailable grip.

As she turned in a full circle, she glimpsed James, tall and slender in his tailcoat and breeches, running his fingers through his gold-brown hair, leaning against the wall with an insouciant slouch. He seemed to be looking directly at her.

Her knees weakened, and she stumbled. Sir Francis had to steady her.

Bloody blazes. She was in serious trouble if James could elicit this kind of reaction in a ballroom.

Very serious trouble.

James studied Mrs. Catherine Lovelock as she danced with Thomas. After several minutes, he made himself turn away and search for a face amongst the throng in the ballroom. There was a man he was looking for, a man with whom he meant to ingratiate himself, and the man should be here. But his eyes kept coming back to the dainty blonde dancing with his friend.

James had no one to blame but himself. This situation was the result of his own lunatic idea. He was the one who had urged Thomas to woo Mrs. Lovelock. Thomas was in dire need of funds, and James had proposed marrying a rich widow as the solution to Thomas' problems.

But he never would have suggested Mrs. Lovelock to Thomas if he had known.

Known what, exactly? Known that, upon meeting her, he would feel he already *knew* her. That quick uplift of the chin. That intelligent gaze roaming over him. That quirk of the brows. That sparkle.

She reminded him so much of…what?

The vague memory itched at him. Itched at the back of his brain, even as he felt the front of his groin also take notice.

Because she was more than familiar. She was perfection, breathtaking perfection. And that was not hyperbole. He had felt the air leave his lungs as he bowed to her. And then a true pink blush had tinted her face, her neck, the top of her bosom, and his brains had gone giddy.

That bosom. Generous and round and lush. Even though her husband had died some time ago, Catherine still wore the lavender of half mourning, but the current fashion meant even a modest widow's ball gown displayed a good bit of the top of a woman's breasts, especially when a man stood above her. And Catherine was tiny, so all men stood taller than she did.

James clenched his hands into fists and scowled at the thought of other men, including his friend Thomas, gazing down at Catherine's chest.

No, no, no, no. All wrong.

He relaxed his brow and forced himself to grin. He was well-known for his even temper, his good nature, being amenable to anything and everything. There was no place in his life for a possessive passion for a woman he had just met. Was he going mad?

Catherine looked up at Thomas and smiled.

Some men were lucky in how they had been made. Well-favored men like Thomas just seemed more masculine than the ordinary fellow. Given how James' own sisters simpered and flirted with the broad-shouldered earl, Thomas was clearly desirable to women. And would likely be so to Mrs. Lovelock.

But James should not begrudge Thomas his charm and good looks. His friend was facing a grave financial crisis and had nothing else to trade on, except maybe his title.

Besides, it was other men who had the kind of luck James envied. Those fortunate second and third and fourth sons who had been allowed—nay, encouraged—to fight in the now-ended wars against Napoleon. Although his father could have easily bought him a hundred commissions, James had not been allowed to go to war. While others had met adventure and gained glory, James had been safeguarded in the name of the bloodline of the Duchy of Middlewich.

But regretting his own disappointments and ogling Catherine Lovelock would yield him nothing tonight. He must find his man.

James turned his head to scan the crush once more, only to lock eyes with the Marchioness of Painswick. She was making her way towards him, her hips swaying, her dark hair in an impressive arrangement on top of her head. James leered as he bowed over her hand and asked for a dance after the midnight supper. She arched an eyebrow, appraised him from head to toe, sniffed, and acquiesced. He did not fail to see the frankly salacious smile behind her fan as she sauntered away.

It mirrored his.

James accepted a glass of champagne from a footman's tray. He must keep his wits about him, yet he must be seen drinking. Just a sip, then. And a bit of a stagger as he leaned up against the wall as if for support.

Now the dance was ending, and the breathtaking woman-he-knew-but-couldn't-recall-how curtsied. His friend Thomas bowed as another man walked up to Mrs. Lovelock and took her elbow.

It was the very man for whom James had been searching all night. His quarry, Sir Francis Ffoulkes.

Two

"Just last week, a dun for my tailor had the impudence to approach me as I was leaving Lady Huxley's ball. It could have been a colossal embarrassment." Sir Francis Ffoulkes shook his head and paced the paint-splattered floor with a glass in his hand. "Retrenchment is hopeless. I am doomed to the gutter. Or worse."

Roger Siddons gulped from his own glass of wine and kept his eyes fixed on the canvas in front of him. "Let me finish this picture while I still have the light. I've been having a devil of a time with it."

It was late in the day, and the studio had no west-facing windows. Rooms that received light from the south and west demanded higher rents, and Siddons could only afford this place with transoms that faced the north and east. As it was, he had to eat, sleep, and paint in the same room. However, if he hired an attractive model, the rumpled bed in the corner was very convenient. As long as he had a few extra coins.

Once, Roger Siddons had not required money for women, but now he found he had to pay for his pleasures more and more often. He flattered himself that he was still a lean wolf of a man with his dark eyes, thin lips, and Roman nose. True, his hair had grayed, and years of drink had led to pouches under his eyes, a softening of his jaw line. And a middle-aged artist with no rich patrons would never be as attractive as a young, promising painter.

He moved his brush over the canvas as quickly as he could. An epergne filled with apples. Another uninspired still-life. He had barely been able to afford the apples, but at least he would be able to eat the fruit when he completed the painting.

Finally, he had no choice but to stop when the crimson hues on his palette faded to grays. He would finish tomorrow. One more picture to submit for next year's Exhibition. One more chance to earn a fee. So that he could afford more paint. So that he could paint another picture. And so on.

He started to clean his brushes. "Now. Talk. Tell me."

"What's the use? I am ruined."

Siddons gritted his teeth. "Really? Have you no other friends from whom you can borrow?"

"I can't let my wealthy friends know my situation. There is a man..." Sir Francis hesitated. "Not really a friend, but someone I know, a distant relation. He lent me money. A good deal of money. But it has been spent, and I'm afraid he will ask me to do something unpleasant if I ask for more."

Siddons looked at his boyhood friend. Everything about Sir Francis Ffoulkes reeked of respectability—his upright posture, his elegant clothes, his silver hair cut in the Titus style with the curls pushed forward over his balding pate. The two of them had grown up together on the Ffoulkes estate with Siddons as the steward's son and Francis as the heir to the baronetcy. They had drifted away from each other when they had come of age but had become friends again in the last few years.

"I thought you had made thousands of pounds with all your years of provisioning the Royal Navy," Siddons said.

"I had. I did. And then I spent it. And now there is peace and no profit to be made from the navy. I am overextended and bankrupt."

"And your wife's money?"

"Gone. All gone."

Siddons poured himself more wine. "To the memory of Lady Ffoulkes," he said, holding up his glass.

"Thank you, Roger." The two men drank.

Siddons grimaced after he swallowed. "I'll be glad when one of us is in funds again. I think I could use this dross to clean my brushes."

Sir Francis looked down at his glass and held himself very still. "Roger."

Siddons said nothing. He knew what was next.

"Roger, can I look at her?"

It was cruel, Siddons knew, to make Ffoulkes ask every time he came to the studio. He could leave the painting out and let Sir Francis feast his eyes. But he deliberately did not. He wanted Sir Francis hungry. He wanted Sir Francis to ask. After all, the baronet might one day be of use, and Siddons wanted the man to remember how weak he had been, over and over again, in front of his friend.

Besides, Siddons had no compunction about being cruel.

He sighed and pretended reluctance as he walked to the rack holding completed canvases. Most were from the last year, but there was one that was older and shrouded to protect against what little light came into the studio. Roger Siddons did not want his most valuable painting to fade.

He took the shrouded canvas and unwrapped it and brought it forward. Sir Francis lit several candles as Siddons put the picture on an empty easel.

The large painting showed a golden-haired figure from the back. Naked from the waist up, caught while disrobing.

Surrounded by trees and water. Head turned to look at the viewer. Big, blue eyes.

"Uhhhnh." Sir Francis groaned as he exhaled.

Siddons laughed. "Such yearning! And all for a painting."

"It…affects me."

Siddons looked at the canvas and squinted. "It's not bad, considering I painted it over twenty-five years ago. But it's not my best. The perspective is not quite right." He put his hands on the corners of the canvas as if to remove it from the easel. "Sometimes I think I should just paint over the whole thing."

"No!" Sir Francis shouted. Then in a voice tinged with threat, "Don't even consider it."

Siddons laughed again, but he let go of the canvas and stepped away, turning to look at Sir Francis who was totally rapt, gazing at the picture. Damn, the man was practically slobbering.

"I only wish," Sir Francis said, his eyes not moving away from the picture, not even for a second, "when I was still rich, I had convinced you to sell it to me."

"We both know you are taken by the subject." Siddons refilled his own glass.

"I am. I am. I don't know why, but I am."

"It's the fear. In her eyes."

Sir Francis blinked. "Is it?"

"The fear and the lust. It's a heady combination." Siddons chuckled. "She was the most wanton, wicked minx—"

Sir Francis stiffened. "I have no wish to hear anything more about her or your knowledge of her. It ruins the painting for me."

The germ of an idea came to Siddons. "You must have occasion to meet her from time to time."

"Yes. In fact, I danced the quadrille with her at Lady Huxley's ball. I thought she might be like the painting, but she was not. She was distracted. She is a handsome woman, I grant you, but she does not enthrall me as the painting does."

"She's older, but I doubt she has changed much in the important particulars," Siddons purred. "Whether that be her hair or her skin or her desire. She could be the picture again, for you. I could teach you how to make her that way. And you are a widower now. She could be the answer to your problems."

Sir Francis narrowed his eyes as Siddons went on, "Her dead husband was very wealthy, Sir Francis."

"What are you suggesting?" Sir Francis licked his lips.

Siddons shrugged. "I just hope once you have a heavy purse again, you will remember your good friend Roger Siddons. And that upon the occasion of your marriage to Mr. Lovelock's relict, you might be willing to buy an extremely expensive painting of your new wife as a wedding gift. For yourself."

THREE

The Marchioness of Painswick was already naked, save for glittering ear bobs, bejeweled rings, a plain locket round her neck, and her dark locks cascading over her shoulders. She reclined across her bed, luxuriating in the feel of her skin against the silk counterpane as she admired the smooth golden back of the young man across the room.

She stroked her own breasts, up the sides and across the nipples, which hardened in response to the flick of her nails. When she had begun this flirtation at Lady Huxley's ball half a year ago, she had had no idea it would take so long for a tryst to come to fruition. She had waited a considerable time, and now she was going to enjoy herself. Immensely.

Her husband was away on a shooting trip at their country seat, she was in the midst of a tiff with her occasional and highly august lover, and, after months of heated looks and whispered promises and gropes in alcoves, she had finally convinced James Cavendish, Marquess of Daventry, to consummate their dalliance. James was an absolutely delicious young rogue and well-known to be one of the most devilish of the London rakes. And so amusing.

But he was supposed to be stripping off his own clothes, and he was taking far too long.

"Lord Daventry," she called to him. "Come to bed. I've promised you a night you'll always remember, and, for good or ill, I always keep my promises."

James drained his glass of claret and absent shirt, cravat, waistcoat, and tailcoat, staggered across the room. She caught a glimpse of his youthful and tightly muscled torso at the foot of the bed before he obligingly crawled onto the mattress and over her body and began kissing her navel.

She grabbed two handfuls of his thick hair and lifted his head up. "No, not with your breeches and boots still on. Silly boy."

He glared at her and growled. "I'm no silly boy." He seized both her wrists and lunged upwards to pin them on the pillow above her head, his face inches from hers. His breath was heavy with fumes of wine.

"And if I want to ravish you with my boots and breeches on, Marshens." His tongue was thick, and he seemed to have to force himself to speak clearly. "Marchioness, I damn well will, what? And that will be," he hiccoughed, "a night *you* will always rebember."

James kissed her then, fiercely sucking and biting at her lips, and she responded eagerly to his savage and messy kiss, straining up to meet him, pressing her breasts to his smooth chest, pushing her hips against his groin.

"Stay still," James commanded, his voice harsh and raw. No doubt from the wine, the late hour, and his desire.

She obeyed him, panting in her excitement, small high-pitched moans escaping from her mouth. This was just the kind of play she liked.

He gathered both her wrists into just one of his surprisingly large hands, still keeping them pinned to the satin pillows above her head. As he covered her mouth again with his, he began to range his other hand freely over her body, kneading her breasts and pinching her nipples before roughly pushing her legs apart and tightly trapping one of her thighs between his own legs.

She whimpered in encouragement as he pawed at her sex, but it was a clumsy touch, never quite locating where her *petite mort* lived.

The marchioness was finding it harder and harder to obey James and to stay still. She wanted, she needed, she desired in no uncertain terms that he touch her in the right place. She had guided boorish young men before, taking their fingers and putting them on her hooded pearl, teaching them the rhythm, the stroke, the pressure of the finger or tongue that brought her the greatest pleasure.

But an infamous lothario like Lord Daventry should not need her tutelage. It must be the drink. However, her hands were still pinned above her head, and James had again covered her mouth with his so she could not instruct or demonstrate. Her confinement—at first, so arousing, so dangerous—was becoming tedious.

His hand fumbled over her sex more and more slowly. His body, leaning on her side, became more and more heavy and more and more slack. His head and mouth fell away from hers, his eyes closed, and his grip on her wrists relaxed. His fumbling hand stopped moving completely. He took in a deep breath, and he...snored.

Unbelievable.

She lurched to get out from under James, but he moved his hand from her mound to around her waist, snugging her into him. He was quite strong for a drunken, dozing, useless lordling. She tried to break free again, batting at him with her hands, and again he squeezed her tightly, nuzzling into her, covering her with his body.

She could not call for help. The servants would tell her husband about the young man in her bed. She was trapped.

Sounds in the house. A dog barking. Her husband's dog. Her husband had returned to London. Early.

Her eyes flew open. She was alone, thank God. She heard her bedchamber door begin to open, and she groped, trying to find a dressing gown, a shawl, anything to cover herself.

"My dear," the Marquess of Painswick said from the doorway. "Your lady's maid would be shocked, if not horrified, to discover you slept naked atop the coverlet. Can we agree never again?"

The marchioness finally seized a dressing gown and threw it over her shoulders. As she did so, she felt bare skin between her breasts. She grabbed at her neck, and her hands came up empty. The locket was gone. She looked at her hands. A sapphire ring was gone as well.

Lord Painswick strode to the bed and plucked off a piece of paper that had been pinned to the brocade canopy.

"A note left by whom, I wonder? *Just helping you rebember* —surely, remember, yes?—*turnabout is fair play.* What's this nonsense?"

The marchioness snatched the paper from her husband's hands.

The note was signed with the letter *J*.

Four

Mrs. Edward Lovelock, *née* Catherine Cooke of the London stage, originally Kate Cooksey of the West Midlands, stood on a platform in the frigid fitting room of Madame Beauchamp's shop and rubbed at the gooseflesh on her bare arms.

Seamstresses clustered around her, taking her measurements even though there was no need for new measurements, nothing had changed about her body in the last fifteen years, not since she had recovered from giving birth to Arabella. The seamstresses were wasting their time.

As was she.

It was madness to order a new dress in October in the hope of wearing it in November. Madame Beauchamp and her staff were overtaxed at this time of the year. The shop was a hive of activity; the bell on the front door jangled constantly, announcing the arrival and departure of customers. Normally, Catherine would have had Madame Beauchamp come to the Lovelock house to discuss color and cut, but the modiste was so very much in demand that Catherine, like all other customers, had been forced to come to the shop.

And she had come alone.

Solitude had crept into Catherine's life piecemeal over the last five years. First, her husband had died. Then her oldest stepdaughter Mary had married and gone to live in Wales with her husband, the Viscount Tregaron.

Her other stepdaughter Harriet—Harry amongst family—had wed last spring, just two months after Lady Huxley's ball. Harry now resided with her husband Thomas Drake, the Earl Drake, at his country seat Sommerleigh, where she ardently pursued her one and only love, mathematics.

And Arabella, the only child Catherine had given her beloved Edward, had gone off to see a puppet show today with the Dalrymple family. At sixteen years of age, Arabella was a little mature for such amusement, but the Dalrymple girls ranged in age from seventeen to seven, and the whole family still enjoyed going to see the puppets. Afterwards, all of them would go back to the Dalrymple house and recreate the puppet play in the nursery with a great deal of merriment.

Madame Beauchamp, tall and angular and dressed in a puce-colored frock of her own design, her dark hair streaked with white and scraped into a severe chignon, cast a critical eye over Catherine and spoke to the apprentice seamstress scribbling notes.

"If you can manage it, *idiote*, write that *la Veuve* Lovelock *est très petite*. We would use the child dress form but for the bosoms, which are of a large size. *Comprends-tu, petite sotte*?"

The harassed apprentice bit her lip and nodded.

Success had turned Madame Beauchamp into a petty tyrant. Her dresses might be the most fashionable in all of London, but Catherine would take her custom elsewhere in the future.

"Do you know, Madame Lovelock," Madame Beauchamp said in a loud whisper, "we have a lover's door for this *salle d'essayage*? If you have a gentleman who is interested in your dresses, he can enter here." She strode to a corner and indicated a tall, narrow door, partially hidden by a cheval glass. "He can supervise your fittings, help you select your silks, and no one will ever be the wiser."

Except the modiste herself, of course, and her seamstresses. Who would all be sure to spread the gossip.

"Even my late husband had no say in my clothes, Madame Beauchamp." A polite smile masked Catherine's pique. "He trusted my taste in all things." Now a careful lie. "And there is no gentleman of my acquaintance who is interested in my gowns."

"For now." Madame Beauchamp gestured impatiently at another seamstress who moved a small set of stairs next to the platform. The modiste offered Catherine her hand to step down and then pulled her in front of a full-length mirror and stood behind her, placing her hands on Catherine's shoulders, easily peering over the top of her head.

Madame Beauchamp sighed. "Still so young."

Forced to look at her own reflection, Catherine could admit she did look much younger than her forty-five years. Golden curls, still bright, gathered in a simple twist atop her head with a few loose locks framing her unlined face. Smooth neck and shoulders. And, yes, as Madame Beauchamp had pointed out, her bosom was of a large size in comparison to her height. A small waist, with or without stays, and then the flare of her hips, which were not as pronounced as her breasts. Her legs were hidden by her petticoat, but they were well-shaped, if short. Like the rest of her.

"Madame Lovelock, is it time? Time to shed the lavender, *les vêtements de la veuve*, how do you say, the widow's weeds? You have been in the half mourning for—what?—many years. Far too long. It is time for you to start living again."

Catherine pressed her lips together before speaking. "Yes. Perhaps it is time."

Because there *was* a gentleman who was interested in how she dressed. Sir Francis Ffoulkes had been pressing her to discard her lavender for the last three months, ever since he had proposed marriage to her.

Just last week, in her own drawing room, he had said, "What will it look like if you go straight from half mourning to a wedding dress?"

"Edward has been gone for five years. Surely people can have no grounds to say I didn't wait an adequate amount of time before remarrying?" Catherine smiled. "Would they not say the same for you then?" Sir Francis' wife had only died a year ago.

Sir Francis frowned. "I do not think anyone would find fault in my behavior."

"Of course not, Sir Francis." Catherine stopped smiling. "I myself am very sensitive to propriety. But I have not yet consented to be your wife, so there is no need to worry about what people will say."

He swept her hands to his mouth and kissed her fingertips. "But I must marry you, Catherine. Why do you delay your answer? Do you hope to inflame my ardor for you?"

"No." She withdrew her hands and turned away. No, the baronet's polite ardor was more than adequate. *Her* ardor was the thing that was absent.

But, surely, that was what she wanted. Was that not the primary reason she had encouraged Sir Francis' courtship? She did not want to feel the wicked throb that would lead her down the path to oblivion, the path she had trodden all those years ago.

She had not thought to marry again. Not until her lust demon had awoken and begun clawing at its cage, slavering after James, and she realized she needed to be steered away from the temptation to hunt down and seduce a very-silly-but-oh-so-arousing James Cavendish. The boy-man marquess was pure peril for her, just as Roger had been all those years ago when she had come so close to irrevocable ruin.

That peril, that temptation had been reason enough to accept the attentions of Sir Francis Ffoulkes, whose older and rather solid presence reminded her at times of her husband Edward. Of course, Sir Francis had not the goodness nor the wisdom nor the tenderness of the late Mr. Lovelock. But he seemed safe. Calm. Quelling. She needed to be quelled. Sir Francis, so respectable, could quell her.

Yes, marriage could save her as it had once before. But she had still not agreed to marry Sir Francis.

Madame Beauchamp lifted her hands from Catherine's shoulders and clapped them together twice.

"*Magnifique*. There is a blue silk, when I saw it, I said if only *la Veuve* Lovelock would consent, it is the exact shade of her eyes. Someone bring it, *immédiatement!*"

A lovely rich-blue silk cascaded off a roll and over Catherine's chest.

"*Parfait!*" Madame Beauchamp cooed and named a price for the dress.

Catherine might have appeared serene, but Kate Cooksey, the farm girl who still lived inside her, blanched. Madame Beauchamp had named a sum that was more than Catherine had paid for her last three ball gowns put together. But she could afford it. And, what's more, Madame Beauchamp knew she could afford it.

Catherine nodded her consent.

"*Bien sûr*. And I warn you, it will be *au décolleté audacieux*." With a trace of her finger over Catherine's chest, Madame Beauchamp indicated the dress would be cut so low as to barely cover Catherine's areolas. "It will be a masterpiece of daring. This will bring *la passion* back to your life. *L'excitation!* You will awaken loins and break hearts everywhere you go! You will be *submergée* with lovers. And who knows, *chérie*? Maybe someone will capture your heart, too."

Catherine shivered and turned away, seeking out the seamstress who would help her back into her own dress.

As the familiar lavender wool slid over her head, she reminded herself—as she had many times over the last six months—she had no interest whatsoever in loins or hearts.

She just wanted a new dress. For Sir Francis Ffoulkes' house party next month. When she would likely consent to be his wife. That was all.

For her, *la passion est morte*.

Catherine nodded her thanks to the young woman who had fastened her buttons. She replaced her bonnet, drew on her gloves, gathered her reticule.

She was calm, composed. Unruffled, untroubled. Virtuous widow, worthy mother.

But, deep inside, she could hear the lust demon howling one word.

Jamie.

FIVE

Dread dogging his every step, James made his way up Bond Street towards his family's town house in Grosvenor Square, where the Duke and Duchess of Middlewich had invited him to partake in some early-afternoon tea. It was unusual for his parents to be in town in October, but his father had been feeling poorly, so the trip back to Middlewich had been delayed.

James had not lived at the family town house for years. During the Season, the house was crammed to bursting with his seven sisters as well as his parents, and there was not an ounce of privacy to be had. Much better to be far away from all the family clatter and fuss and criticism and expressions of disappointment.

And the location of his own set of bachelor rooms was ideal—near the soon-to-be-finished Burlington Arcade, right around the corner from his club, and less than a mile from Madame Flora's. He might take a seven-year lease on the rooms, with an option to buy. And why not? He had no plans to marry.

Golden curls and a bosom that surpassed the beauty of all

others flitted in front of his mind's eye. He shook his head as if to clear the vision away. *None of that, now.*

On his way up Bond Street, he passed a bustling modiste's shop with pretty women going in and out. As the door opened for a matron he didn't recognize, he could hear the tinkle of a bell and a burst of lively chatter.

What a shame it would be considered strange for James to go into the shop. He would be sure to hear some gossip there. He was always trying to suck up chat and rumors and whispered confidences. Mr. Bulverton, the man he most wished to please, craved all gossip.

I could disguise myself as a woman, a very tall woman, and go into the modiste's, seeking a job as a seamstress. Rather like a reverse Twelfth Night.

He smiled briefly at that absurd idea before lengthening his stride, hurrying towards what promised to be a disagreeable encounter with his parents.

The sooner this skirmish began, the sooner it would be over.

"When are you returning to Middlewich?" The duke looked over his teacup at James, raising his bushy white eyebrows. "Haven't you been in town long enough?"

"William always used to bring a big party of his friends up to the castle for the shooting in the autumn, didn't he, dear?" his mother asked his father.

His father snorted. "Yes, William knew better than to spend all his time in town with wastrels, getting drunk every night."

Sprawled across a sofa, James looked up from the cooling tea in his teacup and smiled indolently. "Don't forget getting drunk every day, Your Grace." The duke's eyebrows mashed together in fury. "And I'm not William."

"Yes." Derision dripped from the word.

"We are worried for you," his mother said, her voice quavering and her lips twitching. "We hear such stories. Bacchanals. And you have always been so easily led by your friends."

"Weak," his father said.

The duchess wrung her hands. "We know you are still young—"

"I'm eight and twenty, Mother."

"But shouldn't you be done—what is the phrase? Be done with the wild oats."

James, still smiling, set his cup down in the saucer. "I'm sorry you don't approve of my habits."

His father roared, "It's not your habits, it's you! You're not half the man your brother was!"

There. The stab of the knife to his chest. After all these years, James was surprised his father's words could still wound so much. Surely, he should be calloused to it by now.

There was nothing for it but to sneer and grin and infuriate the duke even further.

James stood and made a mock-curtsy to his mother. "Your Grace." He bowed with an exaggerated flourish to his father. "Your Grace. We agree my brother was the ideal heir. But *was* is the pertinent word. William is dead. I'm dreadfully sorry to be such a source of dissatisfaction to you both." He ran his fingers through his hair. "But, as disappointing as I am, I am all you have, what?"

"Good-for-nothing." His father turned his head in dismissal.

His mother dabbed at her eyes with a lace handkerchief.

James bowed once more and left the drawing room. He walked to Madame Flora's, not far from Covent Garden. He climbed the stairs to the parlor where customers congregated and selected their courtesans. It was a comfortable room, strewn with sofas, wing chairs, and tables where men might drink and play cards while they waited for their favorite doxy to become available or for their desire to return.

But the room was largely empty in the late afternoon. Three women in near-translucent gowns sat on a sofa, chatting with their heads together. As James entered, the women stood, pushed their shoulders back, adjusted their shawls so their bosoms were more fully exposed, giggled a bit more loudly. However, when they recognized James, they relaxed their shoulders and pulled their shawls back up. James had a well-known and long-held preference for the almond-eyed brunette Isabella. He hadn't selected a different whore in years.

As he crossed the room, he stumbled and almost fell but regained his footing with a laugh. "Upsidaisy." He bowed extravagantly to the women who curtsied in return. "Good morning, Miss Lydia, Miss Nancy, Miss Sally."

"Good afternoon, Lord Daventry," the three women chorused and giggled.

Sally, the youngest of the three, a busty, plump temptress with very full lips, pushed those lips out into a pout. "Lord Daventry, when are you going to give one of the rest of us a chance? I know tricks that Frenchy Isabella has never heard of."

Nancy elbowed Sally. There was a code of conduct, and the women were not supposed to poach customers from each other.

James fished for three coins and pressed one into each woman's hand as he leered.

"I'm set in my ways, you lovelies, but I can't say I'm not tempted by what's on offer."

"Thank you, my lord."

He nodded and crossed the parlor and opened a gilded door onto a long corridor dotted with other doors. He walked as quietly as he could, knowing many of the women behind these doors had worked all night and were now sleeping.

At Isabella's door, he knocked. Two quick raps, a pause, and a third rap. He heard a key rattle, and the door opened to reveal the dark-haired, dark-eyed, olive-skinned Isabella DuMornay. She wore a thin gossamer-like gown, similar to those worn by the women in the parlor, but had covered it with a robe embroidered with flowers. She tilted her head to the side and waved James into the room. He stepped in, and Isabella closed the door and locked it.

There was a man already in the room.

He was an ordinary, short man of indeterminate age, wearing a very poor sort of wig and simple clothes that were dusted lightly with flour, highlighting the patches sewn on both elbows of his coat sleeves. His fingertips were stained with ink. He looked like a senior clerk and, indeed, he was one. Or, at least, that was his official title in the ministry of the Home Secretary.

The man squinted, stood, bowed his head. "Lord Daventry."

"Mr. Bulverton." James bowed much more deeply than Mr. Bulverton had, and, when the man resumed his seat, James drew up his own chair.

Meanwhile, Isabella had gone into the little chamber that served as her dressing room and was singing softly to herself in French about planting cabbages.

James dug into his tailcoat pocket and took out a silk-handkerchief-wrapped bundle. He handed it to Mr. Bulverton, who opened the handkerchief to reveal a golden locket and sapphire ring, the spoils of last night's escapade. Mr. Bulverton took the locket and put it in his waistcoat pocket, but, with a twinkle in his eye, he handed the handkerchief and the ring back to James.

"Very good. All's well that ends well. Keep the ring, my

lord. You see, the ring is valuable in a monetary sense but has no sentimental value to, uh, the family. And the, uh, person in question was planning to give the lady the ring, but she stole the locket first. Ha! That put a stop to any idea of gifts. But in a moment of weakness, the, uh, person in question allowed a degree of access and the Most Honorable Marchioness of *et cetera* stole the ring. And this, uh, person's mother would be quite upset to find the locket gone, so that was the important item to retrieve. The, uh, person in question wants you to keep the ring. As a reward for your service. Well done."

James knew—and by extension, Mr. Bulverton knew that he knew—the, uh, person in question was actually the Prince Regent. The prince had a well-known habit of ill-advised love affairs, including most recently with the light-fingered Marchioness of Painswick.

"I wondered," James said, shoving the ring into a pocket in his trousers and carefully folding the handkerchief, "whether there might be something else, some other service I could perform for the crown."

Mr. Bulverton raised his eyebrows.

"I know I serve at His Royal Highness' pleasure—" Mr. Bulverton cleared his throat at that, and James added hastily, "And of course, at His Majesty's, his father's, pleasure. I just hoped, after five years, I might be asked to do something more essential than tidying up the indiscretions of my future king."

Keeping his elbows at his sides, Mr. Bulverton shrugged and put his hands up, spreading his fingers. "You are free to put an end to our meetings at any time, my lord. As you know, your service is entirely *sub rosa*, unofficial, and voluntary."

James thought about what his life would be like without *this*.

Empty. Meaningless.

"No, Mr. Bulverton," he said quickly. "No, you misunderstand me. I want to do more, not less."

"Lord Daventry, you are uniquely positioned. Heir to a duchy. You move in circles far above those of other agents. You are of greatest use as you are."

James choked down his disappointment. He nodded, not trusting his voice, and put his hands on his knees as if to stand.

Mr. Bulverton went on, "And your notoriety is a brilliant ruse. No one suspects a debauched marquess." He put his hand on James' shoulder. "I would be lying, my lord, if I didn't admit I have passed many an uneasy hour thinking over you and your situation. You must never forget you are pretending. You must never allow the role to overshadow the man. It would be a grievous loss because the James Cavendish I know is a fine fellow."

James swallowed and blinked his eyes a few times. Mr. Bulverton had never offered much more praise to James than a *well done*. James lived for those *well done*s.

Mr. Bulverton gazed out the window. "And I am sad for you. I think you must be very lonely."

James was startled into a laugh. He had to disabuse Mr. Bulverton of that notion. "Come, I have had to take rooms away from my family's town house just to have some peace. And you know my nights are taken up with all manner of society and socializing. I am never alone enough to be lonely."

Mr. Bulverton leveled his gaze at James. There was no hint of a twinkle in his eyes now. "Yes, you are surrounded by people. None of whom know you. And you are accountable to none of them. It seems to me that might be the loneliest position of all."

James left Madame Flora's and walked west along Piccadilly, back towards his rooms. He wanted a drink. Three drinks. No, he wanted a whole damn bottle.

His friend Thomas, the Earl Drake, still came to town

once a week to use the services of the doxies at Madame Flora's, and James might meet him at their club for a drink. But Thomas was always gone by the next day, and James had missed his friend last night because of the pursuit and seduction and burglary of the Marchioness of Painswick. The earl would not be back to London for another week.

With the chill of autumn in the air, James had hoped Thomas might invite him out to the country, to Sommerleigh. Only with Thomas, only in that sheltered place away from London, could James be as intemperate in real life as he was by reputation. He could lose control, knowing if his façade crumbled, Thomas would still just see his friend.

And if the earl did notice some alteration in James, wouldn't he be the best person to know the truth? Thomas cared for James. Besides his sisters and his valet Enfield, there were few other people James could say that about.

But if James went now to Sommerleigh, it would not be the same as when Thomas had been a bachelor. James would have to watch himself, hide himself, just as he did in London.

Thomas had married Harriet "Harry" *née* Lovelock last spring. Thomas said his wife—an eccentric invalid from what James could tell—did not mind his whoring. That liberalism towards her husband's habits and the one hundred and forty-five thousand pounds she had brought to the marriage were apparently her chief attractions. The wedding had been rushed, coming on the heels of a nonexistent courtship, so desperate had Thomas been for funds.

James, of course, had been one of the two witnesses at the wedding, and the other witness…no. He absolutely refused to think of Thomas' mother-in-law.

One hand toyed with the sapphire ring still deep in his pocket. The stone was a lovely rich blue, quite like the eyes of…but no.

He must rally himself, find some cheer. The Theatre-

Royal, Drury Lane had a production of *Twelfth Night* on. He might go tonight and lose himself in the comedy. The clowns were always so amusing. And the Viola might capture his imagination. He had always had such a weakness for a well-played, intelligent Viola. Witty. Teasing. Strong. Devoted to her man, that fool Orsino, who couldn't see a good thing right under his nose. And even though James had often claimed nothing was more arousing than a woman's bosom, he wouldn't turn up his nose at the erotic value of seeing a woman's shapely bottom in tight breeches. Mmmmmm.

And, see here, the ring was a reward, and he had never actually earned anything before. Even better, the ring was evidence he had actually done something of use, no matter how farcical it had been. No matter how addle-pated he had pretended to be. He had been angling at the seduction for weeks, and it had all come together beautifully. As always, his false inebriation had been perfectly calibrated.

Yes, well done.

James stopped and looked in a haberdashery's shop window. He appeared to be admiring a waistcoat on display, but he was really using the reflection of the glass to see back into the street. No one of suspicion. All was as it should be.

But if all was as it should be and all was well and well-done, what was this feeling of discontent? What did it mean that he craved obliterating his senses and losing himself completely in a bottle of whisky?

Mr. Bulverton was right. James needed to be careful, or he would be in very real danger of turning into an authentically debauched marquess.

Six

"What are you reading, Mama?"

Arabella carried her embroidery basket into the morning room. Upon her return home yesterday evening, she had told Catherine it had been a delightful day with the Dalrymples, but she was really getting much too old for puppet shows. After all, she had already had a Season.

Catherine turned from where she sat at her escritoire. "I'm considering our invitations, darling."

"Invitations to the country?" Arabella plopped down on the sofa and opened her basket.

Catherine smoothed her dress over her lap. "Yes, it was lovely to go to Scotland in August, wasn't it? And I think we have been back in London rather too long. There is a letter from your sister Harry this morning, quite short and smeared and difficult to read. But she is very clear she is not inviting us to Sommerleigh since she is working on her proof of Fermat's conjecture and has—" Catherine picked up Harry's letter and read from it, *"not the time nor the patience for visitors, even of the maternal and sororal variety, while the proof of the conjec-*

ture still eludes me. Mary, on the other hand, has urged us to come to Wales. But there are many other invitations to weigh. We have become popular."

Catherine briefly wondered if they had received so many invitations this autumn because the difficult Harry need no longer be included in their party, but she pushed the thought away as disloyal. She would a million times over prefer to have no invitations and Harry safe in London than the situation as it was now.

Arabella closed one eye, poked out her tongue, and threaded a piece of silk through a small needle. "I do wish we could go with the Dalrymples to Derbyshire. Lady Dalrymple mentioned it again yesterday."

"I had hoped you would come with me to Sir Francis Ffoulkes' house party next month instead."

Arabella groaned and shook her own golden curls. "I think I would find that exceedingly dull, Mama. You should go to Ffoulkes Manor, and I should go to the Peak District with the Dalrymples."

"You want to go to Derbyshire without me?" Catherine tried to keep her voice light and teasing.

Arabella put down her embroidery hoop, crossed to her mother, and leaned down to wrap her arms around her neck.

"What did you do when you were sixteen? I seem to remember you left home and everything you knew and traveled on your own to London to become an actress with just a few coins in your purse. I only want to go to the very respectable country estate of Lord and Lady Dalrymple, where I will be surrounded by five respectable young ladies whom I quite look on as my sisters. There will be governesses and chaperones aplenty and no end of supervision."

Catherine laughed. "You're telling me I would not be missed?"

"Of course, I would miss you, Mama. It's just no good

thinking we always enjoy the same things. You go to Kent and have a lovely time, and I will go to the Dalrymples' and have a lovely time."

Really, perhaps it was best Arabella not accompany her to Sir Francis' house. It would give Catherine a degree of freedom. Not that she intended to do anything untoward with that freedom. There was no temptation in that direction with Sir Francis—which was what made the idea of a future marriage to him so attractive, she reminded herself—but she might find it easier to make her final decision about marrying the baronet.

"Very well."

Arabella giggled in triumph and kissed Catherine's cheek and then spun away, clapping her hands.

Catherine picked up her quill and dipped it into the inkpot. "I shall write to both Lady Dalrymple and Sir Francis immediately."

Arabella stopped spinning. "And I shall take my new tartan dresses to the Peaks. I must start packing immediately! "

Seven

The famed fencing master Antonio had once told James, "Your technique? *Merda*. But like many young men, you have endurance. This is good. Good for you and good for the ladies, eh?" The swordsman had winked and stroked his chin. "And you surprise. When you thrust, you are going for the kill. I never expect it with you. You deceive like a snake asleep in the sun. And then you strike, like an asp."

Antonio had then sighed. "But when you parry an attack, you have no caution. Hit me, you tell your enemy. Hit me, I do not care if I bleed. I do not care if I die. This is *not* good."

Today, as James went up and down the piste with Antonio's son Ernest, he managed to sweat off the two glasses of illegal Scottish whisky he had allowed himself last night in the privacy of his rooms. He had invited his valet to join him, but Enfield, ever sensitive to propriety, had declined. So James had sat alone and gulped down the spirits and then found his bed and gone off into a dreamless sleep.

But the exercise today lifted his mood and spurred him to hope. He must do this more often. Perhaps if he became more proficient with a sword, Mr. Bulverton might let him undertake something with a bit more danger to it than seduction and eavesdropping. And James should polish his skills at other forms of combat. Visit a shooting gallery and improve his aim, regain some of his acumen at fisticuffs. Tutelage in boxing was one of the things his dead brother William had given James—along with Enfield, swimming lessons, and a horror of the French Pox.

James finally had to ask Ernest if he might pause and catch his breath. He leaned over, hands on his knees, heart pounding, sweat pouring off his face. Perhaps that endurance Antonio had praised once-upon-a-time was waning.

James raised his head and saw Ernest—not perspiring, not breathless, damn it!—go over to where his father was instructing a youth wearing a face mask and a breastplate. The boy was doing some rather advanced footwork, but the face mask and breastplate during a lesson, not a match, were curious. Probably an overprotective mother had insisted.

James wondered what it might be like to have a mother who protected her sons. Not out of duty to bloodline, but out of love.

Ernest came back to him. "Ready to go again, old man?"

"That lad is rather good, isn't he?" James nodded to the corner.

Ernest looked over and then back at James. "Yes," he said and smiled and held up his foil in a mock salute. "Again?"

James straightened up and flourished his own foil. "Again."

After an afternoon of rigorous play at Antonio's Academy, James spent the evening at his club, working. At the moment, that work consisted of doing an excellent job of losing at three-card loo. He always lost. Losing had endeared him to countless gentlemen and paved the way for many useful invitations.

He had a small glass of whisky at his elbow and often held it to his lips, but he did not drink. He had already staggered to the necessary three times holding his glass, and, upon his return to the room where the gentlemen sat at their cards, he had requested the barman fill the now-empty glass. "To the top, to the top, to the tippity-top, man."

Most of the young rakes who might be part of James' set were not in attendance at the club tonight. Probably already in the country for the shooting, if not at the theater or Madame Flora's. James was playing cards with older men, important men. Good. They were more likely to spill the type of information Mr. Bulverton wanted.

And James was seated next to one of the men in whom Mr. Bulverton had taken a very keen interest over the last six months.

Sir Francis Ffoulkes, sporting an elegant waistcoat and crisp cravat, was winning handily. And winning tended to make him less reserved, less priggish, more talkative. He was landed gentry, a baronet—he had a sizable estate in Kent, apparently—but he had also made a fortune provisioning the Royal Navy. Very wealthy from that, what with decades of England at war on numerous different fronts. And he had been widowed in the last year or so.

But there must be something more to the man. Otherwise, Bulverton would not ask about him.

Sir Francis Ffoulkes sipped some claret and patted his lips with a folded handkerchief. "Daventry, there is a woman—"

"Yes? Do I know her?" James waggled his eyebrows in a lecherous manner and smacked his lips noisily.

The other four men at the table laughed.

"No, no," Sir Francis said, laughing as well. "I'm going to tell a story. A joke. You must let me tell it correctly, in the right order. Let's see, there is a woman who prosecutes a man for rape, and the judge—"

"Are you *sure* I don't know her, what?" James interrupted again. He knew the joke. This awful joke, once again. Maybe he could derail it at his own expense.

Laughter again around the table. Several other gentlemen walked over to discover the source of the gaiety. Sir Francis could not speak for laughing.

"You must let me finish." Sir Francis wiped his eyes. "I will never get through if you keep breaking in."

James put his hand over his own mouth.

"There is a woman," Sir Francis paused and looked to James, "who prosecutes a man for rape," again he paused and looked at James, "and the judge asks her if she had done anything to fight off her attacker. Oh, yes, the woman says, I cried out.'"

Under his hand, James bit his own tongue until he could taste blood.

"She cried out in ecstasy, eh?" The interjection came from one of the men who had wandered over. He was tall and spare with a large nose, high cheekbones, dark hair flecked with gray. James supposed he was handsome in a rather lupine way. He was almost certainly a guest of someone at the club as there had been no new members admitted in over a year.

The man smiled. James didn't like his smile. Others laughed at what the man had said, but James and Sir Francis Ffoulkes did not.

"You have ruined the joke, Roger," Sir Francis said with anger.

The wolfish man shrugged and walked away. Sir Francis pursed his lips and would not tell the end of the story even though the other men at the table clamored for it.

For his part, James was glad he had been spared the last line. He knew the piece of questionable wit well, having made it up himself two years ago. The joke had circulated widely since then, and he inwardly winced every time he heard it. He was only glad no one present could attribute it to him.

The joke ran as follows: a woman accuses a man of rape. The judge asks her if she had done anything to defend herself. "Yes," the woman replies, "I cried out." Then a witness pipes up and says, "Yes, but that was nine months later."

Riotous laughter ensues. Exclusively from men. Frowns from women. Rape combined with the pain of childbirth. Not occasions for hilarity, to be sure.

James knew it was a despicable joke, and, of course, he had known it was despicable at the time. But it played so well into his character that once he had thought it up, he had felt compelled to recite it.

And now he had to live with hearing the joke at least once every month or so. He had been thoroughly punished.

The onlookers dispersed as James shuffled the cards. Sir Francis Ffoulkes called for more claret by waving his handkerchief. James noted the delicate lace edging of the handkerchief and its small size.

"Is that the favor of a lady?" James said, grinning as he dealt the cards round the table. Sir Francis quickly put the handkerchief away. James leered. "She must be fearsomely beautiful for you to redden this way, what?"

Sir Francis picked up his cards and held them close to his chest. "She is."

"And is she your mistress?"

"She is not. I plan to make her my wife."

"Lucky lady, then."

"I would be the lucky one."

"And the fair lady's name?" James turned over the card that would indicate trump.

Hearts.

Sir Francis shook his head. "That would be indiscreet. Let

me secure our engagement first, and then I will make her name widely known."

"I will hold you to it, sir!" James looked at his cards and considered what he had seen. When Sir Francis Ffoulkes had patted his lips with the handkerchief earlier, it had been folded in such a way that subtle white embroidered initials were visible. Two *Cs. CC.*

Cecilia Cox, daughter of the Marquess of Miltonshire. No, she had married two Seasons ago. Christianna Crampton was only fifteen years of age and not yet out in society. Clarissa —what was her last name?—no, it was Kingman. And she had not the face nor figure to make Sir Francis blush. And there were far too many Charlottes. Come to think of it, his own fourteen-year-old sister was Charlotte Cavendish—

"Your turn, Lord Daventry." The gentleman on his right, Sir Ambrose Crawford, nudged him.

Oh, yes, what would be a losing but believable play? James had not studied his cards at all.

So he overturned his whisky instead and let his cards fly from his hands as he got up from the table, cursing at his clumsiness and pulling at his wet trousers.

"Trust Daventry to make a mess," Sir Ambrose said.

"I'll pass, I'll pass," James said as one of the club's barmen came over to mop up the whisky.

"You can't pass. And we can see your cards," Sir Francis said. Indeed, James' cards were lying face up on the floor in a pool of whisky. "You'll have to deal again."

"Oh, rot," James said and giggled as the barman dabbed at his trousers. "Ticklish on my knees, Chester."

The barman, who was on his own knees, ducked his head. "Sorry, my lord."

James pressed a coin into his hand and winked. "Upsidaisy. Fetch us some dry cards and some of that brown water of life for everyone at the table, what?"

"Yes, my lord."

James sat back down in his chair. "None the worse for wear or for whisky or for women!" He rubbed his hands together. "Now, Crawford, I've been meaning to ask if you have a daughter. Perhaps a younger sister, what? And her name? Could it be Caroline, perchance?"

EIGHT

Catherine shivered. Madame Beauchamp's shop was as cold as ever, even with the glow of a little stove in the fitting chamber and the sunshine from the skylight above Catherine's head. It was probably the skylight that was letting in so much of the chill.

With the worry and fuss of getting Arabella off with the Dalrymples, Catherine had delayed the final fitting of her blue silk gown. Only now, with Sir Francis Ffoulkes' house party looming, had she finally arranged an appointment with the modiste. But when Catherine had arrived at the shop, Madame Beauchamp had been alone, opening the door quickly, causing the bell hanging over the door to jangle loudly, and then shutting the door again just as quickly and locking it.

Perhaps the absence of all Madame Beauchamp's helpers was the reason why the fitting was taking so long?

Catherine had been standing on the platform in the large fitting chamber, wearing just her petticoat, for at least a quarter of an hour. First, Madame Beauchamp had issued a stream of filthy French curses because her seamstresses had made the blue silk dress too long. She had taken shears and viciously slashed a foot from the unhemmed bottom. It was still too long, but Madame herself would pin it as part of the fitting.

No, no, no. Madame Beauchamp insisted Catherine must wear a particular low-cut chemise and special stays with quite daring cups. She would fetch them now for *la Veuve* Lovelock. She, Madame Beauchamp, had commissioned the custom undergarments, knowing Catherine would need them for her new dress. Take off those stays and that chemise *immédiatement*, she had commanded, wagging a long, bony finger before whipping out of the room.

Catherine hardly liked to admit she was afraid of Madame Beauchamp, especially when the woman was wielding scissors. So when the modiste barked "*Restez!*" without even a *s'il vous plaît*, Catherine took her literally and did not even step off the platform to get something to cover her bare shoulders and breasts.

And now she was in this awkward position. Cold. Half-naked. Stranded on the platform. Well, at least there were no pins poking into her. And she should be able to stand on the platform indefinitely. Years ago, she had played Hermione in *The Winter's Tale* and appeared frozen as a statue for quite a long time.

That was all she was good for these days, being a mute statue.

Catherine could hear voices through the thin walls of the fitting chamber and wondered if another customer or another seamstress had arrived. The talk grew louder, more agitated.

The door opened, and Catherine covered her breasts with her arms and turned her head towards the door, ready to smile and pretend she was not vexed by her chilly wait.

But the person who backed into the fitting chamber was not Madame Beauchamp nor any of her seamstresses.

It was the most dangerous man in London.

Most dangerous for Catherine, that is.

Jamie.

He gave her a brief view of his profile before he crouched slightly with his back to her, listening at the crack of the door. James, the boy-man with the gray eyes and the lazy grin. The one who had wandered into her dreams and played with her lust demon there so she would wake up, gasping, wet and clenching between her legs, released.

She had met him several times last spring since he was friends with her then future son-in-law Thomas Drake. That had been—oh, horrors!—when the Earl Drake had been courting *her*, Catherine. And she had foolishly encouraged Thomas' calls, hoping he would bring his friend with him because then she could have a few minutes of being in the same room with James. A few minutes when she might surreptitiously gaze at James Cavendish, Marquess of Daventry, and imagine doing wicked things with him. A few minutes when she might unwisely let the lust demon out of its shackles. Just for an exploratory sniff. A romp. Nothing more.

But Catherine had not tempted James. He had expressed no interest in her, despite his reputation as a rake. And that was for the best, she told herself, even as the lust demon bit and scratched and screamed as she dragged it back into its cage.

Desperate for money, Thomas Drake had proposed marriage to Catherine. She had refused his offer, only for him to enter into a highly profitable marriage of convenience with her frail, eccentric stepdaughter Harry.

Catherine now bitterly regretted ever allowing Thomas or James to call at her house. Thomas, because the well-known libertine had taken the innocent Harry away from Catherine's care and protection. And James, because she was still infatuated with the gorgeous lordling even though she had not been near him since Harry and Thomas' wedding.

She had seen him only in her dreams, and his ongoing presence there was disturbing enough to change the course of her life, to cause her to seek the refuge of marriage to Sir Francis Ffoulkes.

But this was no dream. James stood within ten feet of her. His thick, curly, brown hair with glints of gold. The perfect skin over his jaw. Those square shoulders in his green tailcoat. That youth, that beauty.

And there was something different about him. Something new. She did wonder at…his intentness. There was no sign of the silly fellow. The tipsy fop was gone. He seemed to be all business.

The boy-man had vanished. There was only man.

A devastating wash of desire spread over her, and a pulse began to throb between her legs. Her chill fled as warmth radiated up from her groin to her bosom. Paradoxically, her nipples, previously erect from the cold, became even more prominent with these licking flames, poking into her forearms shielding her breasts.

She had to have *this man*. This James. She must. She was eighteen years of age again, staring into the maw of ruinous lust.

She sneezed. Just a little sneeze. She couldn't help it.

He turned. His eyes, those gray pools that now seemed almost green to match his coat, went from alert and defensive to astonished.

She was immediately enraged. She didn't want him to see her like this, up on a high platform, half-dressed, covering her breasts with her arms, unprepared for him. Better to have been fully naked, she thought, solidly on the floor. *Then I might have some idea of who I am.*

But she knew who she was. A weak woman. A wanton woman. A depraved woman. In lust with a man who had seemed wholly inappropriate before and now only seemed wholly desirable.

But he didn't want her. He had made that clear. She was too old for him. And she flushed with anger all over again.

He closed the cracked door and put his finger to his lips.

He wanted her quiet.

She'd show him quiet.

She very deliberately took her arms from her breasts and put her hands on her hips, elbows out, fully displaying herself. Except for the dratted petticoat.

He gulped. His eyes skittered away.

Ha. She had discomfited him. She had produced the desired effect. Let the rake be on his back foot for once.

James trailed the limping Marquis DuBois de Laval through the streets of Soho. The man seemed to be heading towards Westminster or Mayfair.

He knew the ambassador from France on sight, having met him at various court-related functions, but today he was following René DuBois because James had seen the man enter and then leave Sir Francis' town house this morning. He had no knowledge of a connection between the two men, and it seemed suspicious the French Ambassador would pay a morning call on a rather insignificant, if wealthy, baronet.

Perhaps DuBois' association with Ffoulkes was the whole reason Bulverton was interested in Ffoulkes?

James had been given no direction by Mr. Bulverton in regards to Ffoulkes, just to gather gossip and to stay close. But James was impatient. When was he going to be trusted to do more? Hadn't he proven himself? It was time for him to act independently in matters of surveillance. He had begun by watching Ffoulkes, his house, his carriage.

The Marquis DuBois de Laval was easy to stalk since he had a slow, unusual gait. He used a walking stick and wore a wooden leg, having lost a good part of the original limb while fighting for France under Emperor Napoleon Bonaparte. DuBois' knee had been smashed to pieces by a small-caliber ball, and he had requested the army surgeon amputate the leg on the battlefield.

One story making the rounds in London was that his valet had wept upon seeing his master's injury and DuBois had said, "What are you crying about, man? You have one less boot to polish!"

James thought that was a rather cracking thing to say, even if it had been said by a Frenchman.

James strolled and gazed into shop windows and even went into a jeweler's to inquire about a particular watch, secure in the knowledge DuBois could not get too far ahead of him. Coming out of the shop, however, he almost missed the ambassador turning down an alley. James quickened his pace, and when he reached the alley, he slowed, shooting a nonchalant glance down the length of it.

No sign of DuBois. Blast. Where had he gone?

James walked around the corner to look at the shop fronts and try to determine which establishment would most likely have drawn DuBois. A milliner, another jeweler, a tobacconist, a dressmaker. The very same dressmaker's that had given James pause a few weeks ago.

The sign above the shop proclaimed the modiste was a Madame Beauchamp. He knew the name; his older sisters favored her for their ball gowns. They said Madame Beauchamp was a genius, a tartar, and she actually *was* French. That sounded promising. But unlike the last time he had been here, the shop looked empty, and the front door was locked.

James went back round to the alley and counted off the doors. This one should be for the modiste's shop. And it was ajar.

He hesitated.

Hang it all.

He slipped in the door and could hear an argument taking place at the front of the shop. A man's quiet voice. That was DuBois. A woman's voice, loud. They both spoke in French, *naturellement.*

"—she is here now, but I think we will find nothing. I asked some questions of her, you know, the last time she came. And she never brings her lady's maid with her. I will have to find another way—"

Then DuBois' voice. But James could not make out what he said.

The woman again. "I wish you had told me before. You force me to work in the dark. You see, I encouraged her last time about matters of the heart, and I am making her a dress that will ensure a proposal—"

James crept past empty cutting tables, scraps of lace and satin on the floor, half-finished dresses on dress forms. A set of stays made from a sheer cloth, with scandalously low-cut cups, was strewn across one table.

The woman's voice, louder. "So there is already a proposal? But she has not answered him? Surely, this is a good thing, and it means she will say no—"

The voices seemed to be coming even closer.

He ducked through a door and into another room just as DuBois and a tall woman came around the corner. James quietly pulled the door almost all the way closed and then hunched to listen at the crack.

Madame Beauchamp was arguing she needed more money. She had spent a great deal bribing different lady's maids to get all the letters *Monseiur le marquis* wanted, and she needed to cover her expenses.

DuBois answered the money would be no problem, because the brother of the beef, after all, had twenty million francs. She would be paid. And then they would come to the rescue of the beef…what did he say? No, not beef or *boeuf*, but *veuf. Le veuf.* The widower.

A small sneeze behind him. Almost not a sneeze. The very softest of *kerchews.*

His heart stopped. The room had been empty, hadn't it? He had come in so quickly that he hadn't really looked around.

He turned slowly.

A goddess stood above him on a pedestal, lit by a shaft of sunlight. Her hair was of gold. Delicate brows over large, brilliant blue eyes. A small, finely formed nose. Generous lips. Inch after inch of perfect pink-and-cream skin. True, she wore a petticoat, but above the waist, she was all luscious, naked flesh, just her arms covering her breasts.

Catherine Lovelock.

The last woman in the world he wanted to see.

She was pure enticement. She still distracted his thoughts, even though he had not seen her for months. Not since the wedding of his friend Thomas and her stepdaughter Harry.

He recalled his enormous relief when Thomas admitted Catherine had refused him. It shouldn't have mattered to James. He had no plans to pursue a woman, any woman. He had worked hard to create his reputation, what Mr. Bulverton called his *cover*, and he worked hard to maintain it. James could not risk discovery by getting involved with a female. Any female.

But now, looking at her, his ardor, his admiration—nay, his worship—came flooding back.

Yes, she was a goddess. But she was no placid goddess of love. She was rigid with…fear? Anger? Anger, he decided. She was a goddess of the hunt, perhaps, or of war, absent a metal breastplate.

See how she knits her brows together in fury, how she opens her lush lips as if to curse and castigate me—

But she mustn't speak. He held his finger to his own lips.

She closed her mouth and took her arms away from her breasts.

Those breasts. Full and round and heavy. Large, pale-pink areolas on creamy skin, crowned with darker-rose nipples the size of a holly berry. Everything and more he had imagined when he had looked down at the top of her bosom at Lady Huxley's ball.

Thank God, the flow of French continued unabated outside the room, and the voices seemed to be moving farther away.

He spotted a length of blue silk on the floor and went to it quickly. He did not think he would have enough reason for what might follow unless he could get her to cover her breasts again.

But when he held the cloth out to her and she took it from him and wrapped it around her chest so her bosom was covered, he cursed himself.

He would likely never gaze on those breasts again.

He was only slightly comforted he could still see the topography of her erect nipples pressing through the fine silk.

Catherine could take pity on James, but why should she? His very presence was maddening—*he* took no pity on *her*. But still, she flattened her breasts with the blue silk and then crossed the cloth behind her back and brought it up over her shoulders, tucking the ends into the band she had made.

James stepped nearer and crooked his finger. He dwarfed her by more than a foot when they stood on the same level, but on the platform, she had to lean down for her face to be even with his.

James moved even closer. She saw the merest trace of golden-brown stubble under his nose and on his chin.

Mmmm. So the boyish jaw she had seen on every other occasion was due to his valet's skill. He could grow a mustache and beard, if he chose.

A wide mouth with lips he quickly moistened with his tongue. Long, golden-brown lashes fringed those pellucid gray eyes. His face came even closer to hers but veered at the last moment to the side, almost skimming her cheek. He put his mouth to her ear.

"I must have you—"

An unutterably sweet twinge in her groin as her breath hitched.

"I must have you quiet," he rasped. "I beg you."

She nodded, a small movement of her head.

His breath lightly stirred the curls by her ear. "And I must leave without being discovered."

Her mind raced with questions. Which she answered herself.

Of course. Why else would he be in the shop of a modiste? He had come with a young mistress in order to help select garments, perhaps even clothes for seduction, but he now feared being caught by someone. A husband? A father? Another lover of the girl?

Her lips were by his ear, as well. "Is your life in danger, my lord?" she managed to choke out, trying to give her words the bite of mockery.

"The short answer is…maybe, Mrs. Lovelock," he whispered back. Then he pulled his head away from hers and looked into her eyes.

This was a new man. She hadn't met this man before. This was a man of vigor and potency. The beautiful youth of fantasy had stirred her loins dozens of times in the night, but now she felt a gnawing ache deep in her chest for… this man.

She did not want that ache. She knew that ache. It

heralded pure pain. It meant the destruction of her carefully constructed life of safety, security, and sanity.

She had the sudden urge to cry out in protest, but she bit her lip and restrained herself. She didn't dare make a sound that could bring danger down on his head.

Because if James had accompanied a mistress here and another man caught him because of Catherine, he might have to duel a father or a husband.

He could be injured. He could be killed. He could be forced to marry. All three outcomes were unthinkably tragic.

And it would be her fault.

She nodded and held out her hand to be helped down from the platform, but the portable set of stairs had been kicked away by Madame Beauchamp earlier. James ignored her hand and instead put his hat back on his head and placed both of his hands on the bare skin of her waist and easily lifted her down. He was strong enough—and chivalrous enough—to hold her apart from him as she made the short trip to the floor. She would have welcomed being crushed against his chest and abdomen, even if for only a moment, just as she had been when she tripped on the cathedral steps at Harry's wedding. But no such luck.

Was it her imagination or did he whisper *upsidaisy* as he lifted her down? And did his warm hands linger on her waist even after she was safely on the floor?

Her skin was soft velvet, and his fingers and thumbs touched each other as his hands spanned her waist. And without a corset or stays. So small. He only removed his hands because she leaned over to pull off her heeled slippers, and the blue silk seemed in danger of slipping. But no. The cloth stayed wrapped and tucked.

Barefooted, she tiptoed across the floor, and he followed,

equally silent in his well-oiled boots, admiring her smooth, white back. He almost reached out to stroke her spine as it rose out of her petticoat into the delectable curve of her lower back, but he clenched his fist instead.

A large cheval glass stood in the far corner. She gestured, and they shifted the mirror together. Behind was a narrow door. She put one hand on the knob and the other on his forearm and lightly tugged on the sleeve of his coat.

He leaned his head down to hers, and she whispered, "It's a lover's door."

Despite their surroundings and the danger of discovery, his desire surged when Catherine said the word *lover*. That word in her mouth. Her breath brushing his ear. He flashed on the two of them in a bed, her curls tossed over the pillows, his mouth on her shoulder, her small hands pulling him into her. Her beautiful breasts again exposed to him and his eyes, his hands, his tongue. He felt his groin drawing towards her, aching and wanting. His cock, which had stirred to life at first sight of the goddess, throbbed and stiffened. He should lift her petticoat and scoop her off her feet and impale her on his shaft, thrusting deep inside her, her bare feet dangling. Take her upright, here, his hands groping her buttocks as she moaned, a goddess no longer, but weak flesh. Taking her like a frenzied lover would, with thoughtless haste and abandon.

She turned the knob on the door and shoved him out into the alley.

Heart racing, breath short, face flushed. She needed to calm herself.

Catherine crossed back to the center of the room and put on her slippers. She had just begun looking for the steps to place next to the platform when she noticed how quiet the modiste's shop had become.

"*Finalement*!" Madame Beauchamp proclaimed as she swept into the room, holding the stays and chemise she had promised Catherine twenty minutes ago. She said the word as if it had been Catherine who had kept *her* waiting, rather than the reverse.

The modiste stopped mid-stride when she saw Catherine standing by the platform. She raised her fierce eyebrows and the corners of her mouth curved down.

Catherine stood up straighter.

Yes, I moved off the platform, but I won't be shouted at by a French dressmaker. Nor by anyone. I'm tired of being accommodating. I'm tired of being restful and managing everyone else's temper. Once upon a time, I was the one with a temper. Once upon a time, I was the one who raged. I may no longer have the youth to seduce a Marquess of Daventry, but I am no cringing crone.

However, she was mistaken about Madame Beauchamp's attitude. The modiste crossed to Catherine, tossing the stays and chemise to the table.

"*Tournez-vous, madame, s'il vous plaît.*"

The *s'il vous plaît* startled Catherine so much that she turned. The modiste clucked her tongue, ran her hand over the blue silk wrapping Catherine's breasts, said "*là, là,*" and kicked the portable steps over to the platform and assisted Catherine in ascending to the platform.

Madame Beauchamp drew a pencil out from her chignon and seized a thin board and a piece of foolscap. She began to sketch rapidly, muttering to herself as she did so, "*Quasiment*—how do you say—Queen Anne, but straight across." She seemed almost delighted. "*Oui, parfait,* a halfway turn, *oui*!"

"Has your other customer left?" Catherine asked.

"My other customer?" Madame Beauchamp looked up from her drawing. "Oh, *non, non,* there was no other customer. I only opened the shop for you today. Did you hear something, Madame?" Madame Beauchamp's eyes narrowed.

"Just voices." Catherine shrugged. "Someone was upset. I couldn't really hear anything."

Madame Beauchamp resumed sketching. "Oh, yes, the man who imports my silks came. I was angry *parce que la facture*—the invoice—was wrong. *Je suis vraiment désolée* for any delay, Madame Lovelock."

"Oh, I see." Madame Beauchamp had something to hide, that much was clear. Catherine had never heard the woman apologize. Ever. "What a bother. Men always think they can take advantage, don't they?"

Madame Beauchamp smirked a little in answer.

Then Catherine remembered the very insistent bell that hung on the shop door, the one she had heard ringing over and over again when she had been here last month. She hadn't heard it since she had entered.

It had been silent today.

Anyone who might have come into the shop would have come in from the back. Not like a customer would.

There had been no young mistress as she had imagined, no ballet dancer flouncing into the shop to have James select and pay for her next dress.

She smiled.

Once Madame Beauchamp had her fill of sketching Catherine's improvised bodice, she helped her into the new gown. And then Catherine found herself smiling again. The new dress was stunning. Daring in its cut. In its color, it matched her eyes extraordinarily well. It would be ready in a week, Madame Beauchamp promised. Catherine knew that meant two weeks, but nothing could put a damper on her buoyant spirits.

In this dress, anything was possible.

Only once she was back in her own lavender day dress, did

Catherine have the terrible thought: no mistress in the shop today did not mean James had no mistress.

And the smell of his breath when his face had been so close to hers? It had been sweet. Clean. No trace of alcohol. And indeed he had not seemed drunk. He had been steady and assured, except when she had shown him her breasts.

She had never heard of James Cavendish, Marquess of Daventry, *not* being drunk.

And what other reason could there be for reform than the love of a woman?

Bloody hell.

Nine

Catherine stared out a drawing room window. She paced. She picked up a book and threw it back down.

There were so many reasons why James and she could never—

An affair was an impossibility.

First, James likely had a mistress. Or many mistresses. He was heir apparent to a duchy. He almost certainly had a string of playthings to fill his time.

And James was too young. Catherine would never hold any interest for him. She was well past the peak of her beauty and could not compete with the charms of women a quarter of a century younger.

And besides, he was an inebriate. No matter that today he had not been drunk. He would return to the bottle soon enough. And young sots were the worst kind. Because a young man's passion could become aroused by drink, but when his potency was overcome by the alcohol, he would find other ways to ravage. To dominate. To take.

Oh, Kate, you are a fool.

Because none of those things mattered to the lust demon. After seeing James today, he tempted her more than ever. In the worst possible way. In a way that would almost certainly lead to ruin of the most degrading kind. Infatuation would turn into soul-crippling obsession, as it had once before.

He had been so *different* today. And it was more than just his sobriety. He had been more virile, more alive, more vivid than she had ever seen him.

That was it. Today, he had been sharply drawn when, before, he had always seemed…blurry. Appealing, but a little hazy around the edges. Every other time she had been in his presence, he had been so nonchalant and loose-limbed. That languid smile. His gray eyes half-lidded, sleepy and seductive.

Today, his eyes had been piercing. There had been a fire and a purpose behind them.

Oh, she wanted him. Felt crazed for him in a way that was all too familiar. It was how she had been with Roger, when there had been nothing that could slake her bottomless appetite but the most sordid kind of rutting.

She was right to have considered James dangerous. He made *her* dangerous.

James would transform her again into that girl for whom need and love and desire were hopelessly entwined. That girl who would tolerate being used if it meant receiving a glimpse of tenderness or an arousing touch. The girl who would do anything for her lover and would explode into violence if she could not have what she wanted.

She could not, she would not, she mustn't.

This was exactly why she needed a man like Sir Francis in her life. A man who did not excite or inflame. A man who could calm and soothe.

She had almost made up her mind to say yes.

Two hours remained until dinner, a meal she would eat alone. The house was very empty.

She went upstairs.

"I'm exhausted, Wright. I'll lie down for a rest," she told her lady's maid. Wright made no comment even though Catherine had never taken an afternoon nap in the three years since Wright had entered service. She assisted Catherine in removing the pins from her hair and taking off her dress and hose and shoes and stays and petticoat and chemise.

Catherine realized she had spent her whole day dressing and undressing. This safe life she had chosen for herself had turned dull. How little there was to it, with her beloved husband dead and her daughters out of the house.

Once the nightdress was over her head, Catherine dismissed Wright and lay on top of the counterpane.

The window nearest the bed was cracked open, and a cold draft stirred the curtains and washed over Catherine, lifting her nightdress slightly away from her body. The muslin gently grazed her nipples, and they stiffened immediately.

She put her hands to her breasts and squeezed. They were just as sensitive as they had been when she was sixteen. Yes, when she was sixteen and she had taken the blacksmith's boy's hand and put it inside her dress as they kissed the night before she left the Midlands for London. She had ached for that boy, hadn't she? Ached for him in a simple, sweet way. If only she could be that way with James instead of twisted and crazed. His hands on her breasts, like this, his body atop hers, his mouth on hers…

Oh, Jamie.

She could not tolerate the ache, the longing. She got up and closed the window. She slid under the counterpane and turned on her side, determined to banish thoughts of James, Marquess of Daventry, from her mind forever. But as she turned, her thighs pressed against each other, and she felt a throb, her slick arousal. She thought of the release she might bring herself with her own touch. And there was no danger, surely, here by herself, alone.

She lifted her nightdress above her waist and put her hand against her thatch of golden maidenhair. She dampened her finger in her own dew and found the source of rapture, that pearl above her opening. She thought of the blacksmith's boy. Yes. The most innocent kind of pleasure. She thought of Edward, always so gentle in his desire, so attentive, so eager to please her, so filled with love. Yes, yes. She tried to think of Sir Francis Ffoulkes, but she could not imagine him without a cravat and a waistcoat. No matter. There were others to think of.

Others, like James.

No. No. She had long ago shut the door on any thoughts of Roger. She could do the same for James.

But her mind would not obey. As her finger slipped over her pearl faster and faster, her mind slipped away until gray eyes and smooth skin and James' imagined body, long and lean, hovered in front of her.

His hands buried in her hair, holding her breasts, clutching her thighs. His mouth on her lips, her nipples, her cleft. The friction of his chest and abdomen against hers as he plunged into her over and over again.

She sneezed.

Slow, sweet, clenching waves rolled over her body, again and again and again. And as she shuddered in climax, she heard him demand with his newfound intensity, "I must have you."

She stilled. She was limp, empty. But in a matter of seconds, she was consumed by the twin desires to touch herself again and to think of James. Her temporary peace was shattered.

How weak she was.

She pulled down her nightdress and got out of the bed. She made her resolve. She knew what she must do. She must marry Sir Francis Ffoulkes.

Mustn't she?

TEN

James made his way to Madame Flora's and reported the cryptic conversation he had overheard at Madame Beauchamp's to Mr. Bulverton. Mr. Bulverton scratched underneath his wig and said, "Yes."

He said no more than that, and his reticence frustrated James. But Mr. Bulverton also did not reprimand James for risking exposure by creeping into the modiste's shop. Did that mean James had Mr. Bulverton's implied permission to expand the scope of his investigations?

James decided it did.

But he didn't think it relevant to report Catherine's presence at the modiste's shop. If Mr. Bulverton was going to hold out on James, James could hold back information, too. And somehow that time—those few minutes with Catherine as a half-naked and fearless goddess—seemed far too intimate to share with anyone.

She gazed up at him through her golden curls and shrugged her loose chemise off a milky-white shoulder so one breast was almost entirely exposed. Only the nipple was still hidden. With just a small tug on the silk, the whole breast would pop into view and he would be able to cup and kiss and suckle that breast to his heart's content. And he knew that breast now. He had seen it.

He reached out and teased a finger along the top of the chemise.

"My lord?"

James blinked his eyes several times and rolled over. He was in his bed in his London rooms with late-morning light coming through a window. There was no chemise, no breast, no shoulder, no head of golden hair.

The goddess had infiltrated his dreams, and she was a distraction he damn well didn't need.

"My lord, your parents are departing the town house at noon, and you asked that I wake you at eleven."

Enfield didn't sound happy. He was likely vexed James had only slept for a few hours. He often said young men, especially his lordship, needed more sleep. Enfield clattered the breakfast things noisily to convey even more clearly his displeasure.

James sat up on the edge of the bed. He felt remarkably well. Of course, it would have looked like Lord Daventry had tippled heavily last night at the club, as usual. He had appeared as drunk as a lord. And why not? He *was* a lord. But he had been as sober as a judge.

And he had finally obtained an invitation from Sir Francis Ffoulkes to join his house party. Having noted how much Sir Francis loved to win at cards, James had managed to lose dozens of pounds to him. Then he had hinted he would love to indulge in some real high-stakes card games, but sadly the club had limits on bets among their members. But at a house party? Why, he had been known to lose a hundred pounds at a time on private wagers.

And he loved Kent. Wasn't that where Ffoulkes Manor was situated? Kent was so…bracing.

James even made a point of reining in his lewd jokes. Sir Francis wouldn't want the mysterious Miss *CC*, the future Lady Ffoulkes, exposed to the kind of bawdy stories James usually shared at the club. He dug deep and invented a whole line of puerile donkey jokes, including the gem, "Where do you find a donkey with no legs? Answer: Right where you left him."

Sir Francis loved the donkey jokes. He laughed and laughed, and James realized he must have chosen a donkey as his subject because Sir Francis' laughter sounded like the braying of an ass.

Finally, the invitation came.

"There's some very good shooting, you know, and the ladies do like to go see the seaside, but I think there could be nothing more diverting than some cards in the evening. What do you think, Lord Daventry?"

Lord Daventry thought it all sounded absolutely ripping, without a doubt. He would love to join the house party, what?

He had done it all on his own. He had not told Bulverton. He had not asked permission. He had his own priorities now. He needed to get away from London, from where he might cross paths with Catherine Lovelock. And he needed to dig in and *do something*. Otherwise, why was he wasting his life in pretense?

There must be some reason Bulverton was always so interested in Ffoulkes. And it might have to do with DuBois. Some connection to the French Embassy. And DuBois was involved in something rotten. Maids were being paid to steal letters. And something about a widower. Sir Francis was a widower. He was rich, but did he have a brother worth twenty million francs?

Let Bulverton keep mum. James was going to uncover whatever secrets there were, all on his own.

After some quick grooming by Enfield, James made a rather undignified dash up Bond Street to see his parents off on their journey back to Middlewich.

Three carriages, all sporting the duchy's coat of arms, waited in front of the town house. Two were for luggage and his father's valet and his mother's lady's maid. His parents waited in the front hall, dressed for the journey.

"Late," his father pronounced and blew his nose as James came through the door.

James kissed his mother on the cheek. "I'll see you at Christmas, Mother." The duchess allowed the kiss but turned from him without a word and went out the door.

"I expect to see some amendment of purpose when next we meet, James," the duke said. "Or you might get a feel of my riding crop. I am not too old to thrash you."

James bowed. "Yes, Your Grace."

His father leaned heavily on his valet as he went down the front steps. He needed the valet and two footmen to assist him into the carriage. The duke was unlikely ever to wield a riding crop again.

James stood outside on the top step, and he tried to look penitent rather than pitying. His father did not want his pity. He wanted his fear.

James had been frightened of his father for most of his childhood. His brother William had always been the one to stand up to the duke and his rages. And the duke had loved William for it.

For his part, James had worshiped William. His brother had been better than James at everything—riding, dancing, sport of any kind. He taught James to box and to swim. Of course, William was seven years older than James, and it was only natural he should surpass his younger brother, but James did not realize that, at the time. He only knew William was the epitome of English manhood. His brother would one day be the Duke of Middlewich, and there could be no one more deserving of that noble title.

James had known even then that he was a disappointment to his parents, but he wasn't sure why. He thought all boys got whipped by their fathers for trifles. All boys except perfect ones like William and his friend Thomas, the future Earl Drake.

The Battle of Trafalgar was a decisive moment in James' young life. Lord Nelson and those stirring words: *England expects that every man would do his duty.* Every man, including a fifteen-year-old James.

He became consumed by the idea of joining the Royal Navy, the empire's glorious fleet. He knew he must sign on to a boat. Become a midshipman. Rise up the ranks. Captain his own ship so he might too, one day, protect *this blessed plot, this earth, this realm, this England.*

Armed with his plan of how he might cover himself in glory, James approached his father in his private study. Innocent and optimistic, he fully expected the duke to buy him a commission.

But it was not to be. His father looked up from his newspaper and thundered, "The navy? Are you mad? With William as ill as he is?"

William had been abed ever since his valet Enfield had brought him back to Middlewich from London. James had only seen William for a moment when he was carried out of the carriage, mumbling incoherently. Large suppurating sores and ulcers had covered his face.

An illness brought on by too much dissolution, his frightened mother whispered to James. His father summoned doctors from London. They brought with them vials of quicksilver for application to the skin and for William to inhale. Ostensibly, to cure him of this pox. Or to kill him with the cure.

Caught up in his own plans, James foolishly hadn't realized the situation was so dire. And he had failed to see that his own future hung in the balance.

If William died, James would no longer be a second son. He would immediately become Marquess of Daventry and heir to the dukedom and would be kept out of harm's way. No navy for him. No heroism or fighting in skirmishes or evading capture. Instead, he would marry a woman chosen by his parents. He would lie with her to make more Dukes of Middlewich. He would wait for his father to die so he might take his seat in the House of Lords.

He would be sentenced to a life of endless ho-hummery.

He went to the chapel inside the castle, knelt, and prayed for William's recovery. He loved William and wanted him to live, but he also knew he was making a largely selfish prayer.

"Please God, don't let William die. I'll take all my thrashings from Father, I won't snivel, but please don't let William die."

William died a fortnight later.

The day after James' parents left London for Middlewich, Her Majesty Queen Charlotte, consort of King George III, mother of the Prince Regent, died at Kew Palace with her son by her side. It was unlikely her husband, ill with insanity, was conscious of her demise.

James hoped the locket he had retrieved from the Marchioness of Painswick had given the queen some measure of comfort in her last days. Inside the locket had been a miniature painting of a blond youth and some engraved Germanic script. James did not read German, but he suspected the locket had been a treasure from the queen's girlhood. Perhaps a gift from a sweetheart whom she had been forced to abandon when she left her home country to marry England's king at the age of seventeen.

What had become of that blond boy in the miniature? He might still live, now stooped and gray and wizened. And if he did, would he mourn the queen's passing? She might have lived in his heart for all these years. Or he might have found his own happiness, long ago.

Out of respect for the death of the queen, Sir Francis delayed his house party for a week.

Catherine was incensed by the news. She needed to flee London. She must be away from any place where she might see James.

And she felt it was imperative she not accept Sir Francis' proposal until she saw his house, the place where she would eventually be mistress. How he was in his own home, that was the tell of a man. And, surely, on his own land and in his own house, he would be more himself. And she would be more comfortable with him. She would feel the safety and peace she longed for. Whatever it was that was nagging at her, keeping her from accepting him, would be wiped away.

She desperately wanted the question of her marriage to Sir Francis Ffoulkes settled once and for all. She was so ill at ease. More than ill at ease. She was wild. She stalked around the rooms of her house like a feral animal, consumed by...what?

Ravening, heart-ripping desire of the kind she had vowed never to allow again.

And she was lonely. So very lonely.

She took up a pen and wrote long letters to all three of her daughters, saving the complicated and often baffling Harry for last.

I hope your first months of marriage have provided that which you wished for when you entered this union. Your letters are full of the theory of natural numbers—which you know I cannot understand—but have little mention of your husband, although I am glad to hear you have a marvelous physician in Dr. Alasdair Andrews. But does the earl treat you well beyond engaging this doctor to attend on you? You know I had strong reservations when you decided to marry Thomas Drake, and I still do. Please write and assure me that you have found matrimony to your liking.

Catherine thought of adding to the letter, *Because it is a state I am considering re-entering,* but she did not.

ELEVEN

Sir Francis Ffoulkes left his town house near Fitzroy Square on foot. He headed south, towards the river, and James followed. It was the eve before the house party, and Sir Francis had not yet departed for his own manor in Kent. Odd.

Sir Francis turned into a set of tatty buildings, and James was able to see which door he entered. That one. Those high transom windows were likely part of that particular set of rooms. Would James be able to climb up? Yes.

Criminy. He had gotten a smear of soot on his breeches. Enfield would be livid.

From his perch, James was able to look down into the large, open space. It appeared to be an artist's studio, filled with canvases and easels and rather a lot of mess.

Sir Francis was speaking to a man. And the man looked familiar. He was the one who had ruined Sir Francis' joke at the club. Had he been Sir Francis' guest that night or had that been where they had met? No, it was a well-established relationship. Sir Francis had called the man Roger. Men addressed men by their surnames or titles unless they were the closest of friends. These two men might even have grown up together.

One of the transom windows was cracked open, and the men's voices floated up to James.

"—even more desperate than before—" That was Sir Francis.

"Calm down, Francis. I know her. I know her like I know myself. I have a plan that will back her into a corner. In fact, she'll be so eager to marry you, she'll go to Scotland with you, and you'll have her money before Christmas. I will seduce her—"

A pigeon suddenly became very interested in James and came over to peck at his boot.

"—after you discover us, you will offer to rescue her reputation—"

James tried to shoo the pigeon away.

"—she wouldn't want to embarrass her daughters. Especially the youngest one, the unmarried one. I have heard she cares a great deal about propriety and social appearances since her husband died. And this way, I'll get something, a chance to revisit the pleasures of the past, and you'll get something—"

The pigeon fluttered off, and James missed the first part of what Sir Francis said back to the other man. What was that? DuBois? He had missed what Sir Francis had said about DuBois.

James cursed himself. He was less than worthless as a spy.

The two men were leaving. Together. No time to scramble down, he'd have to stay where he was and hope they didn't look up. There, they were gone. Now to climb down and set off after them.

"Upsidaisy."

What a dreadful phrase he had adopted. He really must scrub that from his vocabulary.

Oh. Oh, no. A rip in his tailcoat.

Enfield would have his head.

The blue silk dress, along with the special stays and the translucent chemise, arrived at the Lovelock town house. How fortunate the house party had been delayed. Otherwise, Catherine would not have had the dress in time. She should not have been so impatient.

And how wonderful to find she could still take pleasure in simple, harmless things, like a pretty gown. Girlish, innocent things, like her daughter Arabella did.

A decision must be made. Should Wright pack any of Catherine's lavender dresses? No. She would go to the house party completely out of mourning. After all, she had many lovely dresses from before Edward's death. Unfortunately, Sir Francis had an eye for fashion, but perhaps he did not know as much about ladies' styles as he did about gentlemen's and would not recognize her dresses as being out of date.

The elegant Sir Francis had been so very solicitous to her since last spring. Respectful letters detailing his intentions. Requests to dance with her at balls. Tender compliments. At the very beginning of his courtship, he had even offered to pay a call on Thomas Drake to induce him to marry Harry "by force, if necessary," when Harry had been seen coming out of Lord Drake's rooms. Catherine had assured Sir Francis the engagement was already announced. No forcing was necessary.

He had been very kind.

And kindness is what she needed.

Kindness certainly had been what she had needed seventeen years ago. She had not wanted love when she married Edward Lovelock. She had wanted affection from him, devotion from him. Safety. No more fear and no more hurt.

She had not thought of what her own feelings towards him might be in their marriage. She had initially, selfishly, only thought of what he could give her. And as she molded herself into the role of Mrs. Edward Lovelock, she discovered there is more than one kind of love. Despite herself, she fell in love with Edward. And when he died, she discovered there is no protection from the agony of loss. Protection from regret, yes. She had had that. She knew she had been a good wife to a good man. But his passing had left an emptiness in her heart.

Sir Francis would understand that emptiness. After all, he had lost his wife recently. And, surely, she could come to love Sir Francis, in time. With him, she would find peace once more. The peace that had been destroyed by James.

No. Don't think on him.

"Mrs. Lovelock?"

Catherine started. "Yes?"

"Begging your pardon, the slippers you want to wear with your new dress, I have just noticed the heel is loose on this one."

Oh, bother. Catherine inspected the shoe herself. It was a little thing of dark-blue satin, made for her five years ago and stored away since then. Yes, the heel was loose and would likely come off the first time she wore the slipper.

There was nothing for it but to pay a visit to her cobbler. She was leaving early tomorrow morning, and it was evening now. She knew Mr. Quinn lived above the shop, but it was not fair to ask Wright to go in her stead and persuade the cobbler to fix the shoe at this late hour. However, sweet Mr. Quinn would not refuse Catherine.

She told Wright to go downstairs and order the carriage to be made ready. She snatched a heavy cloak with a large hood from the piles of clothing she had considered taking to the house party and discarded. She had worn this particular black velvet mantle in the first months after Edward's death. It was quite warm and would do.

"But, of course, Mrs. Lovelock, if one of your wee shoes has a heel off, I must set it to rights. 'Twill be the work of a moment."

The gravy stains on the napkin tucked into his waistcoat showed Mr. Quinn had been in the middle of his dinner when Catherine had knocked on his door and called out to the windows above the shop. She would need to compensate the man well for his trouble. Really, she was quite pampered.

Mr. Quinn took out his tools and murmured to himself, "Oh, yes, I remember this pair," as Catherine gazed out the window of his little shop. She had not realized how unsavory this neighborhood became after nightfall. Several of the men walking about were unsteady, red-faced, intoxicated. A frowsy woman, undoubtedly a whore, was trying to ply her trade on the pavement. And, across the street, a man walked furtively, staying in shadows, darting from doorway to doorway.

That man was James.

He was the same as he had been at Madame Beauchamp's. Alert, intent on something. Serious. Utterly irresistible.

And she was drawn to him like she was a compass needle and he was her true north.

Without thinking, Catherine stepped out of the shop. Her coachman and footman were standing by the horses' heads and conversing in low voices. She didn't think they saw her as she went around the back of her carriage and crossed the street.

She was very glad of her black cloak now. She pulled it around her shoulders and the hood over her bright hair, hoping she would fade into the encroaching darkness.

She had no idea what she was doing. Pursuing a man

through the streets was pure folly. But she needed to be close to James as she had been in the modiste's shop. Her heart thumped wildly, and a sweet, fierce excitement tinged with desperation coursed through her body.

She followed him for several streets. But near Covent Garden, she lost him.

He disappeared, dissolved, vanished.

She knew these streets. The Theatre-Royal, Drury Lane was close by, behind those other buildings. She turned in a full circle, searching the pavement, but she did not see James.

Suddenly, she felt unsafe. A man in working clothes lurched up to her, and she drew back in fear. But he was merely heading to the gutter to vomit. Three other men, dressed as gentlemen, walked past her, and one reached out and touched her cloak. But he continued on with his friends, laughing at "the whore in mourning."

She would go to the theater. She would find the door-keeper Joseph or a stagehand and pay him to go back to Mr. Quinn's shop and fetch her carriage. This alley would take her through to Longacre Street, the shortest way.

She turned, and a hand reached out and dragged her into the shadows of the alley.

It was him. Beautiful him. Beautiful, dangerous him.

"What are you doing?" he hissed, clenching her wrist.

"I—" She tried to pull away, but his grip was too strong.

"You can have no business here, Mrs. Lovelock. I know you followed me—"

James broke off, holding his head up as if listening. The only sounds Catherine could hear were her own rapid breathing and her frenzied heartbeat.

"Forgive me," he murmured and leaned his body against hers, pressing her against the brick wall of the alley. Both of his hands were on both her wrists now, his arms enclosing her, trapping her. Her breasts were pressed against his abdomen. He bent his head down.

He kissed her.

His mouth on hers. Oh. Oh.

Jamie.

His lips were smooth, with just the slightest bristle surrounding them at this late hour in the day. They parted slightly and she could taste—what was it?—apple.

She had not been kissed since her husband's illness. But that lack wasn't the reason for the fire that immediately licked at her core and at the peaks of her breasts. Enormous, yearning lust that pushed her lips open, welcoming, wanting, demanding a deeper kiss.

That deeper kiss never came. James' lips did not open wider. His tongue stayed in his mouth. But he rubbed his lips against hers, at first lightly and then with a growing pressure. He made a grunting noise.

He was giving her a stage kiss. Catherine had had many stage kisses in her career as an actress. A few had not been like this; they had been delivered by leading men who knew she was powerless to stop them from thrusting their tongues into her mouth while on stage. But most had been like this—a simulacrum of passion with a minimum of contact. Respectful.

This kiss was an insult. A rage began to build.

She heard voices and footsteps, and James increased his pressure on her mouth.

"—it can't be helped. We should leave tonight to be there by morning—"

"Hold."

"What is it? Oh, yes, Lord Daventry. How unexpected."

"Ha! Daventry, having it off with some whore!"

She knew that voice. Those voices. Too much was happening too quickly.

James let go of her wrists and put his hands on both sides of her face and broke the kiss and turned her still-hooded head away from the voices.

"Yes," he slurred, "and iffen you," he hiccoughed, "fellows might be good enough to go away, I might manage to get it hard enough to get the job done." He took one of his hands from her face and fumbled with the buttons on the fall of his breeches.

This was met by jeers and cries of "Good luck with that, my lord!" and "See you on the morrow!" and the voices were fading, moving down the street, away from the alley.

James stepped back. She stayed pressed to the wall. Her heart was coming out of her chest. She hungered for the pressure of his body against hers, his mouth on hers, even if it was only pretense.

"Again, my apologies." His voice was hoarse and strained. "We must get you away from this place. Even under normal circumstances, this is not a safe place for a lady—"

This time it was Catherine who heard voices, sensed movement. She did not stop to calculate or think. She launched herself at James, climbing up his body to wrap her legs around his waist, screeching with laughter, and when her face was level with his, she began kissing him enthusiastically, moaning, humping him.

What's fine for the gander should be perfectly fair for the goose.

She heard some male laughter and could make out the words *lusty wench*. Again, the voices faded.

She slowed her thrusts against him. She stopped her histrionic moans. She could feel James' hands on her haunches, holding her, pulling her into him. She loosened her grip around his neck and trailed one hand up into the thick curls she had longed to touch for months. *Oh, yes.* She filled her fingers. She softened her mouth as she pulled on his hair, and she gave him a kiss.

A real kiss.

And then his tongue was in her mouth, and she could feel his hard cock with only the fall of his breeches separating it from her wet, hungry cleft.

James had been deeply aroused by pressing Catherine to the alley wall and feeling her body against his. He had found it extraordinarily difficult to keep his kiss as circumspect as it had been. And, yes, there might have been a better way to hide her from the passersby, a better way to obscure his own reason for being in the alley, but it was *her*. He couldn't help wanting to touch her.

He was genuinely startled by suddenly having his arms full of a noisy, squirming female, seemingly ardent, intent on reducing him to a pile of quivering mush. But as she quieted, he began to realize the hands he had put under her cloak and her dress and her petticoat were cupping the naked skin of Catherine's buttocks. Like all upper-class women, she did not wear drawers, and he thrilled to have his hands on her bare flesh—so warm, so firm, so smooth.

And then an entirely different kiss than those that had come before. So tender. Soft lips on his, the softest he had ever felt, like cushions of silk. He had never had a kiss like this before. Ever. Such a gentle thing that produced such a violent reaction in him. Blood coursed, and his cock grew harder and strained his breeches, reaching towards her. Momentarily, he wondered if her other lips were just as soft.

His tongue was between her lips, exploring her mouth, entering it and withdrawing. Her own small tongue excited ecstasy by dancing over his and pushing back into him. Her hands on his head drew their mouths even closer, and James answered by pulling her hips even closer to his waist.

He was not conscious of much besides her body and his own, but he knew they were in the exact position he had conjured in his mind a few weeks ago when he had imagined taking her in the modiste's fitting room. Holding her, he controlled her entirely in this position. With the undoing of a few buttons on his breeches, her sex would be against his and he could enter her, draw her down on top of his member and plunge into her deeply, just as he had wanted that day. He could take her. She would be his.

But, no.

This was not what he wanted. This was entirely wrong.

For one thing, with both of his hands holding her up, he could not touch her breasts. He was greedy now and wanted all of her. But she was very light. Perhaps he could shift her weight onto just one forearm and free one of her breasts with the other hand.

For a second thing, he had not yet assessed her arousal—he was more than ready but didn't know if she was ready for him, should he touch her, should he kiss her longer and harder first.

And third…what was the third thing?

The third thing was that he was not an animal.

He pulled his lips from hers and gently put her down.

Her breasts heaved. Her breathing was as rapid as his. Her face was flushed, and her lips were wonderfully swollen from their kisses. But her lips flattened now as she gritted her teeth. She rearranged her skirts and backed away from him, one, two, three steps. He thought she might turn to flee, so he reached out and caught her arm.

"I must beg your—"

His words were cut off by a slap.

He barely felt the blow, but it startled him into dropping her wrist.

. . .

No!

She was ready to have him, savagely, here in the alley, her legs around his waist. She was more than ready for him. She was ravenous for him.

And then he put her down. Made it clear he didn't want her, despite the very hard shaft in his breeches.

Her own engorged sex ached. Her lips tingled, and her nipples were pierced with pain. And her pride hurt. Her vanity was in shreds.

He stood apart from her and looked at her with those gray eyes. Eyes she had first thought so seductive and then so intelligent, but now she saw were merely judging. He must be disgusted by her. She had thrown herself at him, participated in his game of deceiving the passersby, and then betrayed her own desire for him. She had been ready to enjoy him in public like the most vulgar kind of whore.

She loathed him almost as much as she loathed herself, and she hated herself profoundly right now.

So when he tried to stop her from getting away, from escaping this hell she found herself in, when he grabbed her arm, she reacted as she would to an enemy trying to hold her captive.

She hit him.

She meant to hurt him. But she knew she hadn't. She was small, and her arm was for taking gentlemen's arms, for holding fans, for writing letters, for arranging flowers. Not for open-handed blows.

But the slap had its desired effect. He let go of her.

"I never want to see you again," she spat out.

His cheek was red from where she had slapped him. He bowed to her and kept his eyes averted.

"There will be no difficulty with your request, Mrs. Lovelock."

She swept past James, out of the alley, trying to remember the best way back to her cobbler's.

She was definitely marrying Sir Francis. As soon as possible. Before she was reduced to subjugation by her own weakness. Before she ruined herself all over again. Before lust became riddled with violence as it had been before. Before her life became ruled by catastrophic obsession and dictated by the aching need between her legs.

She was on the edge of a precipice. She would not fall over. She could not.

PART TWO

TWELVE

James marched back and forth in front of the blacksmith's forge, his boots squelching in the mud. He and Enfield and the coachman and footman and the horses and the carriage itself were all stuck in a Kentish village, five miles from Ffoulkes Manor. Something to do with the spindle.

Blast.

Well, he would rather it was the spindle than one of the horses. And he should be grateful he had a reason to get out of London after his encounter with Catherine Lovelock, the woman who hated him almost as much as he lusted for her.

But he needed still further escape, further distraction. From himself. From his failings. He was restless. As always, he longed to do *something*.

The blacksmith had demanded payment in advance once he had heard his lordship was headed for Ffoulkes Manor. Curious. But James had brought plentiful coins for wagers on cards, so there was no problem there. The blacksmith quickly pocketed the coins as if he thought they would be taken away again.

The blacksmith and James' coachman were working

together now, dismantling the front wheel spindle. The footman had wandered off to the public house to look at the local girls. The horses had been stabled. Enfield was sitting and reading a small book.

"We're only five miles from Ffoulkes Manor, you say?" James called out to the blacksmith.

The man looked up. "Well, three miles by how the crow flies." And he pointed a broad finger to the east.

Three miles. He could be there in an hour.

"I'm going to walk."

Enfield looked at the sky. "It could start raining again any time, my lord."

"What's a little water? A day in a coach makes me so cramped and skittish. Let me stretch my legs so I can feel human again."

"Let you, my lord?" Enfield said with a grave face. "I would never interfere with anything you wished to do."

"Yes," James said and put on his hat. "Let's maintain that fiction."

He walked for almost ten minutes before it began raining again. It had been a rather rough tramp already. This crow of the blacksmith's flies over some pretty uneven ground, James thought. He found himself sloshing through puddles, staggering up and sliding down hills. However, the plentiful stiles helped since he didn't have to vault any of the fences or walls or hedgerows.

After twenty minutes more walking, the downpour lessened to mizzling. A fog rolled in. He saw a small figure in a red tartan coat ahead. Some poor child caught in the rain. He couldn't tell from behind if it was a girl or boy. Oh, yes, he had mistaken a cloak for a coat, it must be a girl. Well, he mustn't startle her.

He was coming up on her rather quickly since she was walking very slowly.

"Ho, there!" he called out.

Rain fell as Catherine's carriage came to a stop in front of Ffoulkes Manor. Her lady's maid Wright laid hands on the umbrella she had brought for just such a likelihood, but one of Sir Francis Ffoulkes' footmen was ready with his own umbrella as he helped Catherine from the carriage.

Under his butler's umbrella, a weary-looking Sir Francis stood in front of the doors to his house. He held out his hands to her as she mounted the steps.

"Mrs. Lovelock, you are most welcome."

Catherine put her gloved hands in his, and he leaned forward and kissed her on the cheek. She was surprised and warmed by the gesture. Sir Francis was normally so proper. To kiss her in front of his butler and his footmen promised Sir Francis would be more at ease in Kent. This was a very good start to her visit.

Sir Francis folded her arm under his and drew her into the house, away from the rain. "I am most anxious for you to see the estate. It's not at its best today because of the weather, but I am assured by those expert in the matter that the next several days should be fine. And, now, something warm to drink? Some tea or chocolate? It will give your maid time to arrange your things in your bedchamber."

Catherine nodded and gazed at the grand front hall with a high, arched ceiling decorated with a cherub-laced fresco and underfoot, a dark and light marble chessboard pattern.

"Beautiful," she murmured.

Sir Francis leaned down. "Not as beautiful as you, my dear."

Better and better.

He took her into a large drawing room, filled with uphol-stered furniture and hung with velvet curtains. A couple—he, in his forties with silvered temples, and she, red-haired and in her twenties—approached for an introduction. Mr. and Mrs. Swinton were well-traveled and sophisticated and apparently mad for whist. Did Mrs. Lovelock play cards? Not much? They hoped they could persuade her because with a lively party, it could be so diverting.

The Marquess and Marchioness of Painswick. Yes, she had met them before. How lovely to see you again, my lord, my lady. And the Marquis DuBois de Laval, the ambassador from France. A hobbling gait even with the use of a walking stick. She curtsied.

The marquis bent low over her hand.

"*Enchanté.* I am most delighted to meet you, Madame Lovelock. You are as lovely as Sir Francis promised."

There was something in his voice. Deep and mellifluous. Familiar. She started and narrowed her eyes. Had he been one of the passersby outside the alley last night? She dreaded even to begin to dredge up that recent memory, given how enraged and humiliated she had been—no, no, it had not been him, but she felt like she *had* heard his voice recently.

A beautiful young woman, Mademoiselle Isabella DuMornay. Smooth olive skin and almond-shaped dark eyes, dark hair. And what was she wearing? Oh, yes, it was definitely a Madame Beauchamp gown in amethyst-purple. Lovely.

A man in the far corner of the room played the pianoforte, his face hidden by the music in front of him. He was quite good, some showy flourishes as he finished the piece. The others applauded, and Catherine joined in the clapping, ready to meet this talented friend of Sir Francis.

The man rose from the pianoforte bench and walked towards her. She recognized his strut before she saw his face. The man who had twisted her, made her beg, made her do things— She could not think on that.

She was still an actress. She stuffed her horror behind a

smile that would show him how amused she was by this coincidence.

"Cath!" he called out as he came forward. There was some wear in Roger Siddons' face, some lines around his eyes and forehead and by his mouth. But the same thin lips. Same aquiline nose. Same dark eyes and sharp cheekbones.

And the same wrenching pain in her midsection. But only pain. Not desire. No, at least she was spared that. The lust demon was consumed by the unobtainable James, distracted by its pretty new toy, far away in London, out of reach.

Siddons bowed. She inclined her head slightly. Sir Francis was at her side.

"I'm so glad to see old friends meeting again," Sir Francis said heartily, smiling.

Catherine turned her own smile up at him and then at Siddons. "Mr. Siddons." She kept her hands at her sides, relaxed and still.

"Cath and I knew each other in our youth, didn't we? Before she went off and married that banker. Lawdy, you landed in a vat of trifle there, didn't you? And never a word again to your friends once you left us."

Catherine continued to smile.

Sir Francis frowned. "I think Mrs. Lovelock prefers to be called Mrs. Lovelock, Mr. Siddons."

"Oh, yes, of course, my apologies, Mrs. Lovelock." Roger stuck his tongue out at her and winked.

Several large trays were brought into the drawing room, and Catherine was able to break away and have a small cup of chocolate handed to her by the butler. It was hot, creamy. Both sweet and bitter. Bracing. She gulped down her cup as quickly as she could without being unseemly and replaced it on its saucer.

"Sir Francis, thank you for the refreshment. I think I will go to my room and make sure all is well…with my trunks."

"Of course, my dear. I know ladies cannot be comfortable until they are sure all their precious things are in place. I'll have Rowley show you to your bedchamber."

On her way out of the drawing room with the butler, she was stopped by Siddons. He did not touch her, but he leaned close and said, "It does me good to see you, Cath."

She could smell the oil of roses on him.

She almost broke in that moment.

The room to which she was taken was an elegant one, with an extensive view of the grounds. Wright was already deep in the trunks, clucking and unfolding tissue-wrapped gowns, lost in her own world.

Agitated, Catherine walked to the window and looked out. It had stopped raining.

"Have you unpacked my other cloak yet, Wright? And the boots I brought in case I went along for the shooting?"

"No, Mrs. Lovelock, but I will." Wright looked at Catherine's face for the first time. "Pardon, are you quite well? You're so pale."

"I must get out of here, Wright. Outside and away. Alone. Can you get me the cloak and the boots?"

Wright did as her mistress asked and put the red tartan cloak around her shoulders.

"Mrs. Lovelock, I have never seen you— Is there anything that might help?"

"A walk, Wright." Catherine laced one boot while Wright did the other. "Now, show me the servants' entrance."

Catherine walked far away from the house before she picked up her skirts, wet and heavy at the hem, and tried to run. But the grasses clung to her and pulled her down so she could not run. Instead, she had to content herself with walking as quickly as she could and pulling in great gasping lungfuls of air.

She would not cry.

Roger Siddons couldn't hurt her. She was strong. Stronger than she had ever been when she was with him. And even if he could hurt her, she wouldn't show him that. She still had her stagecraft. She could pretend anything.

The rain started up again, and she held her face up to the sky. No tears for her. Never any tears.

She turned around and started back. Not because of the rain, but because she didn't want to worry Wright and she needed time to dress and primp and dry her bedraggled hair before dinner. She wanted to look her best. Sir Francis would have no reason to hesitate in asking her to marry him. Roger's presence here changed nothing. If anything, this ghost from her past should make her even more determined in her course.

A mile from the house, she tried to run again, but her sodden skirts betrayed her, and she fell. How foolish. She went to get up and felt pain in her left ankle. Wretched ankle. It had been weak ever since she had twisted it two decades ago when she played Imogen in *Cymbeline* and did all that fencing onstage.

She managed to get up and take a few steps, but the ankle hurt dreadfully. If only she could find a branch for a crutch, but there were no trees in this rolling field.

The rain had slowed, but she was already so very wet. And so very cold.

She heard a voice call out to her. Rescue at last. Catherine turned, wincing as her left foot made contact with the ground and she put some weight on it. She saw the gentleman approaching.

No. No.

First, Roger. Now, *him*. Evil, cruel happenstance.

He stopped ten feet from her, took off his hat, and bowed. He was staying out of range of her fist, she imagined.

"Mrs. Lovelock."

"Lord Daventry."

She nodded, unable to curtsy. He replaced his hat.

"Rotten luck. So sorry to have to break my promise to you, what?" He smiled, and his eyes crinkled. "You are, despite your wishes, seeing me again sooner rather than never."

He had gone blurry again. This was the old James, the one she had craved in her dreams, not the one who had driven her mad with desire and rage. James as a jester.

"What are you doing here, Lord Daventry?"

"I am on my way to Ffoulkes Manor. And you, Mrs. Lovelock? Why are you in Kent? Here to see St. Botolph's Priory? Or Hadleigh Castle?"

Catherine's teeth chattered until she ground them together. "Those sights are in Essex, as I am sure you are aware." James smirked. "I am also a guest of Sir Francis, my lord."

He stepped closer to her and took off his greatcoat.

"You are cold, Mrs. Lovelock, what? We can't have that when I happen to know you are a very warm creature, at your bottom."

He sniggered, and then Catherine did grow warm with embarrassment, remembering how he had held her last night, under her dress.

James threw his greatcoat over her shoulders. It dragged on the muddy ground. He stepped back and seemed to take in her stance for the first time, how one leg was bearing all her weight, the other bent at the knee so only the toe of her boot touched the ground.

Catherine observed the shift then. The jester was gone, and someone else had taken his place. Someone effective. Competent. Devastatingly competent.

"Permit me?" He was down on his knees in a flash, raising the hem of her dress and unlacing her boot and removing it with the utmost delicacy so he could lay his warm hand on her left ankle. "Does this hurt when I press here? And here?"

She put her hands on him to steady herself and felt the muscles of his back and shoulder girdle flexing and moving as he examined her. After a minute—a minute in which Catherine discovered his touch thrilled her more than ever—he put one arm under her knees and one around her back so when he stood, she came up with him in one easy motion.

"Upsidaisy," he said.

She said nothing. There was nothing to say. He was her only means to get back to the manor. She had no choice, and she might not choose differently even if a different choice were available.

He smelled of rain and something else—something that was him. Something James. Some essence of man. To her, it was the smell of paradise.

But it was maddening to be so helpless on so many fronts, all at once.

In his arms, she was inches from his face as he started walking through the mist. She saw the transition at close range, his lids dropping to half mast, his lips curling into a sardonic smile. The jester was back.

"What? No maidenly protests? I am shocked. Shocked."

"I am not a maiden, Lord Daventry." She steeled herself for a barrage of innuendo and blatant lewdness, how she had certainly not been a maiden last night, har-har, what fun. But the jokes never came.

James felt this was very hard going.

Carrying Catherine was easy. She fit snugly into his arms; her weight was balanced perfectly. His hat was keeping the mizzle off his face for the most part. He didn't miss his coat as he was quite warm with walking. He was having no physical difficulties, whatsoever.

But he was having a very hard time controlling his thoughts. Even when he was assessing her ankle, he had imagined raising his hand higher to those soft velvet thighs he had felt yesterday but had not seen. Or even higher still.

Stop.

He had become the lecher he played. A woman in distress and he could only think of fondling her. How foul he was. How angry he would be if someone like him carried one of his sisters with thoughts like these racing through his head.

But how glad he was that the woman in his arms was not one of his sisters. Even if she loathed him.

He thought she might put her arms around his neck, but she didn't. She kept her arms by her sides, her hands folded over her abdomen. But to have her body so warm against him, her breasts and her lips so close to his mouth even though she was stiff with rage.

A terrible thought rocked him.

"Mrs. Lovelock?"

"Yes?" she answered sharply. "Are you fatigued, my lord? I might be able to walk the rest of the way."

"No. I just wondered…what was your name before you married?"

She cocked her head. "I was born Cooksey but changed it to Cooke for the stage."

"Catherine Cooke."

"Yes, that was my name as an actress."

James said nothing more for the rest of the walk to the manor.

THIRTEEN

James carried Catherine through the front door of Ffoulkes Manor into fuss followed by uproar.

First, there was the mess of the mud and the rain dripping off both of them and onto the marble floor.

Next, they encountered Sir Francis' blustering concern and Mrs. Swinton's shrieking distress, with both parties talking over each other.

And then there were introductions needing to be made, some of them quite bewildering to James. It was difficult to take in the presence of René DuBois de Laval, the French Ambassador and the man he had trailed to the modiste's shop. And Isabella DuMornay, the courtesan and James' fellow operative. And the Marchioness of Painswick, she of the stolen locket and sapphire ring. James anticipated this particular lady might cause him a good deal of trouble.

He covered his confusion by giving a detailed description of how the axle on his carriage had failed, which resulted in his expedition over the fields of Kent. All the while, Catherine was explaining she had needed a walk and hadn't wanted to bother anyone, so she had just slipped out and, consequently, slipped on the grass.

Through this, James continued to hold Catherine in his arms despite Sir Francis and the butler Rowley encouraging him to set her down on a chair in the hall.

"If you'll just show me to Mrs. Lovelock's bedchamber," James said in an undertone to Rowley, who seemed a sensible sort.

"Yes," said the man James recognized as Roger, the one in the artist's studio with Sir Francis last night. The lupine man who had some kind of plan for seduction. He had been introduced to James as Mr. Siddons.

Siddons raised his eyebrows and leaned towards Catherine. "I'm sure Cath wants to get out of her wet clothes."

Catherine's shudder set up a vibration in James' chest, and he involuntarily adjusted his grip on her body, holding her more tightly and pulling her closer.

"And I am sure Mrs. Lovelock wants her lady's maid," he said, abandoning his mask and glaring at this Siddons fellow who dared to smirk back at him.

James followed Rowley up the stairs, the butler wincing a bit at James' muddy boots on the marble treads. At last, James deposited Catherine in a chair by the fire in her bedchamber as her lady's maid readied a stack of warm linen and asked the butler to send a chambermaid to the room. Rowley and James bowed and exited.

"Lord Daventry, shall I take you to your bedchamber?"

"Yes, certainly. Although all my clothes and my valet are still stuck five miles away."

"I will have a dressing gown brought to you, my lord, and I will send a carriage to the village directly in order to retrieve your luggage and your valet."

"And, perhaps, a physician? If Sir Francis has not already made the request. For Mrs. Lovelock's ankle."

Rowley bowed and took him to his bedchamber.

James' mind was in a pother as he stripped off his wet clothing. He thought it had been bad enough to find out Catherine Lovelock was the *CC* of the handkerchief and Sir Francis' intended, but what the devil was Isabella doing here? And with René DuBois? And the marchioness as well? Yes, he had always known he would eventually have to face Lady Painswick. He just preferred it weren't here, during this house party, when he had so many other irons in the proverbial fire.

Blast. James had really put his foot in it this time. No wonder Mr. Bulverton thought he was only good for seducing marchionesses and retrieving stolen jewelry.

Catherine was warm and dry, wrapped in her own wool dressing gown, and glad to have the small glass of brandy Wright had asked the chambermaid to bring.

"My ankle is just a little swollen, and the poultice is helping it along splendidly. Now. My blue dress. It didn't get too wrinkled in the trunk, did it?"

"No, Mrs. Lovelock." Wright held the dress out for Catherine to inspect.

"Good." Catherine sat back in the chair. Her hair was drying quickly in front of the fire. Not all was lost.

"Did Lord Daventry really carry you for a mile, ma'am?"

"Yes, or more," Catherine said grimly.

"He doesn't look like he would be strong enough for that, begging your pardon."

"He has more muscle than one might imagine," Catherine said, remembering his lifting her down from the modiste's platform while keeping her body apart from his. And his arms holding her up under her skirts last night in the alley and the hard muscle of his chest against her breasts as she had kissed him and the muscle of his shoulders and back as he had knelt in the mud to examine her ankle today.

"Oh, it wouldn't be my place to imagine anything, ma'am."

Wright sounded flustered. Catherine looked up and saw her young maid's face had reddened. So it wasn't just Catherine. Other women were susceptible to James, as well.

Of course, they were. And he was susceptible to them, too. Especially to young, beautiful ones like Mademoiselle DuMornay. Oh, yes, Catherine had felt James start when Isabella had been introduced to him downstairs in the front hall. His breathing had become more erratic, his heart beating faster through his wet waistcoat.

"Wright, please remember to get Lord Daventry's greatcoat back to his valet when he arrives."

"I'll be sure to clean and press the coat of the marquess, ma'am."

"He is not *the* marquess, Wright. He is just James Cavendish, Marquess of Daventry. It's a courtesy title until his father dies. Then he'll be *the* Duke of Middlewich."

"Yes, ma'am. So many names for one man."

And so many personae. And how badly she wanted to bed every single one of them.

The banyan the butler Rowley brought James had been made for a stout giant. Yards of cloth hung off of him and flapped when he moved, like loose sails in a weak wind. If Enfield were here, he could have done something with a few folds or tucks to make it sit right on James. But Enfield was not yet here.

Meanwhile, James had haphazardly spread his wet garments on various pieces of furniture in the room. His boots sat by the fire, the mud hardening on them. Enfield was sure to make James pay for the difficulty involved in cleaning those boots, one way or another.

Isabella opened the bedchamber door and slipped into the room. Today was the first time James had ever seen Isabella in a dress rather than in an embroidered robe. She looked very respectable. Almost prim.

"Jacques!" she hissed. "Are you mad? What are you doing here?"

"What are *you* doing here?" he hissed back at her, hauling up handfuls of his banyan so he wouldn't trip on it as he crossed the carpet to speak to her.

"I was sent by Monsieur Bulverton. You know I have been the courtesan of DuBois many times since he came to London—"

"No, I didn't know."

"Well," Isabella waved her hand airily, "Bulverton thought I should try to get an invitation to this house party. He thinks DuBois is going to press Sir Francis into doing something *dangereux*. I usually get what I want, as you know, and I convinced DuBois to bring me. He says it's a good joke to have me at Sir Francis' house party, some kind of nose-thumbing at the English. And now I think the marquis actually wants me to seduce Sir Francis—"

"How do Ffoulkes and DuBois know each other, anyway? What the devil is going on?"

Isabella shushed him. "Ffoulkes' *maman* was French, you know. DuBois' sister's husband's sister. Do you follow? But I must go. I will see you at the dinner. But when we get back to London, I think you will be in trouble with Monsieur Bulverton, *chéri*."

She patted James' cheek affectionately and went out the door as quickly as she had come in.

· · ·

Catherine chose to wear one of her older dresses, a wine-colored silk with a saffron band at the hem. Wright arranged her now-dry hair in the Grecian style—gathered at the back of her head in a large knot with a few golden curls pulled down around her face and neck.

Leaning on Wright's arm, Catherine stepped out of her bedchamber to go down to the dinner. The ankle still hurt when she put her full weight on the foot, and this created something of a quandary. It wouldn't be usual for a lady's maid to walk down the main staircase with her mistress. However, if Catherine held to the banister, perhaps she could support herself well enough without Wright's help.

"Cath?" It was Roger, in his evening clothes. "Might I offer my assistance?"

Without waiting for her consent, he stepped to her left side, smoothly replacing Wright, lacing his own arm with Catherine's. Again, she could smell the oil of roses on him. For some reason, that scent provoked her worst memories, those of pain. Not the physical pain, although those memories lingered, too, but the devastating pain of refusal and abandonment. And of knowing herself to have been a weak and ravening creature, driven to do anything Roger demanded.

Catherine couldn't see Wright. She had retreated somewhere, likely back into the bedchamber.

Bloody blazes. Catherine again had no choice, unless she wanted to make a scene, and that was the last thing she wanted to do. She had already caused quite enough trouble for Sir Francis by going out walking in the rain, unattended, and injuring herself.

She took a step forward, trying to lessen any weight she put on Siddons' arm.

"Cath," he said, his voice husky.

She concentrated on the steps she needed to take to get to the top of the stairs.

"It seems like it was only yesterday since last we met."

Catherine kept her eyes on the carpet. "It was just a few hours ago."

Siddons laughed. "My dear, always such a literalist. It took me by surprise in our younger days. Such a clever little actress. Such a succubus in the bedchamber. And still such a prosaic chit in the world."

She colored. She knew she did. She could feel the blush spreading from her face to her bosom.

"Oh, Cath, how sweet. I've made you pink."

They had finally reached the top of the stairs. Catherine wrenched her arm away and pushed past Siddons to grasp the banister with her left hand.

"I am perfectly capable of descending the stairs on my own."

Siddons held his hands up. "As you wish, Mrs. Lovelock."

She started down. One, two, three, four, five, six stairs. She had difficulty putting enough weight on the banister because of her short stature, but the additional discomfort was preferable to leaning on Roger.

He followed, just a step behind her. "I must thank you. The view is quite a bit better from here."

She stopped and turned. He stood on the step above her, looking down at her bosom. How glad she was that she had held the daring blue silk in reserve.

"It is of interest to me how unwanted attentions can be so perilous," Catherine began, gratified her voice sounded cool and detached.

Siddons moved down two steps so he was a step below her and put his arm around her waist.

"You are in peril of being ravished, you mean? Or you are in peril of surrendering to your desire?" His hand slid from her waist to a buttock and squeezed.

"Or she is in peril of taking a tumble down these steps,

what?" A lazy laugh from James, coming down the stairs behind them.

Siddons hastily removed his hand from Catherine's bottom as James somehow got between Catherine and the banister and took hold of her left arm.

With her body between these two men, these two troublesome men, Catherine could feel how each affected her. How her body was repelled by Roger and drawn to James. Even now, when James was at his most foppish and almost certainly foxed, she only wanted to press herself to him, feel his arms around her. And, yes, kiss him again as she had in the alley last night. Kiss his mouth and more.

"Upsidaisy. Now a step down. Brilliant. And another one? No, don't put your full weight on the foot, just lean more on me here. And what did the doctor say, Mrs. Lovelock?"

Doctor? "I have seen no doctor, Lord Daventry, but I assure you it is just a sprain. It's my weak ankle, you see."

James frowned, and, for a moment, he seemed sincere. "There isn't a single weak thing about you, Mrs. Lovelock."

She took another step down, and the fop returned, chortling.

"Splendid, what? And then another step down. Isn't she doing splendidly, Mr. Siddons? A word or two of advice, sir— for an ankle, an arm under an arm is of far more assistance than a hand on an arse."

Catherine did not turn to look at Siddons, but she heard him grunt as he passed them, storming down the stairs, his tailcoat flapping.

"Oooh, temper, temper. Mr. Siddons seems the explosive type, doesn't he? All that rage cannot be good for one."

Catherine took another step down. "He is a man who does not like to be thwarted."

"It seems to me he is exactly the kind of man who *does* like it. Nothing like a little thwarting to get the blood going, eh?"

Yes, James was right. How aroused Roger used to become when she raged at him. How he had desired the provocation and then desired her body afterwards. And how resistance had only inflamed him further.

And what of her own violence last night? How she had struck James. And how surprised and chastened he had been.

She looked at James, but he was looking down at the stairs and watching her feet. Catherine cleared her throat.

"Mr. Siddons is constitutionally less capable of dealing with frustration than other men."

"You have frustrated him, then?"

"Once upon a time."

James smirked. "You know what they say? The shorter the fuse…the shorter the fuse."

She had to stop this. Catherine pulled her arm away and turned on the tread to face him.

"I don't know what your game is, Lord Daventry, but if you think your lewd remarks are a pleasant escape from Mr. Siddons' lewd remarks, you are mistaken. And if you think I need rescuing from a man I know perfectly well how to manage, you are mistaken there, as well."

James chuckled. "It seems to me the lady needs frequent rescuing. On the streets of London last night and in the fields of Kent earlier today. And now on the stairs of Ffoulkes Manor."

Catherine drew herself up. "And I would remind you that at Madame Beauchamp's," James whipped his head around, scanning the staircase and the great hall, seemingly worried someone might hear, "a fortnight ago, you were the one in need of rescuing. And the only rescue I needed last night was from my loss of sense. Because, as I was about to say to Mr. Siddons before you interrupted, the peril of unwanted attentions is that it makes the unwanted one look a fool."

Catherine walked down three steps and turned. "And,

since you mentioned it, I'll have you know that *the fuse*?"
James raised his eyebrows. Catherine gave her best leer. "Is not
that short."

She walked down the rest of the stairs on her own. She
could not stomp, as she wished to do, but she hoped she at
least did not limp too pitifully.

James grinned until Catherine disappeared into the drawing
room, but his grin faded as a despairing confusion swept over
him. What had she meant? Was he the fool, or was she? Did
she know how much he thought of her? And in such a yearning, hopeless way? Or could *she* be the fool who thought her
feelings were unreciprocated? Could he hope for that? Could
she want him?

That kiss she had given him in the alleyway. That unprece-
dented and remarkable kiss.

And who was this Mr. Roger Siddons to place his hands
on her? Catherine knew him; she had said so. And her remark
about Mr. Siddons' fuse and its length—no, no, no, he could
not think on that. It implied an intimacy between the two that
James could not bear to consider in this moment.

But the effrontery of the contemptible man!

Then he remembered how he had put his own hands in
that exact same place on Catherine's body last night but under
her dress. How he had taken an advantage and pressed it, even
as he had pressed his cock against her. James was every bit as
disgusting as Siddons. He had lost control. He had only barely
pulled himself back in time.

He had been a debauched marquess, ready to take his pleasure where he wanted. He must heed Mr. Bulverton's
warning.

And why had the doctor not come? True, Catherine could

walk, but the pain might be more than she conveyed. She needed an examination by a physician. Had he or had he not told the butler Rowley to fetch a doctor?

The Swintons came down the stairs, and James made himself smile and converse about the weather and the next day's shooting and tonight's cards. All three of them descended the rest of the stairs together and went into the drawing room.

The butler stood at a table to the side, pouring small glasses of Madeira for a footman to offer. James went to him directly and spoke in a low voice, not wishing to embarrass the butler or his host.

"Rowley, why did no doctor come to attend on Mrs. Lovelock?"

Rowley looked nervous. "One could not be found."

James was astonished. Could not someone have gone to the next town, not two more miles up the road? A doctor could surely have been found there. Could not the blacksmith at the village been prevailed upon to come, at the very least?

Rowley stammered. No, Lord Daventry. It was most unfortunate. Certainly, yes, tomorrow someone might be sent to find another doctor in the next town. But perhaps the lady might be recovered by then? Just as my lord wishes.

James suddenly realized he had been quite stern with Rowley, so he winked and staggered a bit and took a glass of Madeira and joined the other guests. He observed Isabella laughing at a remark made by the Marquis DuBois de Laval, throwing her dark head back and exposing her long throat, drawing admiring glances from all the men present, including Sir Francis.

How really well she cleaned up. Not that she had been dirty, but in a proper dress and her hair done correctly, she very much looked a lady. An elegant lady from the Continent.

No one would ever guess either of her professions or that she had been born and raised in East London. James could learn a thing or two from Isabella about subterfuge.

FOURTEEN

Devil it.

James' open appreciation of Isabella DuMornay had not escaped Catherine's notice. Catherine laughed at something Sir Francis said. He had said nothing amusing, but she laughed anyway.

Sir Francis smiled and leaned closer. "How lovely you are tonight. I am so very pleased you decided to join me this week. Your acquaintance, nay, your friendship has sustained me during these difficult times."

Catherine patted the back of Sir Francis' hand lightly. "The loss of a spouse can be very painful, indeed."

She might be mistaken, but he almost looked shocked by her comment. Or had it been her touch of his hand?

"Yes, yes. Of course. And I must tell you, my dear, I have a little surprise planned for you. Later tonight."

He might press his suit to her this very evening.

Good, let's settle this troubling thing. Let's be done with it. Let my darkest fallibilities be vanquished by matrimony.

She took Sir Francis' arm and went into dinner, knowing she would soon be the mistress of this house. Marriage to

Edward Lovelock had saved her, years ago. Marriage to Sir Francis would do the same.

After the substantial meal, Catherine laid her spoon down next to her empty syllabub glass, and Sir Francis Ffoulkes stood and nodded at the butler Rowley, who left the room.

"Normally at this time, the ladies would withdraw to a parlor, and we gentlemen would partake in some port. However, before the rest of the evening commences, I hope I may prevail on all of you to join me in the gallery."

The party, of course, could be prevailed upon to do so. Catherine started gamely up the stairs she had descended two hours earlier. Sir Francis took her right arm. He had not noticed the injured ankle was on the left and it was that side in need of support, and Catherine did not like to bring it to his attention. Soon the rest of the party had passed them on the wide staircase.

"Upsidaisy." James was at her left elbow. "How jolly. Nothing like a little stroll after dinner, even if it's indoors, what?" He did not take her arm or touch her, but as she put all her weight on her left ankle to take the next step, she clutched at his rigid arm that had been bent and locked into just the right position for her.

"Thank you," she said to James.

"You are most welcome, my dear," Sir Francis said. "And I think you will thank me even more when you see what is in store."

"How amusing," James said and tittered. "A surprise for Mrs. Lovelock, what? I can only hope for a surprise for myself at the card table tonight. All the trumps!"

On the next step, Catherine gave up and securely linked her arm with James'. As Sir Francis and James spoke over her head about the gaming planned for later, she could not help but lean into James and test the unyielding muscle and bone and sinew she found there. *More muscle for me and Wright to appreciate.* And no matter how hard she pressed, how much weight she put on his arm, it held in its locked position and his voice flowed over her head uninterrupted, without strain. He was so…solid.

Sir Francis and James moved on to discussing the dogs for the hunt tomorrow.

Oh. Oh. That was it.

James looked like a whippet, acted like a Maltese, but had the strength of a mastiff.

He was a breed all his own.

She looked up at James, at his clean jaw and the brown-gold lashes around his gray eyes, and forgot herself for a moment. She smiled.

He looked down at her, and, although he kept speaking to Sir Francis in the same light tenor voice, she saw something else in his eyes. Something inscrutable.

He knows how he destroys me.

The rest of the party waited in the gallery, laughing and talking pleasantly, relaxed after the meal of rich food and wine. The gallery itself was well lit, almost blazing, with candelabras all around. Clearly, there was something that demanded viewing in good light. A large area of one wall was covered by a red velvet curtain. Sir Francis walked ahead of Catherine and James and stood in front of the curtain. He clapped his hands.

"My guests, your attention, please."

Everyone quieted and gathered in front of the curtain. James helped Catherine to a chair at the front of the group and then stepped to one side.

Immediately, she missed his arm, his close presence.

Her mastiff.

"As you may know," Sir Francis began, "I am an admirer of beauty of all kinds. Including, of course, the present company." He bowed to Catherine. "Long have I admired the painting under this drape. Mr. Roger Siddons, the artist, has agreed to loan the painting to me temporarily. But he has promised that when a certain happy event occurs, he will sell it to me. I will say no more but invite you to feast your eyes."

Sir Francis pulled on a cord, and the red velvet curtain fell away.

Catherine sucked in a breath.

The rest of the party made appreciative murmurs. "Lovely," and "Quite striking."

Roger Siddons folded his arms across his chest and stared at Catherine. She forced herself to stare back with an expression that did not betray her dismay, she hoped.

The Marquess of Painswick began to clap. "Very good," he called out. "Very good." He walked closer to the painting and leaned in as if to examine the brushstrokes.

"Not too close, my lord," Sir Francis said.

"No, Sir Francis." The Marquess of Painswick licked his lips and stepped away. "Not too close. Just close enough."

Catherine felt ill. In seconds, she would vomit. She stood up and walked blindly out of the gallery to the corridor that led to her bedchamber. She sensed someone behind her, keeping pace with her as she limped away as quickly as she could. The someone did not speak, did not touch her, but stayed just behind her until she reached her room, opened the door, and closed it behind her.

She did not turn as she closed the door. She knew James was the one who had followed her. She did not think she could face anyone right now, but particularly not him.

James had felt Catherine's distress coming off her in waves. He waited outside her door, unsure what to do next, as Isabella brushed past him and entered Catherine's room. She turned when she shut the door, and he saw her frowning face and the shoo of her hand.

He returned to the gallery and the rest of the guests.

"Ha! I believe Mrs. Lovelock had rather too much of that syllabub, Sir Francis. Just some dyspepsia, she said. Mamselle DuMornay has her well in hand, what?" James hoped that last sentence was true.

"Hmm, very good, very good, Lord Daventry," Sir Francis replied, oddly unperturbed. He gestured at the wall. "But what do you think of the painting?"

To James, standing a good twenty feet away, it was a pretty picture. A golden-haired and half-naked youth in old-fashioned ballooning breeches and hose stood in a lush green forest, a pool of water at his feet. The boy's bare back was to the viewer, and he had been caught just after removing his shirt, which he still held in his hands. A blue velvet doublet and a sheathed rapier lay on the grassy ground. Some strips of linen—bandages, maybe?—were strewn about. It looked as if the youth had been about to bathe in the pool before he was interrupted. His golden head was turned over his shoulder, and he was looking directly out of the painting, at the viewer. Or the artist.

But the rest of the group was whispering, walking up to the painting and then pulling back to look again at it from a distance. James walked closer.

Oh.

He knew those blue eyes. He had seen those creamy white shoulders and back, that spine, at Madame Beauchamp's. They were Catherine's. But the picture was not of her, was it? It was someone else. He couldn't recall, but it was someone of significance. To him.

And despite the youth's arms being fairly close to his—or her—sides and the youth's body being turned away, the very slightest curve of a breast peeped from under the left arm as the youth looked over his—or her—left shoulder.

Oh, the barest hint of that breast. He knew that breast. It was also Catherine's.

And now James could see the skin was not completely flawless. He spied red horizontal marks just under the youth's armpit and farther down, below the curve of the breast. The marks were not the lashings from a whip. As a boy, James had seen those on his own back in a mirror. These marks were far too fine, and why would they be only on the upper flank and not the back? Of course, a woman's flesh was soft in that place under the arm and might take an impression more easily than a man's flesh in the same place.

James didn't understand the painting. On close inspection, there was something sickening about it. Some horror in those blue eyes.

One could imagine a monster, a dragon just outside the frame, threatening the innocence and the beauty.

Siddons sidled up to James as if they were friends. "It's good to get the thing framed. I remember when Cath sat for it. She dressed in costume for most of the sittings but agreed to show her back and shoulders. And why not? After all, audiences of all kinds had seen that and more. Of course, eventually I convinced her to show me everything."

James swallowed back repugnance and rage. He gritted his teeth. "Doesn't look a thing like her, what?"

Sir Francis stepped forward, grabbed James' arm. "You don't think so?"

"No." James laughed. "It's some boy, isn't it?"

With a disdainful smile, Siddons said, "It's Catherine as Cesario."

"Cesario? An Italian?"

DuBois stepped forward. "Shakespeare, Lord Daventry. *Twelfth Night.*"

James shook his head, continuing to play the fool, while

his mind raced, his heart thumped, and suddenly so much made sense.

Of course. No wonder he had been drawn to and devastated by Catherine. Cesario was Viola's boy disguise in *Twelfth Night*. Perhaps he had even seen Catherine play the role once upon a time. Viola, his cherished ideal woman. The brave adventurer who covered her passion with wit.

But this painting bore no relation to the *Twelfth Night* James knew. *Twelfth Night* was a comedy. With those waggish clowns and some sweet misunderstandings and disguises, some mild anguish over unreciprocated love. But one knew it would come right in the end. Viola would get her man Orsino, the Duke of Illyria. Olivia would fall in love with Viola's twin brother Sebastian. A double wedding in the fifth act.

This painting had naught to do with that. It induced dread. Revulsion. Terror.

Finally, he had to turn away.

Fifteen

She had escaped. Wright was not in the room, and that was a blessing, for once. Catherine sat in the chair by the fire and put her head in her hands. She heard the door open.

"Go away, Lord Daventry."

The door closed. "*Non,* it is not Lord Daventry, Madame Lovelock. It is Mademoiselle DuMornay."

Catherine raised her head, her eyes dry. "I'm sorry, Mamselle. I don't feel well." She attempted a smile.

Isabella crossed to her and sank down on her knees next to her. "Of course, you are not well. That painting is an atrocity."

"You think so, too?"

"*Mais, oui!* Anyone who can't see that is an *idiote!* That poor child *est traumatisée.*" Isabella reached out and brushed one of Catherine's curls with a finger. "But such beautiful hair."

Catherine looked at the fire. "Thank you, you are kind. Of course, that poor child is me."

Isabella turned her head to one side. "*Non, pas vraiment.*

Perhaps it once was, but I have a hard time believing even that. I cannot think you were ever to be pitied."

Catherine met Isabella's eyes. "I hope not."

"But I must ask," Catherine held her breath, dreading the question, "what are the lines?" Isabella touched Catherine lightly on her ribs, under her arm.

Catherine laughed, relieved. "They're from the wrappings, the bandages. I had to compress my breasts, you see, to flatten them for the role."

"Oh, your poor bosom!" Isabella sighed in sympathy.

Catherine shrugged. She had liked playing Viola, a woman who managed to have some power over her destiny even if she had to dress as the boy Cesario to do so. She had liked the world of the play, a fantastical place called Illyria where a woman could survive alone. Where a woman could be spurned and still, somehow, magically wind up in the arms of the man she loved.

And she had not minded the pain of her breast wrappings. She had welcomed the bite and the ache and even the control she had to use to get in a full breath. It had distracted her from the other pain in her life, the pain caused by Roger Siddons and her own despicable weakness.

"I think I will leave tomorrow," Catherine said abruptly. "My ankle."

"*Bien sûr.*"

"It is a lovely house, but the atmosphere is not…conducive."

Isabella laughed. "Lovely?" She looked around the room. "Well, yes, this is quite the nicest room, I believe. You are a favorite."

"Your bedchamber is…?"

Isabella waved a hand. "It is *sans conséquence*. Yes, I agree you should return to London, away from that bad Mr. Siddons."

"And Lord Daventry."

Isabella looked surprised. "Lord Daventry? Why Lord Daventry?"

Catherine was at a loss. "Well, I…uh, he…uh…"

"*Peut-être* his lordship has done something he should not have?"

"No, no, of course not. It's just— He is very drunk all the time, isn't he? And silly?"

"You don't like silly men, Madame Lovelock?"

"I suppose," Catherine said slowly, "I don't like *his* being silly." Although his being silly was perhaps the only thing keeping her safe from the terrible jeopardy she felt when he was in earnest.

Isabella stood. "You should tell his lordship that."

Catherine could feel the heat of the blush coloring her cheeks. "I'm sure he wouldn't be interested in my opinion in the slightest."

"You might be surprised." Isabella shrugged and pouted. "But it is, how you English say, none of my business. I will give your apologies to our host and the other guests. Rest well, Madame Lovelock."

The door closed behind Isabella, and Catherine was alone. To rest.

Rest.

Catherine got up from the chair, and, despite her ankle, she paced the room. Hadn't she been resting for the last decade and a half? She was not built for rest. She was restless by nature.

Because only a restless, wild Kate Cooksey would have made her way to London at age sixteen, determined not to stay a farmer's daughter or become a blacksmith's wife but to take to the stage. And through ambition and hard work and quite a bit of cleverness become Catherine Cooke, a leading actress of the Theatre-Royal, Drury Lane, where she was famed for her portrayals of Shakespeare's heroines. Spirited Rosalind, rebellious Katherina, loyal Cordelia, wise Portia. And, of course, the brave, passionate, and resourceful Viola. She was all of them, and they were all of her.

There was nothing restful about her back then.

Her husband Edward had fallen in love with her as Ophelia in *Hamlet*. Many men had. She had been forced to wear a brown wig and her maid's clothes every night so she could evade her admirers outside the theater. She had needed to hire a servant to ferry her gifts of flowers out of her dressing room, or she would have drowned in blooms. Some lovely—as well as some perfectly horrendous—verse had been dedicated to her Ophelia.

The actor-manager Mr. Kemble had explained her triumph thus: "My dear, your pain when the prince rejects you is palpable. And fraught. You bring a soul-scouring pathos to the part, one I have never seen before. In their heads, these men in the audience become your savior, and they imagine rescuing you, earning your devotion. They want to hold this little girl with the golden hair and make her safe, tame her madness, keep her from drowning. And it doesn't hurt that your Ophelia is a naughty little minx, eager for all sorts of *country matters* with her beau Hamlet before he breaks her heart." Then Kemble had chuckled and patted Catherine's bottom and resumed taking off his face paint.

Twenty-eight years of age at the time, Catherine was no longer a girl. She knew very well how much her bosom and the damp, sheer gown she wore in her mad scene had made her a success in the role. And her pathos in the role was convincing because it was real.

Because of Roger.

Roger Siddons was ten years older than she, an artist of some note when he first came backstage to ask her to model for him. She was drawn to his hunger for success, which she thought matched hers. And to his sculpted good looks. His aquiline nose, his narrow lips. His devouring eyes, his controlling hands.

Their coupling had been torrid in every sense of the word —hot, ardent, and full of tempests. Their nights together had been marked by passionate love-making and equally passionate shouting matches. Roger had struck her often, but he had never hit her on her face. Mustn't leave a bruise or the manager of the company would have had his head.

Even worse, Roger would be cold to her and not speak for days, and she would be wretched, craving his attention, his caresses. But he would ignore her unless she did as he asked.

He asked her to pay attention to other men—to flirt and to allow gropes and kisses—so he might attract commissions. "It's the same as what you do on stage with those other actors," he said. "You might as well do it to benefit me."

So she had whored, in her own way. For him. For her desire for him. She had permitted things. Things she could not bring herself to name even to herself.

And he would reward her with earth-shattering climaxes. Evil became intertwined with pleasure.

Then, after she had spent eight brutal years keeping daily company with her lust demon, hoping for God knows what resolution to the madness of being Roger's mistress, he had suddenly taken up with a seventeen-year-old opera singer.

It had been the day before the opening of *Hamlet*. At least, the heartbreak had been good for her art. And, in retrospect, it had been the making of her to be shut of him.

As the run of the play was extended over and over again, Catherine used her time alone to think. She was an aging *ingénue,* and this could well be the peak of her career. With her short stature, she would never be a Lady Macbeth or a Cleopatra or even a Duchess of Malfi.

She was tired, and she was hurt. She felt damaged. This moment might be her one chance for a new life, a safe life.

Her most devoted admirer, the kindest of men, the banker Edward Lovelock won out over all others. He helped her lock the lust demon away even as she sought solace in his arms. She married him as quickly as she could and learned for the first time that making love could actually *make* love.

Ophelia was her last role.

Her last role on the stage, that is. Because she soon realized that although Edward had fallen in love with a love-crazed and grief-stricken maiden, he really needed someone else. Someone *restful*.

The role of Mrs. Edward Lovelock was actually Catherine's greatest triumph. She determined what her husband and stepdaughters needed, and she created that woman. She became an oasis from their grief of losing Edward's first wife, Mary and Harry's mother. A paragon of patience who could calm Harry's tantrums and direct her away from screaming and thumping her head on the floor. She became oh-so-very restful, managing everything in the house with very little trouble to anyone else. And now with Edward dead, Mary and Harry both married, there was nothing left to manage.

Oh, yes, there was Arabella. But Arabella—lovely, fiery, playful Arabella—did not really need her. Not the way Edward and Mary and Harry had. Arabella could take care of herself. Arabella was just like Catherine.

She stopped pacing and looked at herself in the mirror that hung in the room.

But who *was* Catherine Lovelock? She had pretended for so long, she no longer knew.

Sixteen

The rest of the party was quite gay that night. The Swintons were astonishingly good at whist when they partnered each other and quite middling at other card games. James suffered his planned losses to Sir Francis and very large, unplanned losses to the Swintons.

He must be distracted. It didn't help that the Marchioness of Painswick looked daggers at him throughout the evening. She caught him in the drawing room during a break in the cards.

"Lord Daventry, I must speak to you about your sisters," she said and took his arm and dragged him into a corner near the pianoforte.

"Marshness," he said and leaned on the instrument. "You are as ravishing as always."

"Speaking of ravishing, you owe me, Lord Daventry."

"Marshness," hiccough, "the items I removed—"

She cut him off with a gesture of her hand, fingers laden with even more sparkling jewels than when they had last met.

"We both know that although those things may not have been given to me, I was owed them. Oh, yes, I apologized quite prettily to Prinny and see here," she pushed her chest forward to show James a large ruby pendant hanging below her collar bone, "I received this gorgeous little gem in exchange. So all is forgiven, at least between me and him. But you, on the other hand," she ran a slender finger over James' hand, "you still owe me."

"I assure you, my lady, as soon as I am capable, you will be the first one to know."

"Capable? You mean sober? I could wait a lifetime for that. And I am not a patient woman, Lord Daventry." She leaned forward and whispered in his ear, "I recommend you stop your drinking. Right now. Or there will be hell to pay in Kent tonight."

She walked away, her hips swaying, her threat still stinging his ears.

An hour later, the Marquis DuBois de Laval limped over to the sofa where James was sprawled and sat heavily next to him, leaning his walking stick against a side table.

The marquis. He was a bit of an enigma. A man of many allegiances. He had lost his leg fighting for Napoleon. But after Bonaparte's first defeat and abdication, René DuBois had sworn loyalty to the new French king, Louis XVIII. And he had stayed loyal to the French crown even after Napoleon escaped exile from Elba and ruled for the so-called Hundred Days.

The Battle of Waterloo came at the end of those days, and Napoleon was banished to St. Helena, that isolated island in the south Atlantic, twelve hundred miles off the coast of Africa. After years of war, finally peace. A peace only achieved by imprisoning Bonaparte far away, on an inescapable rock of an island.

René DuBois, the cavalry commander with one leg, was first made a marquis by the grateful new king of France. Shortly thereafter, he was also made ambassador to Great

Britain, to the court of King George III and the Prince Regent, who ruled in his father's stead due to the king's madness.

"Marquis DuBois de Laval." James stood up and swayed. "Would you like some of this brandy?" He picked up a decanter from the table in front of him. "It's French, of course."

The marquis accepted a glass from James. "*Merci*. We have met before today, Lord Daventry, have we not?" He swirled the amber liquid in the glass.

James waved his hand in the air vaguely as he collapsed back onto the sofa. "In passing, I believe, at court."

"Ah, yes."

James quashed a belch with a fist to his mouth. "I was surprised to meet an ambassador here. Sir Francis made me think this was an intimate gathering."

"You must not think of me as an ambassador. I am merely a guest. Like you." The marquis sipped his brandy. "I was impressed by your gallantry today. To carry Madame Lovelock so far in the rain. I didn't know Englishmen were so robust in their attentions."

James bristled a little at the implied insult to his countrymen but covered it with a shrug. "I've twisted my ankle many times. Especially while getting out of my carriage after too much of this stuff," he held his own glass aloft, "so I know it can hurt like the devil. Didn't want the lady to suffer needlessly."

"And I noticed your attempt to provide succor to the same lady's distress after the unveiling of the painting."

"Looked like she was about to cast up her accounts."

The marquis leaned forward. "I think the lady has some fondness for you."

"Well, I never say no to female affection." James forced himself into a lazy chuckle. But he was startled by the warm sensation in his chest at the marquis' suggestion that Catherine might have feelings for him. It was hardly possible it might be true. She had made it clear she despised him.

Except.

Except *before* she had slapped him.

That kiss.

That extraordinary kiss in the alley. How she had pulled at his hair but so softly pressed her mouth against his. The lips, so sweet and tender, and the hands, so demanding. At the same time.

With the memory of that kiss, James suddenly felt very warm someplace a good deal lower than his chest and had to shift his position on the sofa.

The marquis smiled. "I will be bold and tell you I think you should pursue the fair Widow Lovelock. Stir yourself."

James leered. "I prefer to let the ladies stir me, thank you very much. It's so much easier that way."

"She will be taken before you know it. Our host," the marquis looked around, but there was no one near, "and others. They are greedy men, and you will lose your chance." The marquis put his brandy aside, grasped his walking stick, and stood. "*Bonsoir*, Lord Daventry."

James lurched to his feet and made a sloppy bow. "Good night, *Monsieur le marquis*."

As he watched the gentleman limp across the room and lean over to whisper something in Isabella's ear, James wondered why DuBois might want to encourage a love affair between Catherine and a ne'er-do-well like himself.

It was a relief to get back to his bedchamber and be alone with Enfield.

First, the issue of the physician.

"Do you know why no doctor was fetched for Mrs. Love-lock when you were brought to the manor this afternoon?"

Enfield assisted James out of his tailcoat and laid it flat in the clothes press.

"My lord, after the luggage was transferred to Sir Francis' carriage, we did go on to a doctor's surgery. I heard only part of the exchange between the doctor and the coachman, but, from what I understood, Sir Francis Ffoulkes has not paid the doctor for the months of care he provided to Sir Francis' wife before her death a year ago. The doctor said, and I quote, *If it's just some silly woman's ankle, I'll be damned if I ever go to that house again.*"

"I see. How odd. I mean, what an odd thing for Sir Francis to be mean about, don't you think? Not to pay the doctor?"

"My lord." Enfield stopped and bit his lip.

Lip biting was a signal to James to encourage Enfield to be indiscreet.

"Tell me, Enfield."

Enfield spoke in a low voice as he removed James' cravat. "Almost all the servants have only been here for a month and have not yet received any wages. Yes, this room is a handsome one, but there is paint covering the rot of the window frame, and there are moth holes in the curtains. The food for the servants is made up of scraps. The whole downstairs smells of damp—"

"What does all that mean?"

"Things are not as they should be in this house. Not for a man thought to be as rich as Sir Francis Ffoulkes."

Hmph. James had always heard Sir Francis was wealthy from his government contracts to supply the navy's fleet. But the baronet might have overextended himself and gotten into trouble now the wars were over.

"Let me ask you something else."

"Yes, my lord." Enfield knelt to remove James' boots.

"No, I think I better leave the boots on." James put out a hand to assist Enfield up. "In fact, let me have my cravat back on and my tailcoat."

"Yes, my lord." Enfield began to retie James' cravat.

James lifted his chin to give Enfield access. "Were you with my family, my brother, around the change of the century?"

"I became your brother's valet when he was fifteen. In the year seventeen hundred and ninety-eight."

"I am sure you are hardly likely to remember, but do you recall if the family or if my brother and I went to the theater and saw *Twelfth Night* that year? Or the following year? Or the year after that? Perhaps eighteen hundred, the year I turned ten?"

"I'm afraid you're right. I do not recall, my lord."

James rubbed his jaw and grimaced. "I suppose I'll have to ask my mother."

Enfield helped James back into his tailcoat.

"And may I ask why you are dressing, my lord, instead of preparing for sleep?"

"I have a vigil to keep."

SEVENTEEN

It had all gone terribly wrong. Catherine sighed into the darkness and turned over in her bed and enumerated the ways circumstance had conspired against her.

First, Roger. To be confronted by him after so many years was a blow. Because to see him was to be reminded of how she had been with him and how she could so easily be that way again with James.

And James himself. His eyes, his hair, his body—all of him, really—and the desire he ignited even as she struggled to maintain herself as the proper Widow Lovelock.

These two men. One from her past, one in the present. These two men, who made her so wild that she feared she might be lost forever, who made her feel so apart from her normal self that she resorted to imagining a demon. When it was really just *her* and her own uncontrollable and shameful appetites.

Finally, that contemptible painting. Which brought her back to the girl she had been with Roger and the woman she might be with James.

She had to leave. Go back to London. Retreat in order to

rebuild her composure. Find a way clear to marrying Sir Francis so she could have the safe haven she needed.

Her door—the door she had thought was locked —opened.

"Who's there?" she called out. The door closed.

"Shhhhh." A rustle. The smell of roses. "Cath." A voice rasping with desire. A voice that had seduced her hundreds of times in the past. Now, a voice only associated with the pain of misplaced love, unfulfilled desire, and her own failings.

She fumbled at her bedside table and lit a candle. Roger Siddons stood not three feet from her. He wore only a shirt and breeches.

"Catherine," he said. "You are as beautiful as ever."

"That's a lie. Neither of us are as we used to be. We have grown old. I am an old, respectable woman, and you must leave my bedchamber."

Siddons took a step closer to the bed. "Or what? Or you will scream and bring the entire household into this room to see that you, an old, respectable woman, the intended of Sir Francis, were entertaining a gentleman in your bedchamber?"

"There's no gentleman here."

He laughed softly and took another step closer. "At least we can agree on that. I am no gentleman." He reached out and cupped her breast through her nightdress. "And you are no lady. We should share a bed one more time. Let me make you moan again, Cath, like I used to." He ran his thumb over her nipple, and Catherine hated herself for the involuntary stiffening of that same nipple and the spasm of her trunk that followed.

There was a moment just after her body betrayed her with its tremble of lust, with Roger's thumb still on her hardened peak, when she was tempted to lie back, pull up her nightdress, and let him ravish her. Hadn't she ached for months to be touched in just such a way? Not by him, true, but she knew

James would never touch her that way. That dream must be put to death.

"Suck on my finger, Cath." Roger put the forefinger of his other hand in her mouth.

Oh, now she remembered the vile degradation. His misuse of her. His violence when she had wanted love. She remembered why she looked like a hunted creature in the portrait that hung in the gallery of this house.

She considered biting his finger but did not want any part of him inside her. Instead, she reached up and grabbed his wrist with one hand and pulled his finger from her mouth with the other and began to bend the finger backward, intending to break it.

He gasped in pain and let go of her breast and made a fist with his free hand and was poised to strike her just as the door to her bedchamber crashed open and a body came flying in.

"Ho, ho, ho." James caught Siddons' raised arm. "This seems quite unwise. No fisticuffs in the bedchamber. Tut, tut, tut. Something—or someone—might get broken. We can't," he hiccoughed, "have that, can we?" He laughed.

Siddons tried to pull his arm away, but James kept hold of it. Catherine continued to bend back the forefinger of Siddons' other hand.

"Let go of me, Cath. And you, too, Cavendish, you fool."

"Ah, Mrs. Lovelock," James said, grinning, "I seem to be in the wrong bedchamber. How stupid of me. And Mr. Siddons appears to have made the same mistake, hasn't he? Two of us idiots at the same time. But perhaps if Mr. Siddons promises to leave your room without any fuss, you'll let go of his finger, hmmm?"

"I thought I might break it off and keep it as a piece of licking candy. Seeing how he stuck it in my mouth and wanted me to suck it," Catherine said evenly.

"Mr. Stiddens!" James said in a shocked tone. "How

crude." He giggled. "I suppose you're lucky it's not the little finger, eh? Get it? Or your sugar stick?" He laughed and then stopped and looked puzzled. "Wait, those mean the same thing, don't they?" He sat down on the bed, still holding Siddons' arm.

"Let me go, both of you," Siddons seethed and struggled.

"Shall we let go on the count of three, Mrs. Lovelock? One, two, three."

Against her better judgment, Catherine let go of Siddons' wrist and finger just as James let go of his arm, and Siddons, who had been pulling against both of them, stumbled backwards and almost fell.

"Good night, Mr. Shittens," James said and collapsed back onto the bed. "Upsidaisy."

"You'll pay for this, Cath," Siddons said as he backed out the door, nursing his injured finger in his other hand.

She got up from the bed and crossed to the door in her nightdress and bare feet.

"Then it's a good thing I'm rich, Roger."

She closed the door and pushed a chair up against it, wedging the chair's back under the handle. Obviously, the lock on the door was of no use.

She walked back to her bed. James lay across the foot of it, face up, eyes closed, his legs hanging off the side, feet almost touching the floor. He was fully dressed in his boots and tailcoat and cravat and plainly had not yet been to bed.

"Are you all right, Mrs. Lovelock?" he said with his eyes still closed.

"I'm fine, my lord. And yourself?"

He kept his eyes closed but fluttered one hand in the air. "Oh, I'm five sheets in the wind, quite as usual."

"Not three sheets?" Catherine found her dressing gown on the chair next to the bed and put it on.

"Why settle for three when you can have five?" He rolled

onto his side and opened one eye and peered at her. "I say, that fellow is a nasty piece of work, what?"

"Yes," Catherine said. "And I do wonder at your mistaking my room for yours when your bedchamber is all the way over in the other wing."

He closed his open eye, rolled onto his back again, and groaned. "Yes, I'm such a fool, aren't I? Would you mind if I just lay here for a minute?"

"Lord Daventry, I am grateful for your help, but you must—"

"I'm awfully dizzy and I'll just…lie here…in case that dreadful man comes back…just for a minute. I'll be your guard dog…woof, woof."

Catherine was reminded of the mastiff in the body of a whippet and masquerading as a Maltese.

"Lord Daventry—"

But it was too late. His breathing had become deep and even and sonorous.

"Lord Daventry!"

But he could not be awoken.

In time, Catherine slid off his boots. She found an extra blanket and placed it over him. She got into the bed herself, curling into a small ball at the head of the bed so she would not kick him as he sprawled across the foot.

She wondered at his slurred speech and his sleeping so heavily. Because when she had bent over him to cover him against the cold, she had come quite close to his face. His breath had been clean and sweet, with no trace of alcohol on it. Just as it had been at Madame Beauchamp's. And as it had been in the alley last night, when he had tasted of apple.

Drunk. Yet without alcohol on his breath. As mystifying as the man himself.

. . .

James had no plan when he burst into the room. He had been lolling in a wing chair set in a cozy nook down the corridor when he saw Roger Siddons go into Catherine's bedchamber. James felt sure there had been no invitation issued to Mr. Siddons. Or was that merely wishful thinking inspired by jealousy?

No matter. When he saw Siddons' upraised fist, he immediately assumed a dense state of inebriation as he had found absurdity was the best way to subdue violence. He was quite pleased by how calm Catherine had been as she held on to the vile man's finger. And once Siddons had turned tail and quit the room, she continued to be possessed of a perfect equanimity.

But James had no intention of leaving her bedchamber, just yet. There was evil in this house. His place was here, and he wasn't at all tired. In fact, he felt profoundly awake, lying on her bed with her scent in the air, the soft sounds of her putting on her dressing gown. And so he pretended to doze as he had successfully many times before.

James was surprised to feel his legs raised into the air and his boots drawn off. A blanket over him and a sense she was near. The movement of the bed as she got into it herself. He turned his head away from her so he could open his eyes and look at the embers of the fire.

He was still awake an hour later when his hand was caressed. He turned his head slowly and saw she had moved herself parallel to him in her sleep and was facing him, her eyes shut.

"Catherine?" he whispered and closed his hand over hers.

"Um," she said. "Jamie."

She smiled a little in her sleep and withdrew her hand from his grasp. Then her face went slack, her smile melted away, and she said no more.

Eighteen

The Marchioness of Painswick was more than vexed to find James' bedchamber empty. A nightshirt lay across the bed, but there was no Lord Daventry to service her as was her due.

She took off her dressing gown and slipped into the bed. She would wait, but damn the useless rogue. She fretted. She cursed. The longer she lay there, the angrier she became.

Finally, she got out of bed and put her dressing gown back on. She thought she knew where the shiftless James was hiding. She was going to find him and give him a piece of her mind, hell hath no fury, *et cetera*.

Shivering, she searched the drawing rooms downstairs but did not find him drunkenly asleep in a chair as she had expected.

Of course. That little doxy. She would take great pleasure in bursting in on the pair of them coupling and castigating them both. She had heard from her husband that James favored the minx. And the whore had the audacity to come here?

She flung open Mademoiselle DuMornay's door. The room was dark.

"'Oo's there?"

An East London accent. A scared, sleepy female voice. The marchioness stumbled forward and felt the bed blindly. A lone woman here, one who batted her hands away.

She had another idea.

But the busty, presumably lusty, redheaded Mrs. Swinton was not in her room. How strange. Perhaps she slept with her husband. Deviants, the pair of them.

Bang!

James and Catherine both sat bolt upright.

Bang!

The door to Catherine's room was being forced open against the chair propped under the door handle. Catherine had a moment to observe that the top of the chair was a delicate piece of carved wood and ill-suited to acting as a blockade before it splintered and the door flew open, knocking the chair out of the way.

"You!" screeched the marchioness, beet-red despite the cold.

James sprang off the bed and spoke in a low voice, "My lady, hush and come away with me now."

"No!" Lady Painswick screamed. She pointed at Catherine. "You…actress!"

Isabella DuMornay, wrapped in an embroidered dressing gown, appeared in the doorway next to the marchioness. She put her hands on the marchioness' arms to restrain her, but the incensed woman threw her off, cursing.

Other doors on the corridor were opening. In a matter of minutes, the Swintons, the Marquess of Painswick, and too many servants to count were gathered outside Catherine's door.

There was no hushing this up. It did not matter that James was fully dressed, except his boots. It was more than unseemly. It was a scandal.

"I am surprised. I was going to say horrified, but that is far too strong a word. Disturbed, perhaps. Yes, that's it. Disturbed."

Sir Francis was closeted with a hastily dressed Catherine in his study.

"I hope I have always conveyed my respect for you, Mrs. Lovelock. Despite your origins, your years on the stage, you have always seemed a perfect lady. When others said actresses were no better than whores, I defended you. In fact…well, perhaps I had better not say."

Catherine bit back her anger. "I know how these events appear. But I assure you nothing improper occurred between me and Lord Daventry in my bedchamber. In fact, it was one of your other guests who came into my room last night, uninvited, to importune me. Lord Daventry was only there to assist me in removing the scoundrel."

"And this scoundrel was?"

"Mr. Siddons."

"Ah, yes, Roger. You were his mistress before your marriage, were you not? It seems hard to believe you would reject him now when you had spent so much time in his bed previously."

The very same reasoning used by men, judges, juries when they declared a husband could never rape his wife. Catherine had given her permission once-upon-a-time and that meant she had given her permission, forever.

"Like many others—indeed, like many men—I was a fool when I was young. I wasted myself on someone undeserving.

But because I am a woman, there is some conception that I cannot learn from my mistakes, as if I am the proverbial dog that returns to his vomit. Mr. Siddons may well be vomit, but I am no dog."

"Bitch!" Roger Siddons stood from a wing chair, where he had been hidden from her sight. She was pleased to see he held his bandaged finger at an awkward angle.

She turned back to Sir Francis. "My apologies. Apparently, Mr. Siddons thinks I *am* a dog. I was not aware we were not alone."

"Mr. Siddons is the one who brought me the news that you and Lord Daventry had been found in your bed together."

"I am sure he was delighted to deliver that message."

Behind Ffoulkes' back, Siddons made a vulgar gesture for rutting. "You'll get yours, Cath." Catherine felt the bile rise in her throat.

Sir Francis clucked his tongue. "I think you had better leave, Roger. You've done your part."

Siddons slammed out of the study.

"Now, my dear." Sir Francis put a hand under her chin and lifted it, just as if she were a naughty child. "I see you are quite repentant."

Catherine did not feel repentant.

Sir Francis went on, "Of course, Lord Daventry's reputation is well known, so I am sure you are not wholly to blame. At first, I thought I should send you away. But if you promise to mend your ways, perhaps we might remain friends."

"Friends, Sir Francis?" Catherine felt an overwhelming, suffocating panic. He was going to abandon her.

She would be alone.

She would not be able to govern herself.

She would run mad and destroy her daughters' lives.

Deep breath. Control the quaver in your voice. "I thought we might be more than that."

"Certainly. I don't think it's a secret I have long looked on you with admiration. In fact, as you know, I had hoped to make you my wife."

"And now?"

"I still hope for that." He leaned down and kissed her briefly, a mere pressing of his lips to hers.

She felt empty, and that pleased her. Better to feel nothing than to go up in flames. And the emptiness somehow gave her the strength to make a request.

"I have a condition to our marriage."

"What is that, dearest?"

"You will buy that painting from Mr. Siddons and destroy it immediately."

A hesitation. "Certainly, certainly, I will see it done." He frowned. "But we should marry quickly. I do not want this scandal to spread too broadly before…well, no matter. We will pack and make for Gretna Green straight away."

"Gretna Green? There is no need for that," Catherine protested. "Clearly, we are both of age."

"Yes, but the banns, we can't wait for the banns. Three weeks. Even an ordinary license requires seven days. And, as you know, a baronet cannot usually get a special license."

"You've thought this through, I see," she said slowly.

"Well, we must hush up your impropriety with our marriage. If we marry, people will think there is nothing to the scandal, otherwise I would not have married you. You see?"

Catherine did not see, but in her exhausted state, sensing an impending cataclysm of some kind within herself, she would allow herself to be swept away by the sudden force of Sir Francis' wishes.

After all, she had come to this house intending to agree to the marriage. And she did not want a scandal. A scandal would hurt her darling Arabella, who had not yet made a match. She did not want her daughter punished because James had slept at the foot of Catherine's bed like a guard dog. Punished because her mother had a past that would not bear investigation. Punished because her mother was wicked.

Catherine had been controlling so much, for so long. It was time to cede everything. She was near drowning. Let her be towed along by the protection of Sir Francis, out of the maelstrom her supposed lust demon had left in its wake.

She would get Wright to pack some of her things. She would go to Scotland with Sir Francis and be married. She would be rid of both the loathsome painting and that equally loathsome time in her life.

Forever.

NINETEEN

Enfield quirked a playful eyebrow. "Quite a long vigil, eh, my lord?" He saw James' face and lowered the eyebrow. "A thousand pardons, my lord."

James collapsed onto his bed.

"We had better pack, Enfield. Once the sun rises, I doubt we will be welcome here any longer."

"Yes, my lord. And I apologize. I had not thought to bring any French Letters, so I hope you were cautious—"

"Enfield!" James sprang back onto his feet. "You are my valet, not my nursemaid!"

Enfield looked down, abashed for the first time in all the years he had served James as valet. "Yes, my lord."

James crossed to him and put a hand on his shoulder. "I'm sorry. In truth, you are more father to me than…I mean to say, you are a good man. And I thank you. I lost my temper because the lady…the lady…"

Enfield looked at him closely. "The lady would not have you?"

James could feel his eyes begin to water. He was overtired, damn it. "The lady *should* not have me."

Enfield diplomatically busied himself with James' shaving gear for several minutes before reminding his lordship that his carriage was not at Ffoulkes Manor but in the village five miles away, three by the crow's flight. The coachman and footman were sleeping above the public house, and the horses had been stabled there, as well.

No, a haggard Rowley said when he came to James' room. No, Sir Francis' carriage was not available to carry Lord Daventry, his valet, and his luggage to the village. But Lord Daventry was welcome to ask the other guests if he could have the use of their carriages.

James thought he heard a carriage then, leaving. Likely Catherine heading back to London in disgrace. How was he going to mend this for her?

He wasn't. He would be a fool to try to do so. Not when he was selfishly glad his presence in her bedchamber had put paid to any chance she might marry Sir Francis.

But now she must hate him more than ever.

The Swintons had come by stagecoach. The Marquess and Marchioness of Painswick were, obviously, unapproachable. He would die before he asked Siddons for a favor, and, anyway, he suspected the artist had come to the manor via Sir Francis' carriage. However, the Marquis DuBois de Laval was amenable to allowing James the use of his carriage. Isabella asked the ambassador, and as usual, she got what she wanted.

James went to the stables to make sure the marquis' horses were being made ready. He was surprised to see Catherine's horses, her distinctive chestnut team with white stars on their foreheads, still stabled. And her carriage tucked away.

He growled and grabbed a stable boy by the arm. "What carriage has left the house already this morning?"

"Sir Francis' carriage, my lord." The boy looked fearful.

James released the boy's arm. He really must not be so

fierce. It was out of character. "Where was the carriage going?" He winked and pressed a coin into the boy's hand.

"I don't know, my lord."

James ran back into the house and took the stairs two steps at a time. He knocked on Catherine's bedchamber door and was relieved to have it answered by her lady's maid Wright.

"May I speak to your mistress?" He smiled as his heart pounded.

"No, Lord Daventry," Wright said, bobbing and blushing.

"Will you tell her it is of grave importance?"

"No, I mean, that is to say, she is not here, my lord."

His relief fled and was replaced by a tightness in his chest that had nothing to do with being out of breath.

"She left in Sir Francis' carriage? And she didn't take you? Where is she going?"

Wright hesitated.

"If she told you not to tell me, I would not expect you to break her confidence."

"No, my lord."

"No, she didn't tell you not to tell me? Or no, she did tell you not to tell me?"

Wright looked confused. "She didn't mention you at all, my lord."

James bit his tongue and took a deep breath before saying, "Do you think Mrs. Lovelock would be upset if you told me where she has gone?"

Wright smiled. "No, my lord."

James nodded and waited.

"She has gone to Gretna Green, my lord. She is to be married!"

TWENTY

Catherine could usually manage to sleep sitting up in a carriage. But not this one. She was jounced and tossed about as many smaller people were apt to be when inside a poorly sprung carriage. She wondered why Sir Francis had not sat next to her so she might use his shoulder as a cushion and his weight to keep her in place.

However, Sir Francis preferred not to have her touching him. He liked to have her at a distance and to look at her. As he was doing now, seated across from her.

"My dearest Catherine."

"May I call you Francis?"

He paused. "Certainly."

"Francis," she said, testing the name. Perhaps Sir Francis was better. Nonsense, she could not go around putting *Sir* in front of her husband's name all the time. Could she?

"We will have many plans to make upon our return," Sir Francis said.

"Yes." Perhaps a wedding trip in the new year. She could send Arabella to Wales, to Mary.

"There is the matter of your house and my houses. I shall sell yours immediately. Yes, in Mayfair, I would expect a good price. I will keep my town house, which is more modest than yours, but I imagine we will be spending a good deal of our time in Kent."

Catherine felt dazed. "I'm sorry, Sir Francis, but you can't sell the house in Mayfair."

He smiled and reached across and patted her hand. "Of course I can, and in fact, I have already found a buyer."

"The buyer will have to discuss the sale of the house with my daughters. They will own the house, jointly."

"Your daughters? But it's your house."

"It is my house presently, but once I marry you, it will become Arabella's and Harry's and Mary's."

He pulled his hand away from hers. "What do you mean, once you marry me?"

A chill began to gnaw at Catherine's chest. "My husband's will was most unusual. Upon my remarriage, all that he left me reverts to his children."

"All? All the money, too? The shares in the bank?"

"He wanted me safe from fortune-hunters, you see—"

"Are you calling me a fortune-hunter?"

"Of course not. Who could? Everyone knows how you made your own wealth provisioning the navy. You're a man of commerce as well as a baronet. That is why I have always felt so sure of you."

"So sure of me that you bedded another man last night?"

"I told you, and I thought you believed me. Lord Daventry and I did nothing wrong in your house."

"What about in other houses, other places, mmm?"

She would not lie to her future husband and say she had been blameless.

"Once we are married, you will have my utmost fidelity," she said carefully.

He choked out a laugh. "But not your money." He rapped on the roof of the coach. "Stop at the next coaching inn."

The coachman acknowledged the order, and the carriage swayed onward.

There was silence between them. Finally, Catherine spoke. She would force Sir Francis to say what she already knew.

"Why will we stop?"

"We're not going to Gretna Green. You're getting out. I can't marry a penniless whore."

James stopped to change his horse at Duddenhoe End. As at all previous stops, he asked, "Has a carriage come through with a coat of arms on the door—a red shield with a black falcon on it? Yes, a man and a woman. The woman, small with golden hair?"

"Aye," said the ostler. "Will you be having this white horse here, my lord?"

James knelt and felt the horse's knee. Warm. "You've mistaken me for a fool who can't spot a lame horse. You must have a better mount available. I need speed, and I'm willing to pay for it. Handsomely. How long ago did the carriage with the falcon come through? And did they leave by the northern road?"

"About two hours ago, my lord. And nay."

"Which road did they take? Which road, man?"

"The carriage turned around and went back the way it came."

"Turned around?"

"Aye."

James slumped onto a bench. That carriage he had passed going the other direction about an hour ago. Had he looked at it carefully? No, he had been so caught up in overtaking a carriage headed north, he had not bothered to check any of the carriages heading in the opposite direction.

Imbecile.

But perhaps that meant Catherine had changed her mind.

"And the lady, the one with the golden hair? Did she look upset?"

"Aye, she did but less so once the gentleman left."

"The gentleman left her here?"

"He did."

"Where is she?"

"Inn."

James tossed him a coin.

"Will you be taking the bay then, my lord?" the ostler called after him.

Catherine sat in front of the fire in her room, wrapped in her tartan cloak. Tomorrow, she would send word to Wright at Ffoulkes Manor to pack everything and take her carriage and coachman and footman back to London. And she would find a coach here to take her back to London, as well. Or she could head west and be with her stepdaughter Harry at Sommerleigh. Or keep going north, towards the Dalrymple estate in Derbyshire and be with Arabella until Christmas.

There was a knock at the door.

"Mrs. Lovelock?"

He was here. Why must she alway encounter him when she was at a disadvantage? Half-naked in a dressmaker's. Frightened on the streets of London. Injured and wet in the fields of Kent. And, now, abandoned in Duddenhoe End.

The trollop no one will have unless they can also have her dead husband's money.

"Mrs. Lovelock? It's Lord Daventry."

She didn't want to answer the door. She wanted to throw herself out the window and run away. She wanted to shrivel up and die. But those were not feasible courses of action for Catherine Lovelock. Catherine Lovelock had to face things. Like Kate Cooksey would have. As Edward Lovelock would have expected her to.

"Catherine?"

Go away, Jamie. There's nothing for you in this room but ruination.

"Please," he said through the door.

The assured yet respectful *please* made her rise from her chair by the fire. That quiet word with no hint of supplication in it, no demand. Only expectation. How could she turn away a man who said that word in that way?

She went to the door and opened it. His hat crushed in one hand, tousled brown-golden curls, his gray eyes anxious. Now she was glad she had opened the door even though the alarums in her head became very loud. She didn't want him anxious.

"Lord Daventry," she said and bobbed. She could feel the ache between her legs as she pressed her thighs together to make her curtsy to him.

"I was passing. And I heard you were here."

"From whom?"

"Uh, the ostler, if you must know."

"Please come in, Lord Daventry."

"Are you sure? Perhaps we might go to the tavern or take a walk."

"Do as you wish, my lord. I am staying here."

She walked away from the door, leaving the decision in his hands. She cared nothing for scandal. She had already been caught in bed with him.

And her limp was gone. Her ankle had been cured by

time. Or by the desire to no longer appear damaged, weak, or pitiful in front of him.

"Thank you." The jingle of some coins. "Your discretion will be rewarded." He must be speaking to the innkeeper.

She heard the door close.

Twenty-One

The room had a bed. They were alone in a room with a bed. She had invited him into a room with a bed.

After all that had happened and after all his own dreams and thoughts about her, James expected he would feel a tension. Yet, he felt curiously at ease. Relieved. He had found her, and she was safe, she was not crying or injured, she had not married Ffoulkes.

Catherine stood at the other end of the room, near a window. She examined him.

"You followed me."

"Yes."

"You're not drunk, Lord Daventry."

"No."

"In fact, you're never drunk, are you?"

He looked at her carefully. "Am I such a bad actor?"

"No," Catherine said and smiled a very little bit. "It's just that I am such a good one."

"I see." He grinned. "I hope you'll keep my secret."

She mimed bringing an invisible key to her lips, placing it in her pout, turning it, and throwing it away.

There were many beautiful things about that gesture—the humor of it, the feeling he could trust her, her lips. Those bewitching lips. He was reminded of a soft kiss in a rank alley.

She turned towards the window. "That innkeeper thinks he knows what's going to happen in this room. Between us."

The tension James had thought absent now flooded the room even as blood flooded into his cock.

"He does?" James heard his own voice squeak. Damn, he sounded eight rather than twenty-eight.

"The question is," she almost whispered, "is he right?"

James' breath caught in his throat. "I think a gentleman would say it must be the lady's choice."

"Must it?" Her gaze was still directed out the window.

"When the gentleman was slapped the last time he kissed the lady."

Catherine's head turned, and she met his eyes. "I hit you not because you kissed me but because you stopped kissing me."

He looked at the floor and the distance between them. In three long strides, he could join her at the window and take her face in his hands and kiss her.

"If you had said that at the time," he raised his eyes to her, "things might have turned out very differently that night."

Might he cross to her now?

"I lost my temper. I apologize, Lord Daventry. It won't happen again."

He tucked his thumbs into his fists hanging loosely at his sides. "Which part won't happen again? The kissing or the losing of the temper or the blow?"

He had scarcely finished his question before a small body collided with his.

She had charged him, not waiting for his seduction and the careful kisses he had already planned in his head. And now he could not contain the fierce whirlwind who clawed at his clothes, who pulled his head down and demanded his mouth.

And that anguished moan. He thought he would spend in his breeches from that moan.

She released him and backed away, towards the bed.

"If I am to be accused of being a promiscuous woman," she gasped, her voice hoarse, "I might as well have the pleasure of it."

She pushed her cloak off and with one quick movement pulled her dress over her head. She kicked off her shoes and rolled down her stockings. She was in just her stays over a chemise and a petticoat. And then the petticoat was on the floor, and she turned her back to him.

"My lord." It was a plea. A desperate plea. It was the sound of a condemned prisoner begging for her life.

He walked to her and put his hands on the lace of the stays.

"Shall I?" he asked, almost in disbelief this was happening. To him. With her.

"Yes," she groaned.

He began to fumble with the lace, untying the knot and loosening the stays. But he couldn't resist dipping his head and kissing the skin where her neck joined to a milky-white shoulder. So soft, so warm. But she stepped away in the middle of his kiss and pulled off the loosened stays. She faced him again and brought her chemise over her head.

He saw her round, firm thighs edging into her generously curving hips. He saw her golden maidenhair covering her sex. Her abdomen, which bore the beautiful silvery stretch marks of her pregnancy with Arabella, and her slender waist. And her breasts, full and heavy and round, with their large pink areolas and exquisite nipples. Those breasts he had only seen once before but he felt he knew so well because he had conjured them so many times in his imagination.

He moved nearer to her, put his hands on her upper arms, felt her tremble.

"Catherine," he began.

She put her arms up around his neck and pulled his mouth down to hers.

All she knew was she wanted him. Close. As close as possible. If she could melt into his skin, she would. As they kissed again and again and he slid his hands down her back to cup her bottom, she found herself standing on tiptoe and lifting her leg to wrap around his. She was too damnably small, but she wanted her sex against his sex. She had to have it, and it made no difference he was still clothed. She had no thought except her hunger for him.

As she lifted her leg, he slid his hand farther down to just below her buttocks and lifted her by the haunches on both sides so he was holding her and both her legs were wrapped around his waist.

They were just as they had been in the alley. But, this time, she was going to have Jamie. Now. Nothing would stop her. Nothing could.

She felt the wetness in her crease, the throb of her pearl, and she rubbed her aching sex against the tip of his member that strained against the waistband of his breeches.

He broke off from kissing her for a moment and grinned a devil's grin and shifted all her weight to just one of his arms. He bent his head and used his free hand to bring one of her breasts and its nipple to his mouth. As he sucked, the most delicious, piercing sensation connected Catherine's breast and groin, and she cried out.

"Jamie!"

She could not help herself, could not stop herself from rubbing against his still-clothed member more quickly. The rough friction was almost too much for her, and she thought she might climax at any moment even as her sex was hungry to be filled.

"The bed, Jamie," she pleaded. "I need you. Please."

He released her breast from his mouth and carried her towards the bed. He pulled the counterpane back, slid the bedwarmer out, and put her on the bed. He took the bedwarmer to the fire and placed it on the hearth.

Catherine watched him undress through the haze of her lust. Greatcoat and tailcoat and waistcoat. Cravat and shirt. She saw that beautiful torso. Golden skin to match his golden-brown head of hair. His chest, the flat muscle she had felt through his shirt when she had clung to him. And his long, lean flanks that flexed as he leaned over to take off his boots and hose. He straightened up, and as he put his hands to the buttons of the fall of his buff breeches, she stayed him with a gesture.

"Come here," she said as softly as she could, knowing her voice was graveled with desire. She curled her hand in a beckoning gesture and sat up and put her legs over the edge of the bed.

He came and stood in front of her. On his perfectly flat abdomen, a trail of almost invisible golden-brown hair started at his navel and descended down into his breeches. She touched that hair with one fingertip and followed the trail down to the waistband and over the rigid bulge under his front fall.

He gasped and rested one of his hands on her back. She undid the buttons and freed his shaft. As it sprang out, erect, Catherine was unsurprised to find his cock was long. But she was unnerved by its sizable girth. It was no match for her tall, slender Jamie. This was the phallus of a primitive warrior, a Visigoth, a Viking. This was a battering ram. A crude weapon.

James shuddered as she tried to wrap her hand around

him; her thumb could not meet her middle finger. The end of his cock was already wet. She put the tip in her mouth and licked the end, looking up at him. He was looking down at her, and she could not read his face. It didn't matter. She had his cock in her hand, and she knew he wanted her.

She took him into her mouth.

James was overwhelmed by his view of his shaft in Catherine's small, rosy mouth, her large breasts in the middle distance, and, in the background, her lap, where her body forked into legs and a fine golden fuzz shielded her labia. At any minute, from the image alone, never mind the warmth and wetness and licking he felt on his cock, he would spill like an overexcited boy. This was not how he wanted to bed Catherine. He had to take control of the situation.

"Lie back," he said.

She lay back while he stepped out of his breeches. He swung her legs onto the mattress and got in beside her, wedging his body against hers and sliding her to the center of the bed.

She was on her side, and her breathing was both deep and rapid. As she put her hands on his chest and started kissing his skin, licking his nipples, he could feel her quivering.

And she was making sounds he had never heard before from any woman, sounds of agitated arousal, almost small screams. He put one hand between her legs and felt her wetness, and as he did so, her hands and mouth on his chest became more frenzied, as if she were trying to devour him. One of her hands dragged down his body and grasped his cock. He slid his fingers up her smooth folds to find her hardened pearl and brushed it. She did scream then, muffling it into his chest. He kept his thumb lightly on her pearl and slid his other fingers down and found her opening. He put a finger inside and started rubbing the roof of the opening, just behind her pearl. As he moved his finger in and out of her, softly brushing her pearl with his thumb, her head went back, arching her whole body up off the mattress.

"Jamie," she panted, her voice half harsh whisper, half groan, her hand running up and down his shaft. "I need you inside me."

His arousal had only increased with her frenzy in the bed. He had never felt so hard, nearing the point of pain. He wanted to be inside her, but he thought he might spend very quickly once he was.

But she had told him what she wanted, and it was what he wanted, too. He could not remember wanting anything, any woman more. He took his finger out of her opening and rolled to kneel between her legs. He held himself up with his arms, fearful of his weight on her. Still her hand was on his cock, stroking him, not letting him go.

"Catherine," he said, and she allowed him to replace her hand with his own. He laid his sex against hers, his hardness against her dripping softness. She put her legs up and out, kicking the counterpane off, pointing her toes to the ceiling. Her small hands were on his hip bones, pulling his pelvis towards hers, urging him, wanting him.

The silk of her folds and then her inner warmth and wetness and tightness, and so much of her frenzy was suddenly contained even as she contained him.

"Jamie," she cooed. She was still. Her blue eyes looked up at him. She licked her lips. A drop of sweat ran down her neck and between her breasts.

He was lost in a welter of feeling. He wanted to hold still, to savor this moment, the incredible sweetness of being inside her while he looked at her face and her breasts. But he also wanted to thrust and move and buck.

She made it easy for him. She pushed her rounded hips up off the bed to hold all of him, and she began to rock.

"I'm sorry," she whispered. "I…can't wait."

He joined her then, pulling back when she pulled back, thrusting in when she raised her hips to his. He leaned over to brush his lips against hers when he thrust. Her wildness returned, and she grabbed at his hair, his back, his shoulder blades. He supported himself with one hand and twisted his other between their bodies so as to be able to graze her pearl as he thrust.

"Shall I touch you here?" he asked.

"No, no, no, oh Jamie, yes, yes!" she cried out, looking into his eyes.

She sneezed. She shuddered and stopped thrusting up towards him. He could feel her sex close even more tightly around his, her upper body convulsing in perfect synchrony with the lower body spasms that gripped his member. He stilled his hand and waited.

She stared at him with glazed eyes. Her breath was ragged but became slower, more even. She whispered something that might have been *my mastiff*, but that made no sense to him.

He bent his head to hers and kissed each of her blonde eyebrows. Those marvelously expressive brows. She grabbed his head with both her hands and kissed him deeply, forcing her tongue into his mouth as she started pushing up against him once more.

He began to thrust again. He was so aroused by *her* arousal, her climax, he could not stop himself. Within a minute, he was consumed by pleasure and spilling himself into her, clenching on top of her, looking down at her as she held his flanks. He collapsed on top of her, forgetting himself for a moment, and then tried to raise himself off her in a panic. But she held him tight.

"I won't break. I'm not made of porcelain," she breathed in his ear.

He rolled over, taking her with him so he was under her and she was perched on his chest and abdomen.

"It's crushing you, not breaking you, that has me worried," he said and lifted his head up to put his mouth on her perfect white shoulder. "And you *look* like you're made of porcelain."

She purred contentedly, lying on top of him, her cheek to his chest. He stroked her back, long soft strokes from her shoulders all the way down to her buttocks until he noticed she had some gooseflesh. Holding her to him with one arm, he reached for the counterpane and drew it over them. As he did so, he felt the stickiness at his groin for the first time. Some of it was her, undoubtedly; she had been very ready for him. But most of it was him, his seed.

He had not used a French Letter. He, who had always been the most scrupulous of all the rakes.

"Catherine," he began.

She raised her head from his chest and looked at him. "Kate."

"Kate—"

"Jamie," she hummed and kissed him on the breastbone.

"Kate, I did not use…I had no French Letter…"

She began to shake. She was laughing. She moved herself up his body so her face was above his, her beautiful breasts resting on his collarbone. He was very interested in what she might say when she was done laughing, but he couldn't help taking his hands off her back to bring them to the sides of her breasts. The full, soft globes curved perfectly into his palms. These breasts of his warrior goddess. His unbound Viola. He began to rub his thumbs over her nipples and was gratified to feel the tips grow erect under his touch.

"Jamie." She kissed the side of his mouth. "The advantage," she kissed his chin, "of bedding," she kissed the angle of his jaw, "an old woman," she nibbled on his earlobe and spoke softly in his ear, "is there are no babies to worry about."

He turned his head to hers so they were eye to eye, nose to nose, mouth to mouth. He covered her lips with his and kissed her deeply, slowly, luxuriating in the taste of her mouth, the feel of her tongue, the warm scent of her, all the while rubbing her nipples.

When she broke finally from the kiss to breathe, he whispered, "I don't see an old woman. I see a goddess."

"Jamie," she said, her voice strained. She began to move atop him.

Her transient peace was gone, shattered. He was holding her breasts and rubbing her peaks with his thumbs, alternating between quick, soft brushes and rougher, slower strokes. Her groin throbbed in time to the movements of his thumbs, and she began to feel her sex dampen and widen.

He moved lower down the bed, still beneath her, and took a thumb off one nipple. She felt a pang of loss, which quickly turned into a flash of the most delirious pleasure as he took her breast in his mouth and began to suck. Heavenly, sharp raptures shook her. He lightly bit the nipple and then transferred his lips to the other breast. He kissed, he licked, he suckled. And when he nibbled on her other breast, she raised her head up, neck straining, and sneezed just before her entire body was rocked by a climax that started at the tips of her breasts and spread in ever-widening circles across her entire body, like the ripples from a stone cast into a still pond.

She collapsed to his side.

"My breasts," she said between pants, "are very susceptible."

He took her hand and pressed her palm flat to his mouth and kissed it. He looked at her with those crystalline gray eyes whose corners crinkled, and she knew he was smiling under her hand. She moved her hand to his cheek, and, indeed, the smile was there.

"Kate," he said through his grin. "I would say they are exquisitely susceptible."

As she slid her hand off his cheek to fill her fingers with his hair again, a weariness came over her. When one has fought against something for months, as she had, even a temporary surrender was exhausting.

She thought of sending him away to find a room and a bed of his own. To draw a line. It was this one time and this one time only. They were not lovers. They would never be lovers. That was an impossibility.

But she did not think he would understand. And what harm could there be in letting him stay close for a few more hours?

Every harm. Every danger. But for the moment, she could not bring herself to care about the peril of letting him stay in her bed.

She turned and pushed back into him as he gathered her in, his chest against her back, his arm pillowing her head, his other arm around her body, his hand between her breasts, his knees behind her knees. Once they were positioned thus, he went completely still, save the rise and fall of his chest.

Catherine felt his stillness infect her, and the muscles in her neck softened. And she slept.

She awoke some hours later, having felt something change behind her, although he had not shifted his position.

"My lord?" she whispered.

"Yes?" he said, seemingly fully awake. He did not move.

She nudged back against him, pressing into his tumescence.

His mouth was just behind her ear. "I apologize for waking you, Mrs. Lovelock."

"Mrs. Lovelock?" She laughed. "I think I'm a little naked for that mode of address."

"You called me *my lord*."

Very slowly, she turned to him, reluctant to break the warm touch of his body against hers. But, in turning, there was a thrilling friction over her breasts as he kept his arm in place, his forearm abrading her nipples until she was facing him and his arm was curled around her back, her breasts brushing against his chest.

She had to see his eyes. There they were. Gray, soft, maybe a little drowsy.

"What should I call you, my lord?" she asked. She put her hand to his hair, that hair.

He caressed her spine. He bit his lower lip, as if in thought. "Well, the last time you spoke to me, Kate, a few hours ago, you called me Jamie."

"Jamie," she said and kissed him.

He had slept heavily, surprisingly heavily, considering their circumstances. He would have thought his mind would have been vigilant and alert, but his sleep was dreamless and deep.

As he came to himself, feeling her pressed to him, sheltered by him, he thought that *this*, this position, this flesh-to-flesh contact with *this* woman, this was something worth dying for. Or living for.

He opened his eyes, and all he could see was her head of golden curls. But he felt her chest rising and falling with each breath. His hand between her breasts felt the thump of her heart. Her sweet bottom pushed into his groin. And now, undeniably, his member began to harden. He held still, holding her, coiled around her, keeping himself quiet.

But she woke and spoke to him and turned to him and said his name and kissed him. And when she called him *Jamie*, it pierced him with such sweetness that he kissed her back almost as he might kiss one of his sisters.

But Catherine was having none of that. She put her arms around his neck and filled her hands with his hair, drawing his head towards her, kissing him as she first had in the alley. Soft, so soft, so light. Then forceful, avid, her breasts against his chest, her thighs against his cock.

She moved her lips from his mouth but only to kiss his jaw, his neck, the base of his throat. Quite without meaning to, James had gone from lying on his side to lying flat as if she had tipped him over. This tiny woman had melted him onto his back and was on top of him and moving her kisses down from his collarbone to his chest. She held her pelvis high off of him and with her mouth on his lower chest, her own sex was just above his. Her cleft touched his cock, just the lightest of grazes and then a pressing, a prodding, a rubbing.

He throbbed to feel how wet she was.

She looked up at his face. "I must have you," she whispered. He felt only capable of a nod.

She used her hand to hold his shaft and lowered herself down onto him.

Ahhh.

Penetrating her was impossibly arousing, even more so than it had been a few hours earlier. He was fully erect but only partially inside her. He immediately wanted to grab her hips and pull her down so he would be deep inside her. But he resisted. Instead, he rested his hands on the sides of her thighs as she mastered the depth and speed of their coupling with her movements.

He was rewarded with the sight of her irresistible breasts moving up and down, her alabaster throat as her head was thrown back, her golden hair falling in a ripple. She arched her spine, and he could no longer see her throat, only her breasts and abdomen. He placed his hands on her waist and supported her as she moved on his shaft in a pressured, jerking rhythm. Her walls clenched his cock. Her halting breaths quickened, and she let out a moan.

A moan that was interrupted by a sneeze.

She came out of her backward lean, straightened, gave him a dazed smile that hardened his member even more, and fell forward onto his chest with a little whimper. And even as she seemed to have gone from all straining hunger to all soft satisfaction, her hips kept moving, and she took him deeper and deeper into herself.

"Mmm," she said, humming against his chest. "Mmmm."

"Kate," he whispered.

She gripped his upper arms and sneezed as her body shook again. He thought she might rest, lying on his chest, but she continued the sinuous rocking of her pelvis against his.

He was in the sweetest of agonies. He could not bear it. He had to control the tempo of their coupling, and he could not do that from underneath her.

He held her to his chest and quickly rolled over. He was on his elbows and forearms and knees, and she was lying on the mattress, her upper half completely caged by his body, her legs wrapped around his waist. He hovered over her, and she looked up at him, her mouth open, her skin flushed. Her arms were up over her head, her fingers buried in his hair.

"Kate," he grunted.

"Jamie," she gasped.

He quickened his thrusting. He wanted his whole body on her, but he held back, still worried about hurting her.

She read his mind. "You won't hurt me."

He put his whole body against her then, gave her all his weight, pressing her into the mattress as he released in his own spasm of bliss.

After a short time, she sighed, and he suddenly feared he *had* hurt her. He closed his arms around her back and rolled on his side so his weight was off her, but they were still pressed tightly together, and he was still inside her, just barely.

She moved a little, but he tightened his grip, and she exhaled and stayed still.

"Just a minute more," he said. "Please."

"Of course," she murmured.

He was washed by a flood of emotion. Although they were naked and had just climaxed and he was still inside her, he did not believe this feeling had anything to do with copulation.

"That's been a minute, surely," she said, and he loosened his arms and she rolled away.

"Yes," he said and got up on his elbow and touched her face. "Thank you, Kate."

Later, she curled herself into the side of his body and rested her head on the hollow between his chest and his shoulder, and he put his arm around her body so his hand stretched down below her bottom where he stroked the backs of her thighs with featherlight touches.

She's mine, he thought as he drifted off.

He woke to cold sunshine streaming in the window and an empty room. Her little trunk was gone.

There was a sealed note left for him with the innkeeper.

J—

The mail coach is leaving shortly. I will travel to where my youngest daughter is staying. I must remind myself I am, after all, a mother. Thank you for another rescue, even though I assure you I was not in need of it. Again.

There was so much loveliness in all that passed between us last night, and I thank you for indulging me.
Good luck to you and goodbye.

Mrs. Edward Lovelock

Part Three

Twenty-Two

His whole life changed when his brother died.

With William's death, James' dreams of joining the navy also died. He became Marquess of Daventry in his brother's place and heir to the Middlewich duchy.

He also inherited Enfield as his valet. So when the idle and discontented James began his career as a rake three years later, exploring the pleasures and vices of London, Enfield was ready.

It was Enfield who ensured the young lord always had a ready supply of French Letters. He was not going to let this heir go the way of his brother. Enfield explained to James that the French Pox, also known as syphilis, came from lying with women who had lain with other men who had the pox. Although sensation was thought to be blunted by a French Letter, pleasure was still obtainable, and the sheaths prevented unwanted bastards as well as the transmission of diseases, including the French Pox.

Having borne witness to William's horrible disfigurement and his ravings echoing through the castle in the last weeks of his life, James needed very little persuading. He used a French Letter, without fail, and he took care never to drink so much that he would forget his phallic protection.

When James lectured his friend Thomas on the use of French Letters, Thomas laughed and said he had been using them for seven years and was James only learning to whore now? James had better stick close to Thomas, who knew all the prettiest doxies.

James thus learned to satisfy his masculine appetites safely, cautiously, under the instruction of both Enfield and Thomas.

His two teachers were a study in opposites. Enfield had a wife of thirty years who lived in a cottage on the grounds of Middlewich Castle. The valet said Mrs. Enfield was a lovely, warm woman who had given him five children and who put up with his cold feet and he would be a fool to anger her by wandering into a brothel. He was always content to wait until he got home to lie with his wife. Thomas, on the other hand, was never content, often bedding three whores a night, seemingly insatiable.

James found the middle road. He could take pleasure when it came his way, but he was not driven to it. Drink, women, gambling—he pursued nothing to excess. He chose moderation in all things.

His friends said he was barely a rake. The oft-repeated joke was that the future Duke of Middlewich was a rake by means of courtesy title only.

Then, at the age of twenty-three, James suddenly became more dissolute. His friends came to know him as a dissipated marquess—perpetually tipsy and joking. A lighthearted lothario with a bottomless thirst and an inexhaustible fund of innuendo and salacious stories.

The earnest James was gone.

Rake was a courtesy title no longer.

His sea-change came, amusingly enough, whilst at the seaside. At Brighton in that summer of 1813, James and Thomas and their friends all had gone whoring as they were wont to do. They had escaped the swelter of London at the end of the Season and had traveled down for some fun along the shore, following in the wake of the Prince Regent and his court.

They arrived in the afternoon, and by the evening, Thomas had sniffed out the best brothel. The choice was not extensive since Brighton, even when swollen with visitors, was not a large place. James' friends all claimed the few available courtesans, so he shrugged, bought a small glass of whisky, and settled in a chair in the outer parlor to read a newspaper and wait for his friends.

An older man came in and found his favorite whore occupied with Thomas. The older man grumbled and sat in the wing chair opposite James. James offered him his paper, but the man waved it away politely. He had an accent but spoke English well. He had dark hair, dark eyes, dark whiskers, the olive skin of the Mediterranean. He eyed James' whisky, and James called for another glass and a bottle to be brought. He knew the man would have a long wait since Thomas liked to take his time, had boundless energy, and always tried multiple positions with a doxy who was new to him.

They toasted to the whores of Brighton.

The man's name was Astigar Zubiondoa. He was a Basque, a merchant captain. He currently carried barrels of port wine on his ship but confessed to a personal preference for Scottish whisky. He had crossed the Atlantic Ocean to the Americas many times in his youth but now plied the shorter, but still dangerous, passage between the Iberian Peninsula and England. He liked to come into Shoreham-by-Sea with his ship, leave the unloading and selling to his eldest son so he could make the short overland trip to Brighton for the pretty ladies, more refined than those he would find in a shipping port. He regaled James with stories of his travels, of evading warships and pirates, sailing through monstrous storms. James topped up his glass again and again, and Astigar grew more and more voluble.

The man mentioned San Sebastian, a town held by the French and currently under siege by the British. The hair on the back of James' neck stood up. Before leaving London yesterday, James had heard word of the Marquess of Wellington's failed assault on the heavy fortifications there last week.

Astigar knew San Sebastian well. He had grown up there. There was an island in the bay called Santa Clara. It was a very small island with steep sides. It was thought to be impossible to climb. But he knew how to do that. He had done it many times with his friends growing up. There was a way on the west side. There were handholds. One could get to the top easily.

James laughed. He told Astigar he used to love to scale impossibly high things, but the only climbing he did nowadays was out of bedchamber windows when husbands came home too early. It was a lie, but it seemed to endear him to the merchant, who laughed at the young rogue and drank more whisky.

James then told another entirely false story about climbing Ben Nevis in Scotland when he was seventeen and the fine whisky he had drunk from a leather canteen on the way up and the Highlander's daughter he had enjoyed on the way down. In the telling of his tale, he wove in questions about San Sebastian and the way up Santa Clara's cliffs.

When Thomas was finally done with Astigar's favorite whore, the Basque wine merchant got up, swayed a bit, and stumbled off to have his pleasure with the likely exhausted woman. James escorted Thomas and the other rakes back to their inn, made sure all were snoring in their beds, hired the best horse he could find, and rode out for London, leaving a note to explain his absence. Some problem with an unpaid tailor's bill that his father insisted he handle immediately.

He arrived in London late in the afternoon, and at his club, he found the man who had told him about Wellington's failed assault on San Sebastian. It was a baronet named Fudge. Sir Charles Fudge was a bit of a fool, but he had a brother-in-law high up in the government who was the source of his news. Would Sir Charles or his brother-in-law know how James could reach someone at this hour who might be interested in some information about San Sebastian?

After a series of false leads, bureaucratic blockades, and noncommittal answers, James finally found himself at midnight in a rowboat with empty oarlocks in the middle of the Thames with Mr. Bulverton of the Home Secretary's office. They had been towed there by another boat and then anchored and left.

"This is very private," James said, shivering despite the heat of the August night and the suffocating humidity.

"Yes."

"How are we going to leave this boat? I don't fancy a swim in the sewage of the Thames."

"No, my lord. When you have told me what you know, I will unshutter this lantern, which is a signal for the boat that towed us here to come back and pick us up."

"*If* I tell you what I know."

"Shall I unshutter the lantern now? It's all the same to me." Mr. Bulverton made a move towards the lantern.

"No! I mean to say...I just thought I would be talking to someone in the Royal Navy."

"You tell me what you know, and if it is good information and of use, I'll tell the navy. I am what is called the middle man. The local middle man, my lord."

James hesitated. This ordinary Mr. Bulverton with his ink-stained cuffs was so far from James' idea of a spymaster or a navy hero. On the other hand, a young Marquess of Daventry was likely just as far from anyone else's idea of a spy.

Perhaps that was the point.

James spied a glimmer of hope. He might have found a way out of the dullness that informed his life.

"If I tell you and the information is of use, would you let me help you again? In other ways?"

Mr. Bulverton said gravely, "We are all servants of the crown, my lord. It would be, uh, foolish to deny any of us, even a future Duke of Middlewich, the chance to serve, the chance to be useful."

Mr. Bulverton's words to James were like a swallow of cold water to a man in a desert.

James told him everything about the island of Santa Clara. How it was in the bay outside San Sebastian and would provide a perfect location for mounting guns and firing on the fortifications of the town. How it was thought to be unscalable by almost everyone, including the French, but there was a way up the cliffs on the west-by-northwest side. How it might easily be stormed by two hundred men or so. How it might be the answer to Wellington's problems with San Sebastian's seemingly impenetrable fortifications.

Mr. Bulverton asked many questions. Satisfied at last, he unshuttered the lantern and said, "Not a word of this to anyone, Lord Daventry."

A month later, James read in the newspaper that the island of Santa Clara had been taken at the end of August by a small force of British sailors, and eleven days later the French garrison at San Sebastian had fallen, in part due to guns placed on the island by those self-same sailors who had valiantly crawled up the steep cliffs.

Mr. Bulverton had proven he knew how to pass information up the line. James had proven he could gather that information. And keep his mouth shut.

James was unsurprised the next spring when Arthur Wellesley, already the Most Honorable Marquess of Wellington, was named the Duke of Wellington in reward for being the conquering hero on the Iberian Peninsula.

By that time, James had behaved wickedly at several house parties and hunts—fallen over his feet, slurred drunkenly, told bawdy stories that verged on the obscene, groped a willing and mature countess, and leered at several maidens. The behavior then spilled over into the Season.

Such a flirt, the older ladies of the *ton* said behind their fans. Maybe more than a flirt. He was rumored to be quite a swordsman. Wouldn't he be a fun romp in bed? That slouch. Those tight breeches. Those seductive half-lidded eyes. And terribly amusing when he had gulped a glass or five. Really, Lord Daventry, who had been such a serious young man, was turning into a wickedly dissolute rake. Almost a wit, one might say. No, more of a flirt. One *must* have him at one's rout. He was *such fun*.

James felt he was finally living the life he was meant for. And the deception, playing the naughty boy, was a good measure of the fun. Especially when it was spiced with a little danger. There was not much danger, but there was some, surely.

He welcomed his new, scandalous reputation. His father raged at him even more than previously, if such a thing were possible. James felt badly for his mother, but only a little. After all, she had never stopped James' beatings. His sisters seemed blissfully ignorant of the stories about him, and not a one of them ever looked at him askance or scolded him. For that, he was glad.

Isabella's room at Madame Flora's became the chosen rendezvous point for James and Mr. Bulverton. James, as would be expected of a rake, came openly through the front door of the brothel. Mr. Bulverton came through an underground passage that connected the brothel to a bakery. That accounted for the flour on his clothes when he came to collect James' information and give him his instructions.

Mr. Bulverton would also collect Isabella's information. She was of French extraction on her mother's side, which was the only side she had, really, as the illegitimate daughter of a prostitute. But she had been born in England. Her mother, a notorious Parisian *putain* and mistress to more than one aristocrat, had fled the terror of the French revolution and settled in London. Isabella had been born four years later. She was fluent in French but also affected a French accent when she spoke English. She was well known to male visitors from France—merchants, displaced aristocrats, others. She was their whore of choice and had been successful for a long time in teasing secrets from them. She said she acted like a child and said stupid things and the men couldn't help but explain to her how wrong she was before they tupped her again.

James had bedded Isabella only once. Isabella had insisted. "*Chéri*, you must know me, for *vraisemblance*, for the verisimilitude. After all, all of London thinks I am your favorite, *sans exception*."

They had spent an agreeable afternoon in bed so James knew her birthmarks and her scent and Isabella could faithfully describe his cock and where he was ticklish.

But, in truth, the languid Isabella did not arouse James.

He craved a woman with more spirit, more energy. An intelligence. A wit. A sparkle. A woman of the world who was still sweet. A strong woman who was still vulnerable. And who might be vulnerable to him. Who could both swoon and keep her head.

A woman like Viola of *Twelfth Night*.

Of course, he had never met such a woman.

Until Catherine.

And now she had bolted.

He went back to London and found himself on her street two or three times a day, looking up at windows, trying to spy some movement. He called formally once a day and was always told Mrs. Lovelock was still not at home.

Twenty-Three

James cursed when he got the letter on Christmas Eve.

He was in Middlewich. He had longed to stay in London and wait for Catherine's return, but he had promised his mother to come home at Christmastide, so he had made the journey. He might take some comfort in his sisters' company, anyway.

James had not seen his friend Thomas in London for well over a month, but he did not expect a letter from him. They were not men who wrote letters to each other. The letter forwarded from London and arriving in Middlewich on Christmas Eve was, therefore, a surprise. Thomas had written the missive weeks ago, and it had likely gotten delayed somewhere between Sommerleigh and London and then also *en route* to Middlewich.

The letter was a greeting and an invitation. Thomas' wife's stepmother and sister were coming for Christmas, and Thomas would be drowning in women, and would James like to join the festivities and rescue Thomas since it was well-nigh impossible to drag his wife Harry from her mathematics and all the entertaining of the Lovelock ladies would fall on

Thomas' shoulders? With his numerous sisters, James must surely know how to amuse genteel females? Thomas felt he himself would be hard-pressed to come up with suitable topics of conversation.

James fidgeted through the midnight church services and the services on Christmas day itself. He helped his sisters decorate an indoor tree in honor of Queen Charlotte who had died in November. She was the one who had brought the custom from the continent, still rarely practiced in England, of a decorated tree on Christmas.

On Christmas night, he kissed his sisters and said goodbye to his father and mother.

"Where are you going?" his father asked.

"To see Thomas. The Earl Drake."

"The old Earl Drake was a good man. His son, your friend?" The duke made a grimace of disapproval. "A wastrel, like you. A rakehell. How he could live and my William be taken from us, I will never know. But I have heard the young earl has married recently. A common chit of some kind who is very rich."

"The Countess Drake's father could have bought a dozen knighthoods, if he had wished to," James said evenly.

His father harrumphed. "It's good he did not. It sounds like he knew his place, at least." The duke leaned forward and spoke *sotto voce*. "And I hear her mother was a whore."

James slouched and let his eyelids droop and gave a lazy smile. "The Lady Drake's mother was, I believe, the daughter of a tailor. Her stepmother was an actress before she married the countess' father."

"Like I said," his father yawned, "a whore."

James gave instructions to Enfield to enjoy his time with his wife in Middlewich and to return to London with James' luggage after the new year. No, he was off to see Thomas. No, they did not stand on ceremony at Sommerleigh, he could get by with very few clothes, just a saddle bag. Thomas' man Jackson would be willing to shave him, and, no, James did not want a valet, and he especially did not want the redoubtable Mrs. Enfield angry at him for stealing her husband away early after they had been so many months in London.

And, in truth, James did not want a chaperone. Even one as understanding as Enfield.

At dawn, he saddled a horse. He could be at Sommerleigh by noon.

He left his horse in the stall next to Thomas' stallion Octavius. Two grooms quickly had his mount's saddle off and were currying and watering the horse. Even when he had been faced with financial ruin, Thomas always had the best horsemen in the county in his employ.

James stopped for a moment while still inside the stables and tried, in vain, to use his fingers to arrange his hair. Finally, he gave up. Besides, maybe Catherine liked his hair disarrayed? She had put her hands in it so many times that night at the inn in Duddenhoe End.

As he crossed the stable yard, he heard voices. Women's voices. Catherine's voice. He rounded the corner and saw Catherine walking down the drive towards the house. There were two other women with her and his friend Thomas, but all he really saw was Catherine.

"Jamie!" Thomas called out and strode to him and clasped him in a hug. "I got no message you were coming. Happy Christmas!"

"I was at the castle when I received your invitation quite late on Christmas Eve. Yes, happy Christmas, Tom."

The three women had reached them at this point. Harriet, tall and thin with wild tendrils of brown hair, looking rather fierce but a good deal healthier than when James had last seen her, at her wedding. Some color in her cheeks, some more flesh on her still-spare form.

Arabella, a younger version of Catherine, small and rosy and blonde and smiling.

And Catherine. Kate.

James bowed. "Lady Drake. Mrs. Lovelock. Miss Lovelock. Happy Christmas to you all."

He had met all three of them last spring. No one would think it odd he remembered their names.

He tried very hard not to let his gaze linger on Catherine, but it was extremely difficult. She was beautiful, her cheeks pink, a blue bonnet covering her hair. The blue matched her eyes. She held holly in her gloved hands.

"I see you have been gathering greenery."

She met his eyes and smiled. "Yes, Lord Daventry. We have been having what Harry calls a *good tramp*. The grounds are extraordinary. I think I have never seen a place as pretty as Sommerleigh."

Thomas laughed. "It's plain you have never been to Middlewich then and seen the castle and the gardens there. Someday, when the old Duke Crosspatch is away in London, we'll have Jamie take us up to the castle and show us all around."

Arabella's eyes shone. "Oh, yes, please. That would be lovely."

Harriet—no, she was Harry—tugged at Thomas' sleeve. "Luncheon."

"Oh, yes, my wife is hungry," Thomas said. "Come, let's all go in before hunger leads to a fit of temper."

Catherine laughed and started walking towards the house. "I find it hard to believe Harry is hungry. Lord Drake, if you only knew the trouble I always had in getting her to leave her mathematics and come to eat." Her voice trembled a bit, but James thought it likely he was the only one who noticed.

Thomas thumped his chest. "Country air and long walks, there's nothing for it!"

As they approached the front door of the house, James lingered outside, and after Arabella, Harry, and Thomas entered, he said to Catherine under his breath, "Why did you run away, Kate?"

"Please." She turned to him, her eyes beseeching. "Not now. Let me be happy now."

"I only—" he started, but she had gone into the house. He finished alone, "—want your happiness."

But, during luncheon, he admitted to himself he wanted his own happiness, too. More than anything, he wanted to be near Catherine. Catherine herself was gay at the dining table, suggesting a game of hoodman blind this afternoon to keep their blood coursing. He seconded the notion, knowing he would have agreed to anything she said, but the rest of the group was not enthusiastic.

Harry gazed at the ceiling and said she had something upstairs she must take a quick peek at. Something with a proof she was writing. Thomas said he was tired and wanted to sit in the library with James. Arabella said she wanted to read her novel the Dalrymples had given her for Christmas, *Rob Roy* by Mr. Walter Scott, did Lord Daventry know it, it was most dreadfully exciting, and she loved everything Scottish, didn't he? Catherine laughed and said she was defeated and she would read, as well. But tonight they would play Snapdragon and no one would tell her no.

James ate steadily, realizing he had not really eaten anything since receiving Thomas' letter on Christmas Eve. He needed his strength. He had eleven days in the same house with Catherine. Eleven days to win her. Eleven days to woo her.

In the library, Thomas poured them each a small whisky.

"To your marriage, Tom."

"Yes, thank you. To my marriage and to Sommerleigh." They drank.

James looked around the library. "You know I haven't been here since I told you to marry for money."

"Yes, since you told me to marry my mother-in-law."

James laughed a trifle too heartily. "Well, I was mistaken in that, I agree. But you seem to have settled quite happily with your choice of a Countess Drake."

Thomas flung himself into a chair. "It's the damnedest thing, Jamie. I have only just realized I'd never had a conversation of substance with a woman before I married Harry. You have a mother and sisters, of course, but my sister Jane married when I was very young…"

James knew Thomas' sister Jane was a sad subject for him. "Are you sure you've ever had a conversation of substance with *anyone*, Tom?"

"Well, no, you're right, maybe not." Thomas smiled. "And certainly, with Harry, I can't follow a lot of what she says."

"You've not been to Madame Flora's or to London recently."

A silence. "No."

"That's a change."

"Don't niggle at me, Jamie, just come out and say what you have to say."

James looked down at his now-empty glass. "I wondered if you had found that something had changed irrevocably for you after you bedded your wife, "

Thomas got up and poured another finger of whisky into his glass and came over with the decanter and gave James another finger, too.

"Happy Christmas," he said.

"Happy Christmas," James echoed.

They drank.

"Well, I guess *this* is actually the damnedest thing, Jamie."

Thomas crossed to the window and stared out. "I haven't bedded her."

James kept silent.

"I know, I know, here I am, the biggest whoremonger in London, and I haven't fornicated with my own wife. But it's not to be. It was part of our agreement when we married. I got her money, she got to keep her virginity and her mathematics. This whole Christmas and having her family here is just on sufferance, you know. Otherwise, she would be up in the attic sixteen hours of the day, doing whatever she does with numbers up there. That's what she's doing right now."

"I would have thought those circumstances would bring you to London more, rather than less."

"I would have thought so, too." James couldn't see Thomas' face, but his voice sounded angry. "However, when I go to London, I only long to be back here."

James walked to the window and turned his back to it so he was looking at his friend.

"Do you love her?"

Thomas smiled, but there was a bitterness to his smile.

"Love? I don't know what that is. I know what copulation is. I know what friendship is, thanks to you. But I don't know what love is."

James nodded. "I see."

"And, even if I did, I don't think Harry would ever love me back."

"Because…why? Because you're not good enough?" It was the question James had asked himself every day since waking up alone in the inn at Duddenhoe End.

Thomas looked confused. "No. Because Harry probably can't. She has room in her for only one love and that's mathematics. Do you know she's never told her stepmother that she loves her?"

"That doesn't mean she is intrinsically incapable of love, for God's sake, man."

"I know, I know. But can you imagine falling in love with someone you think will never say *I love you* back? It would be like shouting into the void."

I know, James said silently. *I think I am shouting into the same void.*

They did play Snapdragon after dinner. James burnt his tongue. Thomas burnt his fingers. Arabella snatched the most raisins from the flaming brandy bowl.

"Oh, Mama, that means I will meet my true love within a year!" Arabella announced. Catherine smiled thinly at that.

James thought the blue flames of the brandy bowl were enormously becoming to Catherine.

Later that night, he lay in his bed in his usual room at Sommerleigh, feeling he had made no progress with Catherine.

While he had waited for her to return to London, he had met with Mr. Bulverton in Isabella's room. There had been the mildest of reproofs from Mr. Bulverton about James going to Sir Francis' house party, almost as if he had expected James to do something of the sort. And Isabella had airily told him in passing that Mrs. Lovelock thought he, James, was too drunk and too silly.

Today he had worked hard at not being silly. True, he had had two fingers of whisky after luncheon with Thomas in the library, but nothing more than that despite Thomas' excellent cellar and his own desire for Dutch courage. He could not be accused of being drunk.

But there had been nothing but friendly camaraderie and politeness between him and Catherine.

He rolled to his side. Well, he had ten more days.

Warmth and softness and a pair of arms around his waist, breasts and lips pressed to his back, and she was in his bed with him, naked. He turned to speak to her, and she covered his mouth with hers and gently probed at his burnt tongue.

Later, much later, after he had stroked and caressed and kissed every inch of every curve of her body and she had sneezed three times, and, if he had been a sneezer, he would have sneezed twice himself—after all that, he had said, "Kate," and again she had kissed him. Then, despite his best efforts, he had fallen asleep with her in his arms.

When he woke in the morning, she was gone.

The days passed, and they were the most glorious days of James' life. The daylight hours were filled with his best friend, laughter, stories, exercise, good food, and his nights were filled with Catherine. True, the supposedly long winter nights were still too short. And Catherine came to him silently. Every time he tried to speak to her, she covered his mouth with a kiss, and his attempt to tell her he loved her turned into a yearning and an aching desire to be inside her once again. Every night, he swore if he could just slake his lust for her, he would find the mettle to tell her he loved her.

Because surely that must be what this all-consuming desire to be with her was.

Love.

Catherine had not known of Thomas' invitation to James. If she had known, she would have gone elsewhere for Christmas, stayed with the Dalrymples where she and Arabella were welcome, gone to Wales to visit Mary, or even traveled back to London despite her strong desire to see Harry and make sure she was well.

And she had been so pleased her first week at Sommer-leigh, the week before Christmas, to see how Harry had bloomed. How much weight she had gained, how far she could walk, how much more even her temper was. Catherine had been completely opposed to Harry marrying Thomas, and now she knew she had been wrong. Very wrong. Harry was thriving as much as Harry could thrive in this world that was not built for her. Not for the first time, Catherine's judgment had failed her.

Then her Jamie arrived. No, that was nonsense, he wasn't *her* Jamie. James arrived. All that promise, that youth, that beauty, that tall, rangy body with its ticklish knees.

With his arrival, Sommerleigh became a prison. Every morning, she returned to her own bed, vowing she would not go back to James' room that night. And every night, the throb between her legs and the fear she would never have him again would unite in an irresistible siren song, and she would rise from her bed, tiptoe down the hallway and through his door, shedding her nightdress on the floor of his room, and climb into the bed with him.

And every night had been like the first—tender yet fierce, deeply satisfying yet wild and stirring. But always, always, always dangerous. She dared to let the demon out of the cage every night, not sure she would be able to haul it back in the morning. Perhaps, one day, she would not have the strength.

The threat of that made her tremble in fear.

Twelfth Night was the guests' last night at Sommerleigh. There were cakes, of course. Arabella performed a piece from a puppet show she had seen with the Dalrymples. James told an amusing story about the arrival of the three wise men and the wrong turns they made on the way to Bethlehem. And Catherine was cajoled into performing, as well.

She chose to recite Viola's monologue from Act II, scene two. After all, it really was Twelfth Night, why not do *Twelfth Night*? For her, there were no associations between the role of Viola and that odious painting by Roger Siddons. The person in the painting was someone else entirely. That person still lived inside Catherine and threatened to destroy her life even now, but that person was not Viola, despite the costume. Viola never looked at her lover like that. Viola did not despair at knowing herself and how vile she was. Viola lived in a comedy, and comedies must end in marriage. Happily-ever-after.

When she finished with *O time! thou must untangle this, not I; It is too hard a knot for me to untie,* she saw James staring at her.

When she came to his bed that night, he put his hand over her mouth before she could kiss him.

"I must tell you," he said. "I have loved you since I was ten years of age."

She blinked.

"I saw you. When I was ten. As Viola. First, I thought it might be splendid to be your twin brother Sebastian. And then I thought I'd rather like to have you in love with me. I remember thinking the duke, that Orsino, was a fool to want Olivia when he could have had you. And I remember being jealous. I loved you then, as I love you now."

He slowly removed his hand from her mouth and waited.

She rolled onto her back.

"The seduction of an older woman," she said, "is a delicate thing. *I have loved you since age ten* does not arouse as much as one might think."

"But I don't want to seduce you, Kate, I want—"

She got out of the bed, found her nightdress on the floor, and pulled it on over her head. James got out of bed, too.

"I told you I love you, and you're leaving?"

"No," Catherine said. "I mean, yes, I'm leaving. But no. You didn't tell me you loved me. You told me you loved Viola."

"I meant, I mean, I do love you." He stood naked in front of her.

She hardened her heart. She made her voice harsh.

"You couldn't possibly mean that."

She fled the room.

The next day in the carriage on the way to London, James sat across from Catherine and Arabella. They both kept silent as Arabella prattled about the scenery, their Christmas, what she was going to do as soon as they got to London. Finally, Arabella nodded off and slept.

James leaned forward.

"Please, Catherine, give me some hope you can love me as I love you," he whispered, hoping not to wake Arabella but still be heard over the wheels of the carriage.

Catherine looked out the window. "There are plenty of other women to give you hope, my lord. You don't need it from me."

"I know I need you. Please look at me."

She shifted her blue eyes from the window to his face.

"Once we return to London, please promise you won't run from me or refuse me."

Catherine looked at James for a long time as if she were learning him off by heart. Then she looked down at her lap.

"We're pretenders. Both of us. I've pretended many things. I've pretended our differing ages, our differing ranks, my past, your future—and my weaknesses, particularly my weaknesses —I've pretended none of these matter. But, of course, they do. I know why I've pretended. What else is there for me to do when faced with my Jamie? You make me mad with desire, and so I would have pretended anything, I think, to have you—"

James' mind roiled as his heart leapt into his mouth and his groin ached. He made her mad with desire. Were there any sweeter words in the universe? But she was still speaking.

"—but why you walk around London one tenth the man you really are…it's a waste and a shame, James Cavendish."

She cleared her throat. "I last played Viola when I was nineteen. The company had difficulty finding a short-enough man to play my twin Sebastian and make the role-swapping and mistaken identity convincing. That was the end of my time in the part. You were two then, were you not? Even if your mother or your nursemaid had been crazed enough to take you to the theater, and I have never heard of such a thing —but even if they had, you would not remember. You are in love with quite another woman."

TWENTY-FOUR

James sent Enfield out to buy foolscap, quills, and plenty of ink. He suspected he was going to need supplies for a long epistolary siege.

Unfortunately, he had never attempted a love letter. If only Catherine would respond to a coded message or a cipher. *That* he could write.

To my dearest, to Catherine, to Kate—

We returned to London three days ago, and today is the third time in the new year I have been told by your butler that you are not at home to me.

And so I write.

This letter will be brief. Not because I have little to say but rather because I fear inconveniencing you with my affections.

I love you, Catherine. It does not matter that my boyhood memory is faulty. You are the Viola I always longed to know.

I do not expect you to love me. I only hope you will

allow me to love you. And you will either tolerate me or teach me to be tolerable to you.

There are no insurmountable oppositions. None, except a separation you have imposed, a circumstance which is driving me mad.

Please answer me.

Always your Jamie.

To his Right Honorable Marquess of Daventry, James Cavendish:

I write to you to make it clear your affections and attentions are in no way abhorrent to me. You should know that. You are a man of great worth, and my superior in every way—in rank, in character, and, frankly, in beauty.

But you must give this up. Give me up. Give up this crazed notion we will be together, somehow. We will not. It is pointless to belabor this.

As I said, your attentions are flattering to me, but they are also heartbreaking.

No answer is necessary.

Mrs. Edward Lovelock.

Dearest Kate of my heart—

It is very wrong of me to tell you this, but I am over the moon that my attentions are heartbreaking to you. You must know you continue to give me hope. Heartbreaking means you have invested some piece of your heart, no matter how small, in me.

Yes, I will concede there are differences in rank between us. This is a fact but an unimportant one.

However, I cannot accept your assessment of my character and my "beauty."

You, my goddess, my Minerva-cum-Venus, are so beautiful I could not stop looking at you the first time I met you. Remember? Lady Huxley's ball? I wanted to eat you with my eyes.

You are perfection in every way, and I have begun cataloging all the parts of you that should be classified as meeting the highest standard of feminine beauty. Your eyes. Your skin. Your hair. Your elbows, your neck, your breasts, your blush (which is present right now, is it not? Especially after my mention of your breasts), your hands, your bottom, your navel, your ears, your shoulders, your breasts <u>and</u> your bottom (see what I did there?), your toes, your thighs, your waist, your back, and each of the individual golden hairs that cover your sweet womanhood.

(I have written this letter out five times now, and each time I have hesitated to write the last phrase above, and then I have written it, and then I have scratched it out, and then I have started copying this letter all over again. I want you to know I think all parts of you are, without exception, beautiful, and I do not want you to think I have omitted any. Even if mention of them cannot be the usual thing in a love letter to a lady.)

And my character? I hesitate to detail my flaws as you already have so many reasons to reject me. If, someday, you ever let me back into your bed and promise to let me stay, I will tell you all the reasons your character is far superior to mine.

Tomorrow, please allow me to see you. I know if I could

only hold you and kiss you, you would see reason. Or lose your reason. Whichever results in allowing me to be close to you again.

Always your Jamie.

To his Right Honorable Marquess of Daventry, James Cavendish:

I am glad you acknowledge the fact of your noble birth. And the fact I am a farmer's daughter.

Here is another fact for you—

When you are fifty-three, I will be seventy, if I am still alive.

Mrs. Edward Lovelock.

To Kate, who holds my heart in her fist and ruthlessly crushes it—

I am trying out new salutations with each letter in the hope I will find just the right one that will make you melt and you will consent to see me.

But as to the content of your last letter—oh, Kate, Kate, Kate, I shake my head.

I pray you will reach seventy years of age. And if you do, would it be so bad to have a fifty-three-year-old companion of the heart? It is my understanding that appetites are well matched throughout a lifetime when a decade or more separates the ages of lovers. With the male being born second, that is.

*And as to how I would feel at fifty-three about having
a seventy-year-old lady love? If she were you, I would hope
she still remembered me, she still kissed me, she still
reached for my ticklish knees, and she would lean heavily
on my arm as we climbed the steps to bed each night (or
alternately, that my back was still strong and she let me
carry her).*

Always your Jamie.

*To his Right Honorable Marquess of Daventry, James
Cavendish:*

*You are very clever at provoking me into an answer.
Each letter I write to you I intend to be the last, but then
you write nonsense, and I feel I must say something in
response.*

Who will give you sons, Jamie?

Mrs. Edward Lovelock.

Kate—

*What need have I for sons if I can have you?
I thank you for your worry, but my father has a
younger brother. Who has TWO sons. One of my cousins
has knock knees and the other a squint. But they will do.*

*Kate, I can't help but think your stated objections—our
ranks, our ages, the expectation I produce heirs—are not the
real reasons you reject me.*

But I can do better. I can be better.

You already know, to some degree, I am not the feckless cad and inebriate I am reputed to be. But I am still so far from being the man I want to be for you. The man you should have.

I wish you would tell me why you don't want me so I may amend the faults you find most grievous first.

Always your Jamie.

To his Right Honorable Marquess of Daventry, James Cavendish:

If I concede there is another reason we have no future—one that has naught to do with you and only to do with me—will you leave me be?

Mrs. Edward Lovelock.

Dearest Kate—

I have enclosed a key to my rooms. Come to me and tell me this reason.

Always your Jamie.

Dear Catherine—

The best part of every day is the time I spend in walking from my rooms to your house. Hope springs eternal, et cetera. I even have come to enjoy my intercourse with your butler. Chelsom is his name, is it not? The way he varies what he says to me. Sometimes, it is "Mrs. Lovelock is not at home" or "Mrs. Lovelock is not receiving visitors." Sometimes, he breaks all propriety and adds the phrase "at present" to either of the above sentences.

I have heard nothing from you in a week. I had hoped you would come to me, and we would discuss your mysterious reason for keeping us apart. Did you receive my key? Are you well?

Always your Jamie.

Catherine—

Answer me. Please. I am very close to hopping your garden wall if only to catch a glimpse of you and see that you are well.

Always your Jamie.

Dear Mrs. Edward Lovelock:

Please acknowledge this letter in some way. I had thought I was in agony when my only contact with you was by letter, but now that your words have stopped, I know that state was but a pitiful, weak imitation of agony.

James Cavendish, Marquess of Daventry.

TWENTY-FIVE

After a ride across Hampstead Heath, James stabled his horse at his family's town house and walked back to his rooms. The day was unseasonably warm, and he had ridden hard enough and long enough to have sweated through his shirt. He was clammy and wanted nothing more than a hot bath. After that, he would make his daily call to the Lovelock house and be told Mrs. Lovelock was not at home to him.

But Catherine was waiting for him in his rooms. She wore a drab cloak, a plain muslin dress, a brown wig. She was seated by the fire but stood when he came in.

He had not seen her in almost two months and had not received a letter from her in over a fortnight. His entire outlook shifted in an instant at the sight of her.

"Catherine!" he exclaimed and crossed to her, his arms extended to embrace her.

She raised her palm to stop him. He halted three feet from her, his arms collapsing to his sides even as he longed to crush her to his chest. He grinned.

"I'm so glad to see you, I can't even say. Are you well? You look well."

She nodded.

"You used the key?"

"Key?"

"Enfield let you in, then? Good man. He knew you even in your disguise, eh?"

She turned to look at the fire. "He let me in, and he went out. He said to tell you he would be back to dress you for your dinner."

"Hang the dinner." He stepped closer and grabbed one of her hands. "Oh, Catherine, thank you for coming."

He raised her hand to his mouth and kissed the back of it. She pulled, but he held the hand fast. He was not letting go of the one piece of her he now had in his control. He turned her fist over and uncurled her fingers and flattened her hand. He kissed the hollow of her palm.

"Kate," he whispered and kissed her palm again. He felt some strain go out of her arm. Her mouth fell open, and her eyes had a faraway look to them. But then she seemed to come back from that far place, and she curled her fingers closed.

"Let go, Jamie."

He released her hand. She took off the brown wig and laid it in the chair and unpinned her golden curls so her hair went down her back. He thought she might put her face up for a kiss, but she walked away from the fire, shedding the plain cloak and a pair of patched shoes on the way out of the drawing room. In the small stone-floored passage between his bedchamber and the drawing room, she pulled the coarse dress over her head and left it on the stones. He followed her, feeling his cock harden.

Once in his bedchamber, she untied her petticoat. She wore no stays and no stockings, so after she pulled her chemise over her head, she was bare. She had not once turned to look at him since she had started undressing, and she did not turn now. She went to the bed, and he thought she would lie down there and he would be afforded once more the glorious sensation of looking at her completely naked body and the privilege of coupling with her.

But no. She walked to one of the posts at the foot of the bed, grasped it, and leaned over.

In all the times they had pleasured each other at Sommerleigh, she had never taken such a position. He had made excruciatingly slow love to her once from behind, the two of them lying on their sides, his hands on her breasts, her arms pulling at the backs of his thighs, pulling him into her. They had both been sore, he remembered, from some very vigorous and extended copulation the night before, and he had thought entering her from behind might spare her some discomfort. He did not think she had felt any pain that night as her moans were unchanged and she had arched her spine and pushed back into him, seemingly as hungry for him as ever. Although she had sneezed several times that night, they had not repeated the position. James had missed seeing her face as she climaxed.

But, now, he only cared that she was here and wanting him. He went to her and leaned into her and ran one hand down her back and over her beautiful bottom. Her feet were slightly apart. He let his hand slide off her buttock and felt between her legs. She was wet. She shuddered with his touch but said nothing.

"Kate," he breathed and kissed her neck and cupped one of her breasts with his other hand even as he stroked her tender folds and slid a finger into her wetness. She took one of her hands off the bedpost and reached behind her and grabbed his cock through his breeches. He thought he would explode with excitement.

"Yes," he said, "yes." He let go of her and unbuttoned the fall of his breeches. No time to take off his boots, the rest of his clothes. It was enough that he was ready and she was naked and ready. No, not quite enough. He found a cushioned stool and kicked it over to her. "Get on the stool, Kate." She looked down and stepped up on the stool.

She stayed silent as he entered her, and he should have known something was amiss. Where were her groans, her little screams, her soft mews? Even her panting was absent. But he was lost in his own pleasure, the warm silk of her sex, her small body under his, the feel of her breasts swaying under the impact of his thrusts. He reached out to hold her breasts and used them to pull her back into him as he pushed into her deeper still. When he took his hands from her breasts and slid them down her flanks, he intended to use one hand on her slit, to touch her pearl, to contribute to her pleasure, but instead he found both of his hands on her hips, pulling her more forcefully, more quickly, onto his shaft. He lifted one of her legs as she was still too short even while standing on the stool, and he wanted his cock to have complete and unfettered access to her...hot...wet... sweet...cleft.

"Uhnnnnnh."

He arched his back as he spilled inside her, overcome with pleasure. She didn't move, still holding the bedpost. He lowered his arm and let her leg relax back to the stool as his member slid out of her. He leaned over her and kissed her once on her white back, between her shoulder blades.

"You," he breathed, "didn't sneeze."

"No."

Holding her around the waist with one arm, he used the other hand to rub her sex. It took perhaps half an hour before she shook in his arms and sneezed. He had thought to lay her on the bed and use his mouth on her pearl or on her oh-so-sensitive breasts and nipples, but when he moved to pick her up, she held tightly to the bedpost and shook her head.

Still looking away from him, she said through clenched teeth, "Don't…stop."

So he stayed behind her, standing. He whispered endearments in her ear as he fingered her, telling her how beautiful she was, how he had missed her and how he had wanted her, how his life was meaningless without her.

Finally, she said with a strained voice, "Hush."

At last, she hung her head, her legs quivered, and she sneezed.

He thought he would have been hard again, ready to take her once more before Enfield returned. And this time to do it on the bed, properly, face-to-face, kissing her mouth, looking in her eyes, touching her breasts, trying for the magic of a simultaneous climax. To make love to her instead of fornicating with her.

But he was curiously flaccid.

Perhaps he had been bent over for too long. He took his arms from Catherine and straightened his back, stretching.

As soon as his arm had moved from her waist, she was off the stool and putting on her petticoat.

"Wait, wait, wait, wait," he said and caught her arm and lifted her face up with his other hand.

Her eyes were flat, her lips compressed together, her jaw tight under his hand.

"What's this? Kate, what's wrong? Did I hurt you?"

"No, Lord Daventry. I hurt myself." She broke away and went back to tying her petticoat.

"No, Kate, please, come to the bed."

"Why?" She turned to him, her voice angry, her brows knitting together. "You had me, and I had you." She put the chemise over her head. "Where is my dress?"

"I won't tell you until you help me understand."

She stared at him before turning on her heel and going into the passage between the bedchamber and the drawing room. He followed her, feeling like a forlorn puppy, pulling up his breeches and buttoning his fall. She found her dress in the passageway on the stone floor and slid it over her head.

He was desperate and elbowed past her to snatch up her shoes and the cloak that lay on the floor of the drawing room.

She ignored him and walked to the fire and began to pin up her golden hair.

"I have your shoes, Kate, and your cloak."

She shrugged. "I have walked barefoot before, although not through filthy London streets. And it's a warm day."

"Kate, you must tell me you will—"

"You must stop calling me Kate and acting like some lovesick boy."

The tone was so cold. The words so harsh, so close to James' fear that she would never be able to see past the differences in their ages. That he would always be a boy to her.

It was worse than a slap in the face.

He put her shoes and cloak down on the chair and left the room.

She had come to James' rooms to see him one last time, she told herself. To say goodbye since he had stopped writing to her. He must have realized, finally, that there were too many stumbling blocks to a love affair between the two of them. Too many, even without his knowing her shameful past, her fear of herself. She was glad to have been spared having to confess any of that.

But she knew it was a test. She was testing herself.

And she had failed. She had known she would.

She had wanted to see if she could be in the same room with him, alone, with all that had gone between them, and not succumb to her own desires. If she could just *be* with him. The answer was no. His mouth on her palm had sent waves of such sharp want through her body, it felt like pain.

It had been enough to answer the question.

After all these years, where was her wisdom, her control? Gone, when she was with him. She was still the same weak girl but now in a middle-aged woman's body. She had learned nothing.

She knew James would never injure or humiliate her, but she also knew, deep in her core, she would be willing to debase herself out of lust for him. She was just lucky he was her beautiful boy Jamie and not a cruel degenerate like Roger Siddons.

And that's why she had taken Roger's preferred position for her in the bedchamber—the position of a mare, standing and leaning over. She had wanted to be reminded that he held the same power over her that Roger had.

But James had been different from Roger. He had touched her before he had penetrated her. That had not been Roger's way. And James had not held her hair and yanked her head back as Roger had.

And, after James had spent inside her, he had wanted to tend to her, to bring her pleasure. But she perversely had not let him stimulate her the way he wished. She had wanted it to be as difficult as possible for him to arouse her. As difficult as possible for him to bring her to a climax.

And as he had leaned over, holding her, touching her, he had said sweet things to her that tore at her heart. She had been forced to shut him up. And when she had finally released, she had felt filthy doing so.

Of course, it had been a test for him, too. An unfair test. She had designed it for failure. There had been no way for him to succeed once she had failed her own test. He was a young man. Of course, he would do what young men did. Rut his way to happiness.

But there could be no happiness for her with James, only heartbreak.

The day after she had gone to see him in his rooms, she retched several times. She had vomited every day for several weeks, but she thought she had been eating too much rich food, drinking too much chocolate. Or her strong stomach was weakening with age. She had denied what her body was telling her.

She counted on her fingers. She went and walked by the River Thames and thought of Ophelia.

She came home and began the necessary arrangements for Arabella to go to her sister Mary in Wales. As soon as possible. Mary and her husband had a trip planned to Cornwall and Bath, and Arabella could join them on their travels. Arabella would fuss about missing her second Season, but it must be done.

Twenty-Six

Catherine—

You were right. I am a lovesick boy. I wish I could tell you, with confidence, I am a lovesick <u>man</u>, but I am very much afraid it is not true.

But you could be the making of me, Catherine. I know you could.

Would you do me the honor of marrying me?

Always your Jamie.

Catherine—

Are you never to write to me again? Even to answer my marriage proposal? I think I deserve that.

James Cavendish, Marquess of Daventry.

Catherine—

Forgive my last letter. I must have sounded like a needing, petty child—exactly the opposite of the impression I want to give.

I am ashamed, most ashamed, of what occurred when you came to my rooms. I am not ashamed of the physical act itself but instead that I greedily allowed my appetites to supersede what was truly most important—that we speak to each other, that you make me understand how I can earn your love or earn the right to love you.

I have so little wisdom in these matters, Catherine. I know my saying that casts me again as a child, but it is true. I have never loved anyone but you.

Always your Jamie.

He continued to call at her house every day. He had not seen her except for the time she had come to his rooms and offered herself to him and he had done everything wrong.

Finally, on what might be his last day in London for quite some time, she was at home to him. His heart was in his mouth.

"Mrs. Lovelock." He bowed.

"Lord Daventry." She curtsied and nodded to her butler. Chelsom closed the drawing room door.

"Catherine."

She did not answer but met his gaze steadily.

He went on, "I am grateful you agreed to see me. I leave London this afternoon for Middlewich. My father is ill."

"I am sorry to hear that, my lord." She sat. A long pause came here as she smoothed her dress in her lap. "Due to our previous degree of intimacy, my lord, I felt I should inform you that Sir Francis Ffoulkes has renewed his attentions and has again asked me to marry him."

James' vision darkened, and he felt his knees wobble.

"Sir Francis? Surely, after what he did to you, how he abandoned you, you cannot think to accept him?"

She said nothing.

"What made him ask you again?" Despite himself, James' voice was rising in volume. "Did he suddenly realize what every man with eyes and a brain should realize? Namely, that you are the most beautiful and most extraordinary woman ever to...I don't know, grace the empire?" He was shouting.

She spoke back in a whisper. "You are very flattering to me, James."

Hope clutched at his chest. She had called him James. Much better than *my lord*.

Her voice grew stronger. "No, he has not realized that. He has realized I have a sizable personal fortune. Money I earned as an actress and invested long before I married. Money that grew and grew over the years. Money my husband was good enough to keep separate from the injunction in his will."

James gaped, unbelieving. "You know Sir Francis is a fortune-hunter."

"Yes." She rose from her chair.

"You must refuse him."

She snapped back, "What I must do is the same as what you must do. What is best for me and my family!"

He groaned. "Oh, the sins that have been committed in the name of family."

She laughed and shook her head. "Jamie. Jamie. Whatever sins we have committed, they haven't been in the name of family, have they?"

He liked the *Jamie* bit. And her laughing. He wasn't

happy about her use of the past tense. And it hurt she would call what they had done together a sin.

He went to her and folded her into his arms. He leaned over and whispered in her ear, "Kate, you tell me of this proposal to taunt me, I know. There is no need to do so. I will delay leaving London if you will come back to my rooms tonight in that old dress and brown wig. Let me hold you and kiss you and do any number of unspeakable things to you. Let me wash your mind clean of any thoughts of marrying Sir Francis. We belong together, Kate, you must know that."

He did not know what in his words upset her, but she stiffened and pushed him away.

"My lord, I must ask that in the future you tender your affections elsewhere. I am sure your grief over your father's illness has made you forget yourself."

"My grief?" James tore at his hair in frustration. "All my grief is for you, Catherine. I am wild with it. Sick with it."

"Then you must go. Away from my house. And convalesce. And when we meet again, we will meet as friends, I am sure."

A cataclysm of pain tore through his entire body, his mind, his heart, his soul. Worse pain than when William had died and he had lost his brother, his hero, and his future in one fell swoop.

He made it to the door. A shaking hand put to the knob, a shaking voice when he finally spoke.

"I will never be friends with you, Mrs. Lovelock. Never."

TWENTY-SEVEN

Once Arabella had been safely sent off to her sister Mary, Catherine still had a great many tasks before her. One particular thing had been nagging at her mind for months; she felt compelled to find the young woman of French extraction who had been so kind to her last autumn.

She had previously asked acquaintances if they knew a French woman of good breeding named Mademoiselle Isabella DuMornay. All the women had looked at her blankly. Some of the men had showed recognition in their eyes, and a few had even smirked, but all said they did not know her.

Finally, she took her carriage to the alley behind the Theatre-Royal, Drury Lane and knocked on the stage door. Joseph, the very same guardian of that door from seventeen years ago, opened it. He was a huge brute of a man, sporting two cauliflower ears and missing an eye.

"Joseph!" she cried and threw her arms around his thick middle.

"Who is that?" he said, looking down at her. She stepped back.

"It's Cath, Joseph."

Suddenly, she was buried in his arms. "Oh, my goodness, little Cath come back finally to see her Joe." He held her out and surveyed her with his one eye. "Just as tiny and pretty as ever. Wait, it's Mrs. Lovely now, isn't it?"

"Lovelock. But my husband died."

"And will you be coming back to the stage, then?"

"No, no, I won't. I'm here for another reason. To see if anyone knows a young lady I met recently."

"Well, the theater's just gone dark this week, Mrs. Lovely. No one's here besides me and the rats. Who would this young lady be?"

"She is French, and I think from a good family. Her name is Isabella DuMornay. She's about six inches taller than I am, generously proportioned, dark hair, dark eyes. She would make a lovely Helen in Marlowe's *Dr. Faustus.*"

Joseph scratched his chin for a bit.

"I wonder if that might be Izzy. Her name is Dewmorning, same as your lady. But she's not French, although she talks queer, and, well, Cath, she is not what you would call a lady."

"What would you call her?"

Joseph blushed. "She's one of Madame Flora's Cyprians."

Catherine knew of Madame Flora, of course. Her brothel was not two hundred yards from the theater. In fact, it was quite near where she had first kissed James in an alley much like this one. No wonder the passersby had assumed she was a whore.

"I see. Thank you, Joseph."

"She's not in trouble, is she? Izzy is a good girl, she is."

"No, she's not in trouble. And I agree, Joseph. She's a very good girl."

Catherine went home and arranged for her coachman to take a message to Madame Flora's for her. The coachman was astonished and protested. But Catherine insisted. She paid his wages, and she wanted the message delivered.

Two days later, Catherine's carriage waited in front of Madame Flora's. At the appointed hour of two, Isabella DuMornay came out and was helped into the carriage by a dumbstruck footman, whose eyes bulged and mouth hung open. The coachman snapped the reins, and the carriage rolled away.

"You are very good to see me, Mademoiselle DuMornay," Catherine said as the carriage rattled over the cobblestones.

"But, of course. I think I was quite surprised to receive your letter. You uncovered me."

"Yes."

They both were silent for a moment before speaking at the same time.

"I wanted to thank—"

"You mustn't think—"

They both stopped and smiled.

"*S'il vous plaît*, Madame Lovelock." Isabella gestured for Catherine to speak.

"You were very kind to me at a time when I was in a great deal of distress, and I hoped we might meet again so I could express my gratitude. But I could find you nowhere, and I did not like to ask anyone from that house party."

"No. I understand."

"Now I have found you, I would like to help you, if I can."

Isabella laughed a low, throaty laugh Catherine was sure men found enthralling. "Oh, Madame, you are too good. But I need no help. I am happy. And, in truth, I am already leaving my profession because I will marry soon."

Catherine leaned forward. A jealous tug at her heart. "Oh, how wonderful. I congratulate you."

Isabella shrugged and pouted. "I want just to run away together, but the man will not have it. He insists on the marriage."

Catherine smiled. "Not the usual reluctant groom, then."

"I wonder that so many women want marriage. It is all to benefit the man and not the woman. We live in a world run by men. And we live in a world that demands marriage. This is not—how do you say?—a coincidence."

"There are some advantages to the woman, Mamselle."

Isabella scoffed. "Only if there are children, to make them safe. Otherwise, the woman should stay free."

Catherine bit her lip. "Yes. But there are some women who want marriage."

"Of course, but I am not one of them. But I am crazed for this man, and if he says he will not have me without the wedding, then the wedding I shall have. I throw all my rules away for him."

"I'm sure you will be very happy."

"It is good, I think, to find someone who makes you willing to throw away your rules."

The carriage lurched.

"What were you going to say to me, Mademoiselle DuMornay? Before?"

"Oh, Madame Lovelock, I was going to tell you not to think there is anything between Lord Daventry and me. But now you have heard I am to be married, of course, you would not think that."

Catherine sat back. She had no inkling of anything between James and Isabella.

"I know there was always talk because James would come to me so often in the brothel," Isabella said.

Catherine felt her spine go rigid. "I heard...no talk."

Isabella clapped her hand over her mouth. "I had thought, that is, I thought that is why you had asked to see me."

"No, I had heard nothing. And even if I had, Lord Daventry's behavior could have nothing to do with me."

Isabella's eyes became very large. "Oh, no, Madame, you will break his heart."

"Nonsense."

Isabella frowned. "I cannot say what I wish to say. But, begging your pardon, you are a fool."

Catherine smiled weakly. "On that, we can agree." She knocked on the ceiling of the carriage and told the coachman to take them back to Madame Flora's.

Just before the carriage came to a halt, Isabella patted Catherine's knee. "At the very least, you must tell him."

Catherine began to ask what she meant but thought better of it. She compressed her lips into a thin line and shook her head.

Isabella got out of the carriage without waiting for the footman's assistance, but she popped her head back in through the door.

"His father has died, in case you had not heard the news. Jacques is the duke now."

TWENTY-EIGHT

A week later, Catherine had a caller. Her butler Chelsom had become well accustomed to telling all who came to the door that Mrs. Lovelock was not at home. And, certainly, never at home to James Cavendish, the new Duke of Middlewich.

Today, however, Chelsom came to Catherine in the morning room, where she was writing a letter to the man now in charge of the Lovelock Bank. She needed an expeditious transfer of some monies abroad.

"Ah, madam?"

Catherine looked up. "Yes?"

"A Mr. Roger Siddons is most insistent he see you."

Catherine considered. "Show him into the large drawing room, the one nearest the front door. And keep the doors open and stay in the front hall."

"Yes, Mrs. Lovelock."

Catherine took a minute to gather herself as she might have years ago while offstage, in the wings. *Breathe. Stand straight. Speak clearly. Remember what you are doing.*

Siddons was looking out the front window when Catherine came into the drawing room.

He turned. "Not afraid to have me in the drawing room, where anyone might pass by and see me?"

Lit from behind by the window, he might still be the twenty-nine-year-old painter she had desired when she was nineteen. But she hated him now, and she hated herself, remembering what had passed between them. How he had mangled something that might have been good in her and made it malignant.

And then she thought of how she could so easily close the doors and go to him and once again submit to him and to that which still lived within her, her lust demon.

No. No demon. It was long past time for her to stop thinking of her wickedness as something apart from her. There was only her. And she was despicable.

She took a deep breath.

"People know I have a past with you, Mr. Siddons. There is no need to conceal it. And the drawing room doors will stay open. There will be nothing improper. My butler is just there in the hall."

"I think you would probably prefer if the doors were closed, Cath."

"The doors will stay open."

"Fine." Siddons sauntered around the perimeter of the room and looked at the Sir Joshua Reynolds portrait of Edward that had a place of pride on the back wall.

"Sir Sloshua always had a way with bankers, I'll give him that. You can practically see the gold oozing out your husband's pores."

Catherine waited.

"My hand is fine, by the way." He wiggled his fingers at her. "Thank you for inquiring."

"I assumed I would have received a solicitor's letter or a doctor's bill if that had not been the case."

"Well, actually, Cath." Siddons smiled. "The bill is coming due now."

A foreboding chill ran through her body. "In what sense?"

"You know the painting of you? That half-naked portrait of you as a boy that you hate so much? The Cesario-*cum*-Viola picture?"

Catherine clenched her fists. "That is a lewd and evil painting, and you should burn it."

"I should," Siddons said in a light tone and shrugged. "Or I should display it in the Exhibition of the Royal Academy."

Catherine gasped despite herself and sat down. Hard. "You wouldn't."

"I would. And I am. They are already printing the catalog. Portrait of Mrs. Edward Lovelock. I think it will be the talk of the *ton*."

"How much do you want for the painting?"

"Oh, no. No, no. You may be able to buy your way out of a lot of things, but not this. I'm not selling you the painting."

"You must have a price."

"I do. The price is your complete and utter humiliation. I understand you have a seventeen-year-old daughter who looks a great deal like you. I wonder if she looks like you in the picture? After all, when I painted it, you were only two years older than she is now. I wonder what her suitors might think about their future wife's assets being on display in the Exhibition?"

"They would never hang that picture at the Exhibition."

"You forget your breasts do not really show. Most onlookers think you are a boy, at first. Believe me, they'll hang the picture. I think tickets will be in high demand." Siddons went to the door. "And you know how they hang the paintings in the Great Room all the way up to the ceiling so you can barely see the pictures at the very top? Well, you're being hung down at eye level. No one will miss you."

Siddons went out into the hall, and Catherine could hear Chelsom opening the door to show him out and saying, "Good afternoon, sir."

"Chelsom," she called.

He came into the drawing room.

"Yes, ma'am?"

"I need a message sent to Lord Daventry, I mean, the Duke of Middlewich, as soon as possible, and when he comes here in answer to it, I will see him immediately. I'll go to the morning room now and write the letter."

She stood and staggered, and Chelsom took one step forward as if to catch her.

"I'm fine," she said.

But she wasn't.

Half an hour later, the dispatched footman returned. He had gone first to James' rooms near the newly opened Burlington Arcade and then to the family town house on Grosvenor Square. His Grace, the new Duke of Middlewich, was still in Middlewich. There was no telling when he would return to London.

TWENTY-NINE

Six of James' sisters were still in town for the Season, staying at the town house, hoping for matches. His father and mother and his youngest sister Charlotte, who was not yet out, had stayed in Middlewich since the duke had never fully recovered from his illness last autumn. When James arrived back in the duchy, his father had been reduced to hoarse, rattling exhalations and the exhaustion that comes at the end of a life.

"Father." His father opened his eyes. "You know the Earl Drake's wife? We spoke of her at Christmas?"

Had the old man nodded, just a bit?

"And we spoke of her stepmother. An actress."

His father coughed weakly and struggled to take breath in.

"I love her. The stepmother. Her name is Catherine. She is beautiful, resilient, clever, and courageous. And I am going to marry her when she agrees to it."

His father's lips moved. James leaned forward and put his ear to his father's mouth.

"Wastrel," the old man whispered. "Whore."

His last words. A few hours later, the duke stopped

breathing. The doctor listened to the duke's chest and shook his head. His Grace's heart had gone still.

"The duke is dead," the doctor said, looking at James. "There is a new duke, Your Grace."

James hugged his mother. She was pale and hunched, but she did not cry. She pulled away and held him at arm's length and looked up at his face. "You are the duke, James."

"Yes, Mother."

"Once you marry, I will be a dowager duchess. And your father, he doesn't suffer anymore."

"Yes, Mother."

She turned, her skirts whirling, and left his father's sickroom. He heard her go into the nursery. There was quiet and then a howl and Charlotte, tears streaking her face, ran into the sickroom and seized their father's wrinkled hand and sobbed. Charlotte had always been the duke's favorite and, like William, the brother she did not remember, she had never been frightened of the duke, able to tame him by curling her small hand into his and swinging his arm until he picked her up.

James went to stand next to his sister, and she released her father's hand and turned to him and cried into his waistcoat for a long time.

The rest of his sisters arrived the next day from London with their chaperone aunts and their lady's maids. Their Season was over, and they were all in mourning. And now James had the responsibility of ensuring the happiness of six sisters—no, seven, counting the fifteen-year-old Charlotte.

His father was buried. His mother's sixty-first birthday came and went. James headed to London to present himself to the House of Lords, to petition for a transfer of the title. It was really all just ceremonial. No one questioned his legitimacy or his right to be duke.

As the ducal carriage made its way towards London, James

considered his domestic arrangements in town. As the title-holder, he would have to move into the town house eventually. But, for the moment, his rooms still afforded him a degree of privacy that the house in Mayfair did not. He would wait until things were settled between himself and Catherine. After their marriage—for that is what he still hoped for despite their last meeting—they might move into the town house, together.

When he and Enfield arrived at his rooms in London, they were met by half a dozen letters under the door. He recognized the hand as Catherine's. In each letter, she entreated him to come to her as soon as he returned. He ran as he had never run before all the way to her house.

Catherine, beautiful Catherine, was at home to him. She *was* home to him.

"That will be all, Chelsom," she said. As the butler closed the drawing room door, James, still breathing heavily, took a step towards her.

"Catherine, I—"

She cut him off with a deep curtsy and the words, "Your Grace."

"Ah, y-yes," he stammered. "You've heard, I gather." He ran his fingers through his hair.

"You have my condolences on your father's death, Your Grace."

He studied her. She looked tired, but her skin and her eyes had a clarity and a glow to them. A few fine lines were etched by her mouth that he did not remember.

"Tell me, before all else, tell me. Have you accepted Ffoulkes?"

"I have not."

A weight came off his chest.

"And are you well, Kate—I mean, Catherine, Mrs. Lovelock? And all your family?"

"Yes."

"And Arabella. She is well?"

"She is traveling with my eldest stepdaughter Mary and her husband."

"Ah, yes. The Viscount and Viscountess Tregaron."

"You have a good memory, Your Grace."

"Catherine." He stepped forward and seized one of her hands. "I would never forget anything that had to do with you. Certainly, nothing as important as your family."

"You are very kind, Your—"

"Please call me Jamie. Please. I can't bear it. I just can't."

She took back her hand, and he thought there might have been a glistening in her eye.

"You must bear it. It's for the best," she said.

"You say that, but I don't see how it can be. Not for me."

Her voice was ice. "You are young. You will heal."

He folded his arms across his chest and put his hands into his armpits and clamped his arms down and held them there, containing himself.

"I am not raising my voice because if I do, I will be accused of being young. I am not storming around this room because if I do, I will be accused of being young. I am not making violent and passionate love to you as I want to because I will be accused of being young. Yes, Catherine, I am *younger* than you. I am not young."

Something in her face softened. She reached out and stroked his jaw with one finger.

"So clean," she said. "Do you know, the first time I met you, I thought you could not grow whiskers?"

"I can grow whiskers," he growled. "I had six weeks at Lord Bastable's hunting camp once, and I grew a full beard. It was red-blond. I came back from that trip looking like some damnable Viking."

She laughed. "I would have loved to have seen that."

"Oh, Kate." He put his arms around her waist.

"Kate, let's go to a cottage somewhere for six weeks, Ireland or Portugal or the Alps, and let me grow a beard for you."

She did not break away from him, but she did not embrace him. She looked at his waistcoat buttons.

"I need you to do something for me."

"Anything." He kept his arms around her but stooped to try to meet her eyes. "Anything, Catherine, you know that."

"I would feel better if you removed your hands from my person. I suddenly feel I am trading intimacy for your kindness, and I do not want that. I want things to be pure. And right. Between us."

He took his hands off her waist immediately and backed away—one, two, three steps from her.

What did she mean? Were they to be as sister and brother now? Friends, as she had said on his last visit? As if somehow the night at the inn at Duddenhoe End, the nights at Sommerleigh, and, yes, even that disastrous time in his rooms that still filled him with shame (how could he have misread the situation so badly?)—as if all those times together had never happened.

Fine, fine. He could accept that. For now. Anything to get back in her orbit, to be in the same room with her.

"I need you to acquire the painting you saw at Sir Francis' house," she said.

"Acquire?"

"I would prefer if you bought the painting, and, of course, I would pay you back. Mr. Siddons refuses to sell to me, but he may sell to you. But if you have to steal it…" She smiled sadly. "I suppose in encouraging you to perform acts of larceny, I am not really starting this pure and right relationship on a solid footing."

James grinned. A job he was made for. Finally, a good use for his skills at pilfery. "I don't anticipate any difficulty. I'll buy it. The price will be no barrier. And it will be my gift to you. And if I can't buy it, I'll steal it."

"The thing is…" She hesitated. "I don't know where it is. Mr. Siddons plans to show it in the Exhibition at the Royal Academy."

"The upcoming Exhibition?"

"Yes."

"But that opens in," he thought quickly, "four days."

Catherine bit her lip. "Yes."

"Then the painting is either with Siddons or on the premises of the Academy. I'll go at once."

Catherine looked relieved and felt for the nearest chair and sat down, rather quickly. "Thank you, Your Grace."

James took a step towards the door of the drawing room but hesitated and turned to her.

"I would like something in return. I do want to trade for intimacy. But intimacy of a different kind. When I bring you this blasted painting, I want you to sit with me. And for us to speak together. About everything. Truthfully. I will tell you my secrets. You will tell me yours. Will you do that for me?"

She trembled. She folded her hands in her lap in front of her abdomen as if she were shielding herself.

"Yes, Your Grace."

Thirty

James walked east, towards the location he remembered as Siddons' studio. He found the shabby building and knocked on the right door.

Siddons answered, wearing only a paint-spattered shirt. Barelegged, barefooted. He sneered.

"James Cavendish."

James did not wait for an invitation to step inside. A young woman stood naked on the far side of the studio. She made no move to cover herself when he entered. James averted his eyes.

"Pru!" Siddons barked, and the girl started as if she had been asleep. "Put something on. You're embarrassing Lord Daventry."

James saw no reason to correct Siddons with his new title.

The girl Pru moved slowly, dreamily, as if she were wading in deep water, and picked up a drape from the floor and began wrapping herself in it.

"I was expecting someone at some point, but I thought it would be a solicitor. I didn't know it would be you, Daventry." Siddons picked at the paint flecking his hands. "Perhaps I should have. You always seem to be bursting in where you're not wanted, trying to save the day, but only making things worse for everybody."

"I want to buy the painting."

Siddons look surprised by James' directness. But, of course. the man would expect him to be drunk, mocking, unable to approach a subject head-on. Well, too late now.

Siddons recovered and laughed. "Of course, you do. So many people do. The painting is not for sale."

"Name your price."

Siddons smiled. "The painting is not for sale."

"A thousand pounds."

Pru squawked, "Lawks!" and almost dropped her drape.

Siddons felt the bump on the bridge of his nose. "The painting is not for sale."

Had there been some hesitation there? "Five thousand pounds."

"The painting is not for sale."

"Ten thousand pounds."

"You think you can buy anything." Another sneer. "The painting. Is. Not. For. Sale."

"Is it here?"

"If it were, do you think I would have opened the door? It's gone to the Exhibition. It's too late."

"I see." James went to the door.

"Farewell, Marquess, and thanks for the laughs."

James stopped and turned around. "It's Duke, actually. The Duke of Middlewich."

"Oh, it's Your Grace, now, is it? Well, Your Grace." Siddons leaned forward as if to tell James something in confidence. "The painting is not for sale."

James stared at Siddons. Siddons took a step backwards.

"What are you looking at, Cavendish?"

"Ten thousand pounds is a lot to lose just for the opportunity to hurt someone."

"Yes, well, I was never very clever about money, was I? Otherwise, I wouldn't live like this." Siddons gestured to the squalid studio.

"No, I suppose not. You are driven by other things. Things even more ignoble. How wretched you must be."

James turned on his heel and left. He walked south towards the river. Eventually, he found a hack and rode the rest of the way to Somerset House.

James paid the driver, and the hack pulled back out into the busy traffic of the Strand. He turned to face the building. The part of Somerset House facing the street, this section, housed the Royal Academy.

He noted five uniformed and armed Royal Marines standing at attention outside the building. He walked through one of the three arches and into the vestibule and out into the large courtyard. Across the courtyard, at the South Wing, the building that faced the Thames, he saw more Royal Marines. Ah, yes, the Navy Board was there.

When he had first taken up his work for Mr. Bulverton, James thought he might someday report to an admiral or some person of importance at Somerset House. But it had never come to pass. Perhaps because only his very first piece of intelligence, the one that had led to the rout of the French at San Sebastian, had been related to foreign affairs. Since then, all of his endeavors had been domestic concerns.

And, if he were honest with himself, rather trifling domestic concerns. Carrying a coded message from one place to another, reporting the gossip of the *ton*, informing on those who voiced sympathies with the Americans or Bonaparte or the Irish. And, yes, stealing jewelry and love tokens and indiscreet letters that should never have been sent by important men with too much time on their hands.

Well, that part of his life was over. He must tell Bulverton. He was a duke now. He had responsibilities to his sisters and mother, to the people on his estate and in his duchy.

And to Catherine. He must find this painting quickly.

In the offices of the Royal Academy, James seemed to be the only visitor whose hands were not covered in paint. Several clerks and functionaries tried to placate a seething mob of artists, all expostulating loudly about the positioning of their paintings in the Exhibition. James elbowed his way to the front.

"I am the new Duke of Middlewich," he roared over the clamor. "And I demand to see the man in charge of this madhouse!"

For pity's sake. He was turning into his father now.

The artists murmured and withdrew, leaving several empty feet of space around him. In a matter of moments, James was ushered into the private office of the secretary to the President of the Royal Academy of Arts.

The secretary stood, bowed. "Your Grace." He looked harried.

"I wish to procure a painting."

"Yes, Your Grace, the Exhibition will begin in four days, and, at that time, you may purchase a painting at your leisure."

"Yes," James said. "May I sit?"

The secretary frowned. "Certainly." James sensed the man was under a great deal of pressure and wanted him out of the office with as much haste as possible so he could get back to the stack of papers on his desk.

"Have all the paintings been delivered to the Academy?" James asked.

"Yes, they're being hung at this moment by the Hanging Committee. The Varnishing Days start tomorrow and will go for three days. Then the Exhibition will open."

"The painting I want, well, I would rather it was never hung. I would like to buy it and take it with me now."

"That would be most irregular, Your Grace."

James leaned forward. "But would it be impossible?"

The man thought. "Yes. It would. There are over thirteen hundred paintings to be hung. We cannot interrupt our work to go looking for one painting, in particular. And then, of course, you would have to apply to the artist for the purchase. My advice to you, Your Grace, is to come back very early on the first day of the Exhibition and buy the painting then."

James stood. "Very well. I will do so."

Blast. Hellfire. Damnation. He was going to have to steal the painting.

He walked back out into the courtyard and looked around. There were so many armed marines about. Of course, they were not there to protect the Royal Academy, but he wondered how they might react to a duke slipping out of a window, carrying a large painting.

James came back that night. Royal Marines at the Strand entrance. He could see beyond them into the courtyard where torches were lit. Still more uniformed Royal Marines.

Tricky.

He had no idea what to do next.

He went back to his rooms, sent Enfield to bed, and paced. What a sham he was. For almost six years he had considered himself a covert operative and had delighted in fooling those around him and having secret meetings with Bulverton. And now, when he needed to do something of import for the woman he loved, something that actually mattered to *him*, he was useless.

But he still had one tool at his disposal.

One he had never used.

. . .

Catalog and ticket in hand, accompanied by Mr. Deedles, his father's longtime London agent, James pushed to the front and was among the first to enter the Great Room on opening day of the Exhibition.

There, on the far end. Eye level. Siddons' painting.

And what luck. The secretary he had met four days ago was in the Great Room, surveying the press of people.

"Sir!" he accosted the secretary.

The man bowed. "Your Grace, you're here. Very good. I hope you find your painting."

"I've found it. I'm ready to buy it. This is Mr. Deedles. He is ready with payment."

The secretary stammered. "B-b-but you must make application to the artist, Your Grace. The Academy has nothing to do with the purchase of paintings."

"Come with me." James put his arm around the man's shoulders and walked him across the Great Room to Catherine's portrait. Most of the viewers were still on the other side of the room, looking at the pictures near the entrance. Mr. Deedles trailed behind, carrying a small metal box.

"What is your name?" James asked, keeping his arm around the secretary's shoulders, keeping him facing towards the picture.

"Harris. Mr. Elias Harris, Your Grace."

They stood in front of the painting, and James released him.

"Oh," Mr. Harris said. "Oh, this is the painting you meant. I see."

"My sole aim, Mr. Harris, is to remove this picture from public view and save a lady from embarrassment."

Mr. Harris fidgeted.

James went on, "I think you would agree there would be no great loss to the world of fine art if this painting disappeared."

Mr. Harris nodded. "I seem to remember this painting was chosen by the selection panel almost purely," he lowered his voice, "to provoke offense and bring in curiosity seekers. Not what I would wish for."

"No, certainly not. It is immediately apparent you are a man of taste and the highest aesthetic values. Now. The artist is not willing to sell to me, personally. Not at any price. Have you ever been in love, Mr. Harris?"

"Your Grace, I…yes."

"There is a Mrs. Harris, then?"

"No." The man blushed. "But I have hopes."

"Well, I sense you are a man of enormous sympathy, and if I told you, in confidence, I love this lady in the painting and I would do anything to spare her even the smallest bit of pain, you might think of some way I could obtain the picture. Legally. Without involving the artist."

"Well, there is a rule…"

Thank God. "A rule?"

"The Academy has the right of first refusal on any painting displayed during the Exhibition. But we have very little room for storage and almost never buy anything. Let's see." Mr. Harris leaned forward to examine the card next to the painting of Catherine. "For its size, the price would be ten pounds. Not too dear. I suppose the Academy could buy the painting and sell it to you?"

"Excellent. And the painting can be removed immediately from public view?"

"It's most irregular," Mr. Harris dithered.

James snapped his fingers, and Mr. Deedles approached. "I think five hundred pounds would be a good price for the painting. And a letter of praise from the Duke of Middlewich regarding your good work here and the need for your advancement. Or barring that, perhaps a new career as a curator of a personal collection, a position that would surely pay enough to allow for a wife and a family."

It was done.

James took the painting off the wall immediately and covered it with the drape Mr. Deedles had carried under his arm.

Of course, money had smoothed the way and the promise of a letter or a position. But James couldn't help feeling, for the first time in his life, he had solved a problem by telling the truth.

It felt decidedly pure. And right.

THIRTY-ONE

James was bewildered not to hear back from Catherine immediately. She had been so fearful about the possibility of the painting being displayed, and he had hoped when she received his letter, she might summon him or come to him. And, yes, he hoped she would be grateful. But he had tried to have no other expectations. Such as a kiss. Or coming into his bed. Or what he most wanted—a declaration of love.

It should be enough for him that he had relieved some distress for her. And she had promised to talk to him. Frankly. And he might finally tell her of his secret life that had sustained him until he had met her and realized he only wanted to be the man in her bed, at her side, in her heart.

He comforted himself with the fact that he had been the

one to whom she had turned when she found herself in trouble. That must mean something, surely. She saw him as a man who could solve problems, a man of action, not the foolish drunk he had played for so long. *Not* a boy. She had trusted him, and he had proven himself worthy of that trust.

After waiting several hours, he went to sleep. He had an early meeting the next day.

He rose while it was dark and checked on the painting. Yes, it was still there, still covered, leaning up against his fencing kit in his dressing room.

Enfield came into the bedchamber to stoke the fire in order to heat water for his shave.

"Don't touch the object in the dressing room, Enfield."

"Yes, Your Grace."

"It will be removed very soon."

"Yes, Your Grace."

The ducal carriage, normally housed at the family's town house, appeared outside James' rooms just after dawn and took him to Madame Flora's.

"So this is the end, Your Grace." Mr. Bulverton looked much the same as usual. Ordinary. A tight-lipped bureaucrat. Flour on his clothes. Of course, the bakery was so busy in the morning, James was surprised Bulverton was not coated in the white dust, looking like a chalk miner.

"Yes. It's the end for me. I'll be busy in Middlewich. And I think it would be better for everyone if I…grew up. I have to conduct myself responsibly now. Make sure Cather—make sure my sisters know I will always do my best, do my duty."

"That makes sense." Mr. Bulverton rubbed his chin.

"Oh, Jacques!" Isabella threw her arms around his neck and quickly squeezed him. "I will miss you."

James mumbled something and then spoke more clearly. "I wondered if you might want to, perhaps, open a shop, Isabella?"

"A shop? But what kind of shop?"

"Well, maybe for these embroidered robes you make for yourself. I would think ladies would like these a great deal. I could stake you. You could sew them and sell them and—"

"And I wouldn't have to sell myself anymore? It's all right, *chéri*. You don't have to rescue the whole world."

"Well, I wasn't trying to—"

"*Non, non, non.* Don't worry. I have my plans." She hesitated. "And I hope you are making your plans, as well."

Mr. Bulverton stood and stuck out his hand. "Best of luck, Your Grace."

"Yes," James said. "Yes. And thank you."

"Oh, Jacques? Your friend Lord Drake, he came in last night. He is still here, I think. With Nancy."

"Thank you." He kissed her on the cheek. "*Au revoir.*"

Bulverton suddenly gripped James' forearm. Hard.

"You are a man, a good one. Don't forget that. And don't let anyone treat you like a boy. You're not one."

James waited in the parlor of Madame Flora's for an hour until he saw Thomas cross the room, heading for the stairs down to the street.

"Tom!"

"Jamie!"

They embraced and shook hands and went in search of a coffeehouse. Thomas hadn't yet heard of James' father's death.

"So you're a duke now."

"Yes."

"I didn't think you wanted to be a duke."

"I wasn't given much choice, was I?"

"I suppose not. But it probably isn't such a terrible thing, in the end. I'm sure as a duke you won't have any trouble attracting a wife. Not that you would have had any trouble before. My housekeeper Mrs. Dewey always called you Lord Adonis behind your back, you know, and she still asks when you're coming to Sommerleigh again."

James smiled and frowned at the same time. "No, I didn't know."

Thomas leaned forward over his cup of coffee. "And when I was courting Mrs. Lovelock last spring, there were a couple of times we called on her together when I was absolutely sure she was eyeing you like you were some succulent slice of roast beef while being perfectly polite to me. That's why I stopped asking you to come with me, you know? But, back in December, it seemed she had quite settled into thinking of you as a kind of favorite nephew."

James laughed a little too loudly.

"Mature women like you, Jamie. You should remember that. Especially when you go to take a wife."

If only he could talk to Thomas about his feelings. But he couldn't. At Christmas, his friend had said he didn't know what love was. With his chaste marriage-of-convenience and his whores, Thomas could have no understanding of the twinned hope and despair in James' heart.

After coffee, Thomas wanted to buy a book for his wife, and they went in search of a bookseller. Thomas Drake and James Cavendish, in a bookseller's shop at nine o'clock in the morning. It beggared belief.

When James got back to his rooms, there was no word from Catherine. But he still hoped she might come for the painting, so he sent Enfield to stay at the Middlewich town house. Of course, sending Enfield away meant she would definitely not come, he realized that.

He spent the afternoon fencing at Antonio's, determined to distract himself with exertion. He exhausted himself successfully, but he still held his breath when he came back to his rooms. No letter, no note slipped under his door. He threw his fencing kit on the floor of the drawing room. Tomorrow, he would go to her.

In the middle of the night, James came out of deep sleep. He had heard something.

"Catherine?" he called out into the dark. No reply. He went back to sleep, he thought. Then another sound roused him.

Someone was in his dressing room.

He had slept naked, hoping she would use the key he had sent her back in February and come into his bed as she had at Sommerleigh.

Now he cursed himself for a fool.

He got out of the bed and looked for a weapon. His fencing kit was still in the drawing room. Here, the poker from by the fire. And would more light help him or help the intruder?

The question was taken out of his hands as lamplight filled the room. Siddons stood in the door to James' dressing room, holding a lamp and pointing a pistol.

"I'm here for the painting," Siddons said.

"That's theft, Siddons." James kept the poker in his hand. "And if you fire the pistol, it will be assault."

"Oh, no, Your Grace. If I fire the pistol, it will be murder. I assure you."

James said nothing, but he could feel his heart thumping.

"You're the thief, Cavendish. You stole the painting from me."

"I bought that painting. From the Royal Academy. As you know."

"Yes. After you forced them to buy it. After you threw around your title and your money and you got your way. Like I'm sure you always have."

James was silent.

"Drop that poker and light the candle on the mantel. I want to see you clearly."

James let the poker clang to the floor, and he found a tinder box and lit the candle.

"Ha! You sleep as God made you. Rather difficult to be a white knight when you have no armor, eh?" Siddons laughed. "Come here and hold this lamp. And then I am going to take this painting and go."

And in between those two things, you are going to shoot me dead. Because how could you possibly let me live to speak of your crime?

James walked over and took the lamp. Siddons, still pointing the pistol at him, backed his way into the dressing room.

"Come here." He jerked his head. "I want to make sure I have the right thing."

James came into the dressing room and walked to the far end and held up the lamp and removed the drape from the painting.

Suddenly, the golden-haired youth blazed to life. The fearful eyes. The white skin. The ominous forest and the pool.

Siddons walked forward and flipped the painting, looking at its back side. He seemed confused for a moment, but then he shrugged. "You will carry the painting for me. Carefully."

Siddons backed away, holding the pistol out, and James hoisted the painting up with one hand, raising the lamp with the other. He walked out of the dressing room, certain he would hear a shot at any second and feel a bullet enter his body.

When James got to the little passage between his bedchamber and the drawing room, the stone was cold on his bare feet. He remembered the one time Catherine had come to his rooms and how she had pulled her dress over her head in this corridor and dropped it on the stone floor, and he almost wept.

Siddons was going to have the painting, and there was nothing James could do. He stopped walking and stood still. Siddons came up behind him.

"Keep moving, Cavendish."

James turned around to face Siddons and put the painting down, resting it against his own leg. With both hands, he lifted the lamp high above his head and threw it as hard as he could onto the stone floor. The lamp smashed, oil splashed out, and flame spread over the surface of the oil puddle on the stone floor.

Siddons jumped back. "What are you doing? You shitsack!"

The oil and the flames spread closer to James' feet as he took the painting and put it face down on the fire.

Siddons screamed, a wordless cry. James saw a lick of flame near Siddons' outstretched hand.

Oh.

He crumpled to the floor.

He fired the pistol. I anticipated that, didn't I? I just forgot to do anything about it.

THIRTY-TWO

Catherine had heard nothing from James.

Yesterday had been the opening of the Exhibition. No note came. And he himself did not come to her. He must have failed to get the painting and was reluctant to tell her. She thought of sending someone—maybe Wright—to the Exhibition and having the maid report back if the painting was there and what people were saying about it. And about her. But she didn't.

At midnight, as she sat in the dark morning room, writing letters by candlelight, adding things to her lists, making plans for her future and for Arabella's, she finally realized why she might not have heard from James.

"You bloody fool!"

She had told him to steal the painting if it came to that. She had told James, her Jamie, to commit a crime. Was she mad? Anything could have happened. He could have been arrested and been put in gaol. Or he could have had violence used against him. He could have been stabbed or shot. She had been so stupidly selfish.

She rang for Chelsom. She went and got a pair of boots

and put them on. Her butler appeared in his dressing gown and slippers.

"Chelsom, I have to find the Duke of Middlewich. He may be arrested or injured. I want you to go to Tothill Fields gaol and look for him. If he's there, find out the bond and pay it. If he's not there, you must start going to hospitals and infirmaries and looking for injured men."

"Why Tothill Fields and not Newgate, Mrs. Lovelock?"

She went to the front door and opened it. "Because Somerset House is in Westminster, not the City, Chelsom. Can't you think?"

She ran down her own front steps and onto the dark pavement. It was only a few streets from her home to the Cavendish family town house. She banged on the door. After a great deal of time, a footman came.

No, the duke was not at home.

Catherine attempted to calm herself. She knew she appeared wild, and the hour was late. Did the footman know if the duke was at his rooms near the Burlington Arcade?

A nightshirted Enfield appeared at the door. "Mrs. Lovelock." He shouldered the footman out of the way.

"Enfield." She wrung her hands. "The duke, where is he? Why are you not with him?"

Enfield leaned forward and said quietly, "He sent me away, Mrs. Lovelock. He did not say why, but I think he was waiting for you. He's in his rooms."

"He's there? He's safe?"

Enfield smiled. "He was safe as can be when I brought him his dinner this evening."

Catherine stood on her booted toes and kissed Enfield's cheek. "Thank you, Enfield. Thank you."

She dashed down the steps and away, south, to Piccadilly, to the Burlington Arcade.

The windows of his rooms were dark. The door to the

building was open, and, when she reached the door to James' rooms, she found that door ajar as well. Perhaps Enfield was right, and he really had been waiting for her, leaving the door open like this.

But why should he have expected her when he had sent her no word? Was she to be a mind reader?

She took a deep breath, reminding herself only minutes ago she had been crazed with fear over his safety. He was safe, that was all that mattered. He was safe.

She entered his rooms and realized she was wrong. He was *not* safe. Light spilled into the drawing room through the little passage to the bedchamber. In the time since she had entered the building, someone had lit a candle or a lamp in James' bedchamber.

Roger's voice. She could hear him say if he fired the pistol, it would be murder.

Roger was here. And he had a pistol.

The drawing room itself was dark. She stumbled on something. She stopped moving, but the voices in the other room continued. She got down on the floor and felt around. There. She had tripped over something long. It had a handle. It was a sword, a fencing sword.

It must belong to James. She had not known he fenced. In so many ways, she knew very little about him.

Carefully, quietly, she took the foil from its sheath. She touched the blade very lightly. It was sharp. The tip was not blunted.

The light was stronger now, coming through the little hallway into the drawing room, and she could see a naked James holding a lamp and a framed painting, and there was a smash and the floor was on fire and the very loud crack of a shot rent the night and James was down on the floor.

THIRTY-THREE

James felt a tug on his feet, and he was pulled out of the hallway, all the way into the drawing room. He was turned over, and a body, a little one, covered him and beat on him with small hands.

"Your hair, your hair," the little body said, slapping at his head.

It was Catherine. He put his arms up to hold her to him. "Upsidaisy," he murmured.

"Let go of me. I put out the fire on you, but you have to let go of me."

He still held her fast.

"Be not afraid of greatness, Jamie."

That seemed reasonable to him. He allowed his arms to fall to his sides, and she was gone.

When he let her go, she was off him in a flash and feeling around on the floor for the foil she had dropped when she heard the shot and saw James fall into the flames.

She found it, got to her feet, and walked towards the

passage between the drawing room and the bedchamber. A few flames still licked on the floor, but the oil from the lamp had mostly burnt away. It was a stone floor. The fire would not spread.

She could see Roger Siddons beyond the hallway, in the bedchamber, kneeling on the floor, the painting in front of him. She couldn't tell if the painting had been damaged. She couldn't see the pistol.

But then he saw her, and she saw the pistol because he raised and leveled it at her.

"Roger," she said and walked towards him, holding the foil behind her back.

"Cath," he said and stood up and backed away.

She walked through the passage and into the bedchamber.

"You always were very daring, Cath," he said and smiled. "Very much of a risk taker."

"Not really."

"And you've grown out of your fear of me, I see."

"I was never afraid of you, Roger."

"Really? This painting you hate so much says otherwise."

"You're holding a single-shot dueling pistol. I don't think you've had time to reload." She whipped the foil out from behind her back and lunged and a flick of her wrist knocked the pistol out of his hand. "Surrender to me, and I won't kill you."

"Um, Cath," he said. He was looking at her feet. "You're on fire."

It was true she felt some warmth around her ankles. She looked down for a moment. The hem of her dress was burning. She had caught fire from the few remaining flames in the passage. Stupid. She should not have confronted Roger. She should have dragged James out of the rooms...and then what? Would she have been able to get them both to safety?

Some movement. She looked up. Siddons had grabbed a

long object from the floor. It looked like a poker. He swung it at her, and she ducked.

"You better get those clothes off, Cath, or you'll go up like a torch."

She lunged forwards with the foil, but he parried with the poker.

"Know this, Roger. I was never—"

A series of blows, she tore his trousers, she saw blood.

"—afraid of you—"

He was so much taller than she, so much stronger.

"—I was afraid of—"

She lunged and pointed the foil upward towards his neck, as high as she could.

"—myself."

She pulled the foil back.

A startled look on Siddons' face. He put a hand to his neck. The hand disappeared in a fountain of bright blood, and he fell to the floor.

She dropped her sword and fell to the floor herself and rolled, beating at her dress and her petticoat. The flames had destroyed the cloth up to her knees, but she finally put them out. She grabbed the candle from the mantel and ran through the small passageway. There were no flames now. The lamp oil had been consumed, and, as she had expected, the fire had burnt itself out on the stone floor.

"Jamie. Jamie!"

He was sitting up on the carpet of the drawing room, holding his head, but when she rushed to him, he stood and said, "Where's Siddons?"

"He's dead. Where were you shot?"

She saw blood on his legs, his abdomen, his chest, his shoulders, his face. She wanted to examine him, to run her hands over his body to check him for wounds, but he clutched at her and lifted her up and said "Kate, oh, Kate, are you all right?" and covered her mouth with his so she could not answer.

He kissed her. She kissed him back. He kissed her more. She put her hand in protest over his mouth.

"Jamie, put me down and let me look at you."

He complied, and she ran her hands quickly over his abdomen and back, his buttocks, his legs. He stifled a laugh when she touched his knees. Catherine felt a measure of relief. A man who could stand, who could kiss, who could be ticklish was a man unlikely to have a serious injury. "Kneel down." He obediently knelt and rested his hands on her waist as she checked his chest and upper back and shoulders.

Finally, she found the wound in the burnt hair on his head. A four-inch-long graze that was bleeding copiously.

"Help me take my dress off."

He obligingly lifted what remained of her dress and helped her pull it off, and she balled it up and held it to his scalp.

"It looks like a graze. Do you hurt anywhere else?" She saw some areas of redness on his chest and on his thighs. His leg hair was singed.

He was feeling her legs. "Your petticoat is incinerated."

"Yes, but I didn't get burnt. But you did. Oh, Jamie, your beautiful hair."

"It will grow back. How…how is Siddons dead?"

She closed her eyes. "I killed him."

Roger was gone. Forever. It didn't make it easier that it had always seemed inevitable it would end this way. That she would be driven to this. She had never once pictured it the other way round, that she would die at the end of Roger's sword or pistol or chokehold. It had always been *her* killing *him*. Her exacting the price of her torture. Her rebelling against the hold he'd had on her.

Yes, of course, she would have done the same to anyone who tried to hurt the beautiful man who was on his knees in front of her, holding her and bringing her head down to cover her face in kisses.

But it had been Roger. She had been an understudy, rehearsing in her head for so long, and she had finally stepped into the role.

That of a murderer.

The painting was blackened, but James pointed out the face and upper body were still visible and identifiable.

They burnt the rest of the painting in the fireplace in the drawing room. First, Catherine used James' razor to slice the canvas to ribbons, and James used the poker to bash the frame to bits. Catherine made a dressing for James' head out of the remains of her petticoat. James dressed and gave Catherine a pair of his breeches and a shirt, and she put them on and was so dwarfed by them that they laughed together. Their laughter was tinged with hysteria.

They both tried not to look at the body lying on the floor of the bedchamber when they went to get clothes from the dressing room.

The long case clock in the drawing room chimed. Once. They waited. That was all. It was only one in the morning. No one had come in response to the pistol shot.

They left the rooms and walked to Catherine's house. They encountered no one. He held her hand as they walked, something he had never done before. How small her hand was. How good it felt to be linked to her, even in the midst of this horror.

"You won't have been there," he said. "I killed Siddons with my foil when he trespassed to steal the painting, which I had already destroyed. It's all very close to the truth."

"Yes."

"And we will need to stay apart for a while. I want no association between you and Siddons' death. I don't want it to come out that you might have been involved in any way."

She hitched up the breeches she was wearing with her free hand and said nothing.

"What was that you said to me when I was dazed and holding you and you wanted me to let go?"

She shook her head. "I don't know why I said it."

"But what was it that you said? I can't remember."

"It's from *Twelfth Night*. The line is *Be not afraid of greatness*. And you know how it goes on. *Some are born great—*"

"*—some achieve greatness—*"

They finished together, "*And some have greatness thrust upon them.*"

He looked at her. She smiled at him. His Viola in oversized breeches and her little, scorched boots.

A carriage rolled by, one street over. Someone leaving a ball early or going to one late. It might even be Lady Huxley's ball tonight. One year since they had met.

"Thank you for saving me, Kate."

"You and I both know you would have been in no danger if it weren't for me and my stupid wish to be rid of that painting."

He squeezed her hand. "I hope you know I would do anything for you."

She nodded and kept walking and did not drop his hand.

"But why haven't you answered my letters?" he asked.

They had arrived at her house, and she mounted the steps and knocked on the door. She looked down at him standing on the pavement.

"I've answered all your letters."

Chelsom opened the door. "Mrs. Lovelock, I'm glad you're back, I got halfway to Tothill Fields, but I forgot to bring money for the bond and I could not find any ready cash—"

He broke off when he saw James standing behind her.

"No need, Chelsom," Catherine said. "And His Grace was not here tonight, and I never left the house."

"Yes, Mrs. Lovelock."

She turned to James. "After the magistrate, you'll get your head seen to."

"Enfield will make sure of it. Don't worry."

She laid her hand along his cheek, and he clasped it there, reluctant to let her go, wanting to remain close. After long seconds, she took her hand away and went into the house.

Thirty-Four

As Wright helped her dress, Catherine noticed her maid was acting as troubled as Catherine felt. Wright had been changed of late. On edge. Anxious and easily startled.

Catherine scolded herself. She had been so caught up in her own drama of James and her own condition and then the painting that she had had no thought for anyone else.

After Wright had fumbled with the clasp of Catherine's necklace for several minutes, Catherine put her hands up and took the necklace from her.

"I beg your pardon, ma'am." Wright blushed.

"I think no necklace today." Catherine smiled in her mirror at the maid, but Wright was in tears.

Catherine stood and took the maid's hands.

"Wright, what is the matter?"

The young woman shook her head and gave no answer.

That night, Wright took her things and disappeared. She left no word with anyone, and no one knew where she went. The rest of the staff agreed the girl had seemed nervous recently and the chambermaids reported Wright had recently purchased some new and expensive-looking clothes.

Catherine only hoped Wright had landed somewhere safe. She wrote to the vicar in Wright's home village, hoping to hear word that the young woman had gone home, but she received no reply.

Even as Catherine worried over Wright, she was glad James had said they should stay apart. She had plans to make, and they were plans of which James could know nothing.

Time was fleet. Time was treacherous. She would be showing soon.

The magistrate deemed Roger Siddons' death the result of an act of self-defense by the new Duke of Middlewich. James had committed no crime, and, even if he had not been a duke, there was no charge to be made. But once Siddons' body had been removed and the blood had been scoured from the floor, James still did not return to his rooms. He told Enfield to leave everything in place, it all smelled of smoke. He would now live in the town house as befitted the Duke of Middlewich, and he could wear his father's clothes until the tailors fitted him for new ones.

He had never noticed he and his father were exactly the same size.

He got his hair clipped very short, with all the burnt ends cut off. He hoped Catherine would not mourn his locks too much.

Mr. Bulverton asked for a meeting with James and Isabella. But not at Madame Flora's. Instead, they congregated in Mr. Bulverton's office in Whitehall. They might as well do this openly, James thought. The jig was up for him, at any rate. Isabella, too. She said she was retiring from being a *pillow spy*.

Bulverton's office was not the office of a senior clerk.

Unlike Bulverton's appearance, his office was luxurious, a spacious room. Fine carpets, mahogany desk, velvet curtains. Bulverton was a great deal higher up than James had ever suspected. Clever, that bad wig, the patched coat, those stained cuffs.

Senior clerk, my arse.

"I heard there was an incident, Your Grace, in your rooms," Mr. Bulverton said as he shuffled some papers at his desk.

"An intruder, a thief. He had a pistol and shot at me." James rubbed the stitched-together ridge on the top of his scalp. "Had to kill him."

"I see. What was he trying to steal?"

James shifted uneasily. "A painting I had bought from the Royal Academy. He was the artist, and he wanted it back."

"Where is the picture now?"

James licked his lips. "It got burnt, destroyed, when a lamp tipped over."

"I see." Mr. Bulverton shifted some papers on his desk and cleared his throat. "The Prince Regent," he said, looking down at the top piece of paper on his desk, "is aware of your actions over the last many years and thanks you for your gallantry, your courage, and your valor in preserving the safety of the empire and of England. He has asked me to present you with a medal he has named the Cloak and Sword."

James and Isabella stood and received the small golden medal embossed with a furled cloak and a broadsword, held by a crimson ribbon with blue edges.

Bulverton cleared his throat. "And now, I must ask you for the medals back."

James had expected something like this and unpinned the medal from his coat and put it in Bulverton's hand. Isabella gave back her medal, too, and James saw a ring on her left hand. Good for her.

It was over. What had been the best part of his life for many years was done. He thought he would feel devastated, but he didn't. If he could only get Catherine to marry him. All this was nothing in comparison to that.

As he left the building, someone grabbed his arm, and he was pushed against a wall.

"You eejit," a woman's voice hissed. It was Isabella. Normally lazy and languorous, she was practically spitting in fury.

"Mamselle DuMornay," he got out.

"Dontchoo *mamselle* me, Yer Grace!" Her French accent had fled, replaced by that of her native East London. "Yew 'aven't got the sense Gawd almighty gave a feckin' 'edge-'og, yew doan't!"

A few passersby stared, curious.

James pulled his arm from Isabella's grasp and tugged at the sleeve of his tailcoat. "I don't have the slightest idea to what you are referring. But I am sure you are prepared to illuminate my deficiencies. So let's cut this short, and you tell me exactly where my sense is absent."

"What I want ter know is, Yer Grace, whenjoo last see our Mrs. Lovelock, eh?"

He hedged. "A while ago."

"Whatchoo noticin' about our Mrs. Lovelock then, hmm? 'ow she look?"

"She looked much the same as usual."

"Did she, Yer Grace?" She threw her hands up into the air and broke into a stream of French so rapid and curse-filled James could not follow it. He did catch *stupid man* and *wouldn't know his penis from his nose.*

He waited.

"Did Yer Grace not see 'er skin? Glowin', I'd say. And 'er buzooms? Fuller and bigger than before. And 'er woom?" Isabella clutched her own lower abdomen.

James opened his mouth, and it stayed open while he stood on busy Whitehall Street and his mind struggled to catch up.

Glowing skin. Larger breasts. A very gentle rounding of the lower abdomen he had felt the night of Siddons' killing, when he had knelt for her inspection and put his hands around her waist and his thumbs and his fingers had not met each other. As they had before.

But she had said…she must have believed…and then he remembered his own mother had just turned sixty-one years of age. And his youngest sister was fifteen. *Subtraction, James, subtraction.*

Isabella folded her arms and nodded.

"Ah, *Monsieur le duc*, he sees at last, I think." Her French accent had returned.

"I m-m-must," he stammered. "Find a hack." He went to the curb and looked helplessly up and down the street.

"*Bonne chance*, Jacques," Isabella said and disappeared into a throng of government office seekers.

Sweating, he arrived at her house, mouth dry, cravat askew. Chelsom eyed the duke and said Mrs. Lovelock was not at home.

"Tell her she owes me a conversation. She promised. To sit. And talk with me. Tell her."

"I am sorry, Your Grace, but Mrs. Lovelock is not at home."

James backed down the steps in frustration and swore out loud in the middle of the Mayfair street.

He walked away from the house. She was almost certainly at home and just refusing to see him. Perhaps he might be able to scale the house from the back and break into her boudoir.

No, no. That was no way to convince her. She would

think him juvenile and presumptuous. But he must find a way to convince her to see sense. She must marry him. She had refused him before, but this time, he would overwhelm her.

Wait. Had she refused him before? Refused marriage from him before? He stopped in the middle of the pavement. Had he actually ever asked her to marry him?

Yes. In a letter. Which she had not answered.

But she said she had answered all his letters. Which meant she had never received *that* letter. In Catherine's world, he had never asked her to marry him.

He had asked her to share his bed. To partake in mutual pleasures of the flesh. But he had never said out loud *will you marry me* or *will you be my wife* or any of the dozen other blasted ways there must be to tell a woman you wanted her forever, legally and carnally.

She must have thought he wanted her to be his mistress as she had been for Siddons. No wonder she had turned from him. And she was carrying his child. How horribly alone she must have been these last weeks.

He saw now that if he wanted her by his side, he had done everything wrong. Because some deep part of Catherine must crave convention. She had married a banker, for Christ's sake! He had mistaken the woman who aroused him like no other— the fierce, brave, desire-driven Viola—for the woman whole. And, yes, even Viola had wanted to marry her duke.

What did conventional lovers do when they wanted to marry their lady loves?

Flowers. He must find flowers. He considered raiding the central garden of the square, but all he could see were shrubs and grass.

And that is how the thirteenth Duke of Middlewich found himself in the back garden of his family's town house, pulling up sweet peas and delphinium and pricking himself on thorns from roses. At one point, one of the footmen, still wearing a black armband for James' father, came out with a pair of cunning snippers and took over holding the flowers while James amassed every bright bloom he could find. The footman's face was lost behind the flowers by the end.

"Good, good, but I must clean up. And find a ring. I need a ring. Get someone to make a bouquet of those, there's a good chap." James darted into the house.

A ring, a ring, a ring. James was glad to have the house to himself, barring the servants, as he stripped and ran from room to room, Enfield following and picking up his discarded clothing. James was hoping to find some suitable piece of jewelry in his mother's room or one of his sister's rooms. Alas, all the jewels had been taken back to the country seat in Middlewich.

He would go to Rundell & Bridge. The jewelers. The goldsmiths. He could barely stand still long enough to have Enfield help him into a fresh shirt and tie his cravat.

"Ahem."

"Yes, Enfield?"

"Some months ago, you asked me to take possession of an item for you. I have kept it with your cufflinks and watch fobs. I think it might be of use to you now. Perhaps. It does match the lady's eyes."

With a flourish, Enfield presented the sapphire ring.

James crushed Enfield in a hug and clapped him on the back. "Excellent! Perfect." He put the ring in his waistcoat pocket and rushed down the stairs.

Enfield called down after him, "The flowers, my lord."

James stopped halfway out the door and turned back. "Yes, yes, the flowers. Where are my blasted flowers?"

The footman ran up the servants' stairs from the kitchen, carrying an enormous bouquet. James grabbed it from him.

"Yes. Good." He ran out the door and down the front steps.

. . .

She was gone from London.

That's all he could discover from Chelsom. "My Grace, I assure you, she really is not at home. Not just to you, but to anyone."

James believed him.

He went round to the rather elegant lane that constituted an alley in Mayfair and found an idling stable boy. The boy worked for the house next door but said he had been talking to Mrs. Lovelock's coachman and footmen early in the morning.

"Off to Kent, but I think the mistress plans to stay there a good long while because she took two trunks, but Dawson, one of the footmen, says the carriage will be back tomorrow without her. Which is good because Dawson owes me a half a shilling."

Kent.

She must have changed her mind.

She must have accepted Sir Francis' proposal.

Of course, she had. Above all things, Catherine loved her daughters, and, although Mary and Harry were settled, there was still Arabella. Catherine would not give birth to a child in an unwed state if for no other reason than it would fatally damage Arabella's prospects of a good marriage. Even if that meant a bad marriage for Catherine.

There was no problem with the timing. If a baby was born after a wedding, no matter how soon after, the child was legitimate. Yes, there might be a few months of gossip, but that would pass. The matrons of the *ton* would eventually shrug and move on to discussing some new *on dit*. So? The engaged couple had been a trifle eager and consummated the marriage early. This was common enough to be only a minor scandal. The whispers and knowing looks engendered by a baby born fewer than nine months after a wedding would in no way compare to the censure Catherine and Arabella would face if Catherine gave birth to a child while still unmarried.

James shoved the bouquet at a young nursemaid accompanying a little girl rolling a hoop down the pavement and ran the two streets back to his town house.

But it was his child. She must be made to see it was only right he be allowed to take responsibility for the baby. And for her.

Even if she did not love him, she must see that.

He would trap her with the baby. And once they were married, he would make her fall in love with him. He had to believe it was possible.

He left for Kent immediately on the fastest horse in his stable.

THIRTY-FIVE

Catherine gazed out the window of the carriage. She had managed everything as efficiently as she possibly could have. She had enough clothes, enough money. She had even sewn coins into her cloak to thwart pickpockets in case of a crush getting on the boat. She would write to Mary, Harry, and Arabella once she had settled somewhere on the Continent. Likely deep in the countryside, in Brittany, far from Paris, far from where she might see anyone she knew.

She would be in Dover tonight and Calais by tomorrow.

She would have the child and leave it in France with a wet nurse, a woman who would take money for caring for the baby. She would return to London and ensure Arabella had a good match. Once Arabella was wed, then and only then, she would return to France for the child. There would be whispers, of course, about her adopted ward, but with Arabella safely married, Catherine could withstand that.

And she would have left James an unhampered future. He would never know, and there would be no bastard to haunt him.

Or to make a future bride turn away from him.

She shuddered. She could not think on that hypothetical bride, that future Duchess of Middlewich, that virgin of the *ton*. That beauty unmarked by age, that innocence unstained by evil. How jealous she was of that imaginary girl already, that girl who would only ever know one lover in her life and it would be James.

Jamie.

But, no, she would not think on that girl. Or on James. Or on Roger and how she had killed him.

Despite her circumstances, a smile twitched at her lips. There were so many things on which she could not allow her mind to dwell that she was surprised she had anything left she *could* think about.

But she was Kate Cooksey, Catherine Cooke, Mrs. Edward Lovelock, and she was made of strong stuff. As Kentish villages and meadows moved past her carriage window, she conjured up all the good things that could occupy her thoughts.

A future love-match for Arabella. Harry's improving health and her mathematical ambitions. Mary's ongoing wish for children with her husband. And this child growing within her, this child that could not help but be beautiful since it was James' child, too. She would surround this child with so much love, he or she would never miss a father.

Catherine would think on these pleasant things, and she would close the door on that part of herself that had always been so intemperate, so difficult to control, so maddening. So prone to fornication and violence. So weak, so unable to make decisions that weren't influenced by lust. Yes, there had only been two men in her life who had brought that part of herself to the fore, but they were two too many.

And one was dead now. At her own hand.

She had lied to herself for so long, naming it as something apart from herself. But it wasn't. Yet, she had to believe she could still excise it. From this time on, she would live as a nun, at least in respect to her desire. It was the only solution.

Besides Ophelia's solution. And she would never undertake that. Never.

There would be no cold, dark water covering her over, smothering her breath, snatching her life away. Catherine Lovelock would die in bed of old-age, her hair silver, her face lined, her children and her grandchildren surrounding her.

James galloped up to Ffoulkes Manor. Something looked different about the house, but he couldn't place it. He dismounted and ran up the steps to the front door. He pounded on it. No answer. He tried it. Locked.

He looked back at his horse, foamy with sweat, nibbling on some long grass on the side of the drive. That was what had changed. The grass was long, likely uncut the entire spring. Weeds were springing up through the gravel of the drive.

He went down the front steps and around the side of the house. In the back, he found a recessed door and forced it open. It was the servants' entrance that led into a warren of rooms and passages, including a kitchen. There was a foul odor here—yes, the damp Enfield had mentioned last autumn but also something rotten. There was no one about.

He found stairs and climbed them.

"Catherine?" he called out.

He discovered the large hall where he had carried her in, out of the wet, and the large main staircase where he had helped her both down and up.

"Catherine?"

He heard a noise. *Plink*. He went into the drawing room where he had drunk Madeira before dinner and played cards after dinner. It all seemed so long ago.

The room was desolate. The rugs were gone as were the

curtains. The sofas, the chairs, the mahogany tables for the cards—all gone.

Mysteriously, the pianoforte was still here. And Sir Francis Ffoulkes was sitting on the bench, head resting on the music shelf, playing the same note over and over again.

"Sir Francis!" James strode across the empty room.

Sir Francis raised his head. His eyes were bloodshot. His Titus curls were flat and greasy. He had aged perhaps ten years since James had last seen him.

"Good day." He stayed seated and bowed from the waist. "I would stand, but I would likely fall." James could smell alcohol from where he stood.

"Is Mrs. Lovelock here?"

"Mrs. Lovelock?" Sir Francis gazed at something invisible across the room.

"Yes."

"There's no one here. Except me."

Thank God. But where else would Catherine go in Kent?

Sir Francis' eyes came to rest on James. "You!" He tried to stand. "You. You killed Roger. My friend." He collapsed back onto the pianoforte bench.

"He broke into my rooms and shot me, Sir Francis. I am surprised you would call such a man your friend."

"Well, he was. I told him to go get the painting. I gave him the key, and he went. And now he's dead."

Sir Francis had been behind Siddons' invasion of James' rooms. But why would Sir Francis care about the painting? Except that, of course, it was a painting of Catherine.

"How did you get a key to my rooms?"

"It doesn't matter." Sir Francis waved his hand. "I got it from René, if you must know. He was going to pay me a lot of money for the plans. But you took the picture away and we had to get the plans back. I mean, I wanted the painting, too. Badly. But the plans were worth a fortune."

René DuBois. The conversation he had heard at the modiste's shop between the Marquis DuBois de Laval and Madame Beauchamp came flooding back. The bribing of the lady's maids to get letters—Catherine's lady's maid must have been one of those bribed. That's why so many of James' letters had gone astray, including his proposal of marriage. And, of course, the letter containing a key to his rooms. James had also sent a letter to Catherine saying the painting was in his dressing room. Siddons had known exactly where to search.

But why Catherine?

"What plans are these, Sir Francis?"

Sir Francis was silent.

"You said it didn't matter. Why don't you tell me?"

Sir Francis leaned over and vomited on the floor. When he sat up again, James stepped forward.

"What were the plans for?"

Sir Francis raised a bottle to his lips and swigged. "An underwater ship. Madness. René has been after me for a year to get him the plans out of the Navy Board archive. I got the plans, but…"

"But what?"

"I saw all the marines, and I thought I might be searched when I tried to leave the courtyard. I went into the Royal Academy. It was the first Varnishing Day, and there were artists everywhere…"

But not Roger Siddons. He had completed his painting twenty-seven years ago. No finishing touches for him.

Sir Francis looked down at the pianoforte keyboard. "I saw it. Roger's painting. I knew he didn't intend to sell it, so I thought I would put the plans behind the picture and when he took the picture home at the end of the Exhibition, I could get the plans back. And I wouldn't get caught."

James said slowly, "But when I bought the painting, I took these plans."

"Yes."

James thought hard. When he and Catherine had taken the picture apart, they had found no plans.

"What did they look like, Sir Francis? The plans?"

"Oh, I folded them. They looked like folded papers. White papers. Long and thin."

James shook his head. He had seen no papers. "Mrs. Lovelock has come into Kent today. Do you know why she would do that?"

"Kent is a beautiful place, Your Grace, as I am sure you are aware. Indeed, I will miss it."

James had tarried too long. "I must go. Is there anyone here looking after you?"

"Just me, Your Grace. But you go on."

James did. He felt a degree of worry and pity for Sir Francis, but he had to find Catherine. He unlocked the front door and came out and found his horse still nibbling on the grass. He took the horse around to the well outside the stable and pulled up several buckets of water for the horse. James drank several dippers of water, as well. He was about to lead the horse back out to the front and let the horse graze again when he heard riders and a coach coming up the drive. He tied his horse to the well and walked back to the front of the house.

There were six riders, all armed with pistols, and a coach. The riders dismounted as the coach door opened, and Mr. Bulverton got out. Just as he was about to go up the steps, he saw James and paused.

"Your Grace." Mr. Bulverton inclined his head.

The sound of a gunshot punctured the air. The dismounted riders had been standing on the steps, waiting for Mr. Bulverton, but now they ran through the front door of the house. Mr. Bulverton and James followed.

Sir Francis Ffoulkes was found on the floor of the drawing

room, next to the pianoforte. A pistol was next to him. A bullet was in his brain. He was dead.

James sat on the grass in front of Ffoulkes Manor, hunched forward with his legs in front of him, knees up, forearms resting on his knees, forehead resting on his thumbs. His horse grazed nearby.

Mr. Bulverton came over and stood next to him. One of the riders brought over a small stool, and Mr. Bulverton sat.

James said nothing.

"It's been an odd business all along the way," Mr. Bulverton said. "I set you onto Sir Francis Ffoulkes because of his association with the Marquis DuBois de Laval. And because I knew he had overextended himself and was in debt and, hence, vulnerable."

James squinted and looked up at Bulverton on his stool. "Not because of Mrs. Lovelock?"

"Mrs. Lovelock? No, she is entirely incidental."

She's not incidental to me.

"You'll remember I asked you to watch Ffoulkes before you ever met Mrs. Lovelock."

James thought. "That's true."

"Indeed, if Ffoulkes had married Mrs. Lovelock, I might have halted surveillance of him because he would have had the money he needed. He would have been unlikely to do DuBois' bidding."

"But why would DuBois steal Cather—Mrs. Lovelock's letters? Why would he want to know what I wrote to her?"

"He didn't. He wanted to know what Ffoulkes wrote to her. The maid in question simply pilfered all the letters she could get her hands on before her mistress opened them."

"I don't understand why DuBois would go to all this trouble for some plans for a ship."

A rider brought a hamper basket over to Mr. Bulverton and set it down. Mr. Bulverton opened it and took out two glasses.

"Here." He handed the glasses to James and took out a jug and uncorked it. He poured two foaming glasses of ale and took one back from James and drank deeply. He wiped the foam from his lip. "Go on and drink, Your Grace."

James drank.

"The strangest thing about all this? The man who drew up the plans was a painter when he was younger and actually shared a studio with Roger Siddons around the time he was painting Mrs. Lovelock's, uh, portrait." Mr. Bulverton drank more. "It seems, however unlikely, a scrap of chance. Serendipity. The man's name was Robert Fulton. Have you heard of him?"

James shrugged. "No."

Mr. Bulverton poured them both more ale.

"An interesting man. American. Miniature painter who got interested in steam ships and canals. Was painting here but then went to Paris and built an underwater ship for Napoleon in eighteen hundred. But Napoleon didn't pay him, so Fulton took the ship apart for scrap. That was the *Nautilus*. Then he came back to England in oh-four, and the navy hired him to design another underwater ship. But when Nelson won Trafalgar, it was clear the British Navy was so dominant, an underwater ship was deemed unnecessary, and it was all given up. Fulton went home to America. He died there three years ago. The plans Fulton had drawn up for the British underwater ship were put into the archive at the Navy Board."

"Why would DuBois want the plans for an underwater ship?"

"It is called a sub-marine. Quite clever, that." Mr. Bulverton drank. "Why do you think, Your Grace?

"The war is over."

"Yes."

"So…?"

"A ship that can be under water and invisible for a day or more at a time. A ship like that might be the ideal way to approach a heavily guarded island that has four ships patrolling it at all times."

"St. Helena's?"

Mr. Bulverton said nothing but took another swig of ale.

"DuBois is a Bonapartist?"

Mr. Bulverton raised his eyebrows.

"DuBois means to rescue Napoleon from St. Helena's?"

"Yes, Your Grace. That is my theory. I first got an inkling of what DuBois might be conniving at based on what you overheard at the modiste's. *Le veuf,* you heard, correct?"

"Yes."

"At first, I thought *le veuf,* or the widower, referred to Sir Francis Ffoulkes. After all, he had been recently widowed. But some more recent work on coded messages passed among Bonapartists taught us *le veuf* is a code name for Bonaparte."

"But his wife still lives. Bonaparte's, that is."

"Yes, but his first wife, Josephine, the older woman he divorced because she could not provide heirs, the one he truly loved, she died while he was in exile on Elba. He would not come out of his room for two days after he heard the news. That is when the Bonapartists started calling him *le veuf.*"

An older woman he loved but whom he had abandoned because she couldn't give him sons. No wonder Catherine had thought their love affair doomed from the start.

James cleared his throat. "You know I burnt the painting, and I saw no plans."

"I'm not surprised. Wedging the sub-marine plans into the frame at the back of the painting was an impromptu decision, and like most schemes born of impulse, it failed. The plans could have fallen out anywhere. On the floor of the Great

Hall, on the Strand as you carried the painting to your coach, in your coach itself, or—"

"—in my dressing room."

"Yes, after learning this morning you had bought a painting from the Royal Academy, an institution that shares a building with the Navy Board, and the painting had been Siddons' target, I sent someone to search your rooms before I set out for Kent. But I felt I should not wait to question Sir Francis. As you see, I had already waited too long." Mr. Bulverton shrugged and poured more ale.

"I feel badly about Sir Francis."

"Yes, money is a devil of a thing, isn't it?" Mr. Bulverton drank.

James lay back on the grass and watched some small white clouds scudding across the sky.

"I just wonder where Catherine has gone to."

"Ah, Mrs. Lovelock. You don't know?"

James sat up. "You know?"

"I know a great deal. Of course, I know that."

James got on his knees and grabbed the lapels of Mr. Bulverton's much-patched coat.

"Where is she?"

"She's gone to Dover, Your Grace. She means to cross the channel to France."

PART FOUR

Thirty-Six

J ames had to acquire another horse, so it was close to midnight when he arrived in Dover. He went to one of the public houses abutting the harbor and discovered the next ferry crossing would be in the morning.

"Is there a Mrs. Lovelock staying here or a Miss Cooke or Cooksey? Small, fair-haired woman, traveling alone?"

"No, not here. And it's a good thing, too. This is a rather rough sort of place. Not good for a woman traveling alone. She should be in one of the inns farther from the harbor."

"Which are those?"

"Well, there are close to a dozen of them. But those people won't tell you if she's there or not. Not at this hour. Is she going to make the crossing? Be at the harbor at dawn. You'll see her there. Now, do you want a room or no?"

James took the room even though he did not sleep but paced up and down, too afraid of missing the dawn, too afraid of missing Catherine. Finally, he saw a lightening of the sky in the east, and he left the public house and went to wait at the harbor. It was cold there, with a brisk offshore wind towards the Channel. But the sea was not rough, and James thought it likely the *Bonny Bess* would leave in a timely fashion.

With each woman who approached the harbor, James' heart set up a tattoo. But they were all too tall, too stout, too old, too young.

The sun was up, and the boat would be leaving within the hour. There were more and more people coming to the harbor, and James had to stand directly next to the wharf where the *Bonny Bess* berthed to make sure he would not miss Catherine.

Unless, of course, she had arrived at Dover in time to take the last crossing yesterday. That was unlikely. Or she had hired a private packet boat to take her across. That was more likely. Catherine could afford it. James stayed by the wharf but craned his neck, trying to see if a woman of Catherine's size was heading towards any of the other boats.

And then he saw her red tartan cloak and her golden curls covered by a lace cap, a small figure directing two men carrying her trunks. She was headed directly towards James.

A man bumped into him. A limping, well-dressed man with a tall woman with gray-streaked hair. James recognized the man and grabbed his arm.

"DuBois!"

DuBois tried to wrench his arm away but then looked at James' face. "Your Grace," he said and smiled. "Are you making the crossing, too?"

Catherine and her luggage were getting closer.

"Might I ask what you are doing here, *Monsieur le marquis*?"

"I am going home, Your Grace. To France. There is something I must attend to."

"Is it possible you have something in your possession that belongs to the British government?"

"I am at a loss. I don't know of what you speak. But I

must insist you let me go so I may make this crossing. As your Chaucer wrote, time and tide, *et cetera*."

But James did not let go.

"Two men are dead. Siddons and Ffoulkes. Do you have the plans stolen from the Navy Board? Did you find them in my dressing room?"

"You are mad, Your Grace. I know nothing of this. Release me."

Catherine was upon them with her stevedores, trying to get past and onto the wharf to board the ship.

James turned towards her. "Catherine."

"Jamie." Catherine had no smile for him. To James, she looked very tired.

The tall woman with the gray streaks in her hair pulled at James' arm to get him to release DuBois, but James held fast.

Catherine had a look of recognition on her face. "Madame Beauchamp?"

Madame Beauchamp gave up tugging on James and instead grabbed Catherine and pinned her arms behind her and started dragging her down the wharf towards the boat. The two stevedores blinked and put the trunks down.

"Release René!" Madame Beauchamp shouted as Catherine struggled against the much larger woman.

"Your Grace, I am not your enemy," DuBois hissed. "Unhand me and *la Veuve* Lovelock will be safe. I have read your letters. I know you love her."

James let go of him.

Of course, he did.

What had he been thinking? There were no possessions of the British state that surpassed the importance of Catherine and Catherine's safety.

DuBois hastened down the wharf, limping as fast as he could. When he reached Madame Beauchamp, she let go of Catherine.

Catherine had been pulling against Madame Beauchamp's grasp, so when the woman released her, Catherine lunged forward, tottered on the edge of the wharf, and, as James watched in horror, she fell into the water.

She was immediately lost to view, sucked down by a great force as if Scylla herself had snatched Catherine from the surface.

James dived into the sea.

The water was cold and murky. He should have taken off his boots. But he kicked as hard as he could and swam towards the spot where Catherine had sunk. The harbor was deep. He swam down and touched bottom and couldn't see her. Surely, he should be able to see her red-tartan cloak.

His lungs burning, he surfaced and gasped and saw he was a good fifteen feet beyond where she had fallen in. He swam back and dived down again.

And there she was, on the bottom, struggling to undo her cloak, a look of panic on her face. James caught her around the waist and kicked. Up, up, up. He issued a prayer of thanks to his brother William who had insisted he learn to swim and dive in the lakes and ponds of the Duchy of Middlewich.

Catherine was limp now. And she was so heavy, far heavier than she should be.

He surfaced with her, and there were arms reaching down from the wharf. With his last bit of strength, he shoved Catherine's body up and into those arms. Only once he saw she had been laid down safely on the wharf did he accept a hand up out of the water himself.

An old salt was leaning over Catherine and listening to her chest. Catherine started coughing, and the sailor turned her on her side, and she vomited.

James got on his knees next to her and took over holding her.

"I hope Mrs. Lovelock is all right."

James looked up into the face of Mr. Bulverton. He squatted down next to Catherine and James.

"Be sure to give her some good thumps on the back so she gets all that sea water up. She'll be right as a trivet in a minute."

The old salt was hovering nearby and handed James a knife. James cut the cords of Catherine's cloak, and it fell to the wharf with a thud and a clank.

"Ah, she sewed guineas into the lining of the cloak," Mr. Bulverton said. "No wonder she sank straight to the bottom."

James thumped Catherine vigorously on her back several times. After the fifth thump, Catherine said, "Stop, Jamie," and turned and put her arms around his neck and buried her face in his chest.

"Upsidaisy," he whispered into her wet hair.

James got his arms under her and stood. He carried her back down the wharf, followed by Mr. Bulverton. The Marquis DuBois de Laval and Madame Beauchamp were being forcibly moved away from the shoreline by Mr. Bulverton's men.

"A rider came after you left Ffoulkes Manor. He brought word the plans were not in your dressing room, but someone had clearly conducted a search in the rooms recently. DuBois left London for Dover yesterday, and suddenly someone high up became very anxious about the, uh, papers. We were dispatched to bring DuBois back to London for questioning."

James stopped in front of the stevedores who were still standing next to Catherine's trunks at the end of the wharf. "Go get that cloak on the wharf and bring it and those trunks along to the public house over there."

Catherine looked up at him, and James looked down at her.

Mr. Bulverton said, "I wager the plans will be inside his wooden leg, mark my words."

James was still looking at Catherine. "Good luck, Mr. Bulverton." James strode off, the stevedores following.

"Goodbye, Your Grace," Mr. Bulverton called after him.

James gripped Catherine tightly. There was so much to say. "You're very wet, Mrs. Lovelock."

Her teeth chattered. "As are you, Your Grace."

"You know," he said, "this reminds me of a certain walk we once took together across the Kentish countryside."

"Being carried by a handsome duke sounds very romantic until you realize you have to be injured and soaking wet and cold every time it happens."

"I will endeavor to make sure," he said and kissed her forehead, "that the next time I carry you, Kate, you will be dry and warm and unhurt."

He took her to his room in the public house, which was even more grim in the light of day. But there was a bed. There was a fireplace. The stevedores brought the soaked cloak and the trunks to the room, and they must have told the innkeeper that the very wet man with the very wet woman had been called *Your Grace* by another man at the harbor, because the publican appeared at the door of the bedchamber.

"Does Your Grace need anything else?"

Coal and tea and towels. But, first, some privacy. After the door closed, James deposited Catherine in a wooden chair by the fire and peeled off her dress, unlaced her stays, removed her petticoat and hose and chemise. Her cap and her slippers were gone. She wasn't shivering anymore. Her skin was pale but not blue with cold.

He saw the roundness of her lower abdomen and wanted to place a hand there and say the word *mine*, but he restrained himself.

She pointed at one of the trunks, and he opened it.

"I don't trust the linens at a place like this. Give me my nightdress, there on top," she said. She took it from him and dried herself all over with it. "Now my dressing gown." She put it on.

"Now you, Jamie," she said. He undressed and also took her damp nightdress and dried himself all over.

"The salt water has made pretty much everything except my boots unsalvageable, but Enfield will have packed something, I should think." He opened his saddle bag and put on the dry shirt and the trousers he found there.

Catherine was spreading the soaked nightdress over the chair.

"This is a truly terrible room," she said gazing at the stained walls, the coarse sheets on the bed, the dust in the corners.

"Yes."

The coal bucket and tea and towels were delivered. The publican laid and lit the fire as James poured Catherine a cup of tea.

James pressed a coin into the man's hand and got him out the door.

Catherine looked at James over the top of the crude pottery cup.

James looked at Catherine.

Catherine put the cup down.

Then they were kneeling in the middle of the bed, both having clambered up on it to meet the other one there. He held her face in his hands and kissed her. Hungry, deep kisses. She kissed him back, grabbing at his shirt with her small hands, pulling him into her. He pushed her dressing gown off her shoulders, and she lifted his shirt over his head. He got off the bed and removed his trousers. Now they were just as naked as they had been five minutes before.

"Jamie," she said.

"Kate," he said and got back on the bed and put his hands on her waist and pulled her down to the mattress.

He lay next to Catherine on the bed and ran his hands all over her body as he kissed her face over and over again. She tasted salty, like the sea, and he knew he must taste the same. She moved closer to him, and he wanted to cover her with his body, keep her there, under him, safe.

She reached down and took his member in her hand. She stroked, and James groaned. He put his hand between her legs and touched her wet folds. He grazed her pearl, and she shuddered.

"Please, Jamie," she whispered, and he felt his cock become even harder. He withdrew his hand from between her legs and positioned himself over her. She did not release him but spread her legs wider still and guided him into her.

Sweetness. Wonder. Joy. He was adrift in an ocean of pleasure. She put her heels behind his knees and rocked her hips as he thrust into her, and she sneezed and sneezed again as her body shook. "Jamie!"

He would never tire of hearing her say his name.

"Kate," he said and used one hand to brush a wet tendril of hair from her face. With very little warning, he reached his own crest and released. Rapture rolled through his body for a long time.

When it was over, he lay on her. They breathed together. His neck was bent and his face was buried in her wet hair. She had her head under his chest, her face turned to the side. He had a flood of emotion, lying on top of her as he had months ago, when they had first coupled. And this time, even though she shifted slightly under him, he did not get off her. He stayed on top of her, and he stayed in that wash of feeling.

How grateful he was that she was under him right now, breathing, living. How frightened he had been with her in the water. How sure he was that if she had stayed in that cold, dark place, he would have felt forever alone.

She must have felt him shake or heard the quiver in his

breathing because she put her hands to his head and stroked the short hair she found there.

Finally, he rolled off her and summoned words. "Don't go to France. We must talk. You promised me that. In exchange for the painting. We must talk."

"Yes," she said and stared at the cracked ceiling. "But not in this room."

THIRTY-SEVEN

He hired a carriage and took her to a coaching inn just outside of Canterbury. The inn reminded Catherine of the places where she had slept on her long, slow journey to London when she was sixteen. Small and snug and clean. It was not unlike the inn at Duddenhoe End. Perhaps that was why James had chosen it. He wanted to remind her of their first coupling.

As if she needed reminding.

As if she hadn't spent the coach ride from Dover to Canterbury longing to sit astride him, to kiss him, to undo his cravat and run her hands over his chest and lower still, to touch his cock and make it hard again with her hands and her mouth. To lose herself with him inside her.

"Jamie Cooksey and wife. Kate, she is," James said to the innkeeper. A few coins, a wink from the innkeeper, and five minutes later, she and James were alone in a room with a hearth, a table, some chairs, and a bed. And her two trunks.

James took the key that had been given to him by the innkeeper and locked the door and handed the key to Catherine.

"Will you sit?" he asked her.

After she had sat in one of the chairs, he sat as well.

"You used my birth name," she said.

"Yes."

"Why?"

He shrugged. "Because suddenly I wanted to be a Cooksey, an ordinary man. With my wife. With you."

"You want to worry every day of the year about the rent or the roof or the hens that won't lay?"

"I want *not* to worry the woman I love won't have me." His eyes were calm even as his voice betrayed some emotion with a very slight quaver. "You must know I want you to marry me."

No, she didn't know that. Not with certainty. She had hoped he wanted that, even as she had known it was impossible. Her chest ached.

But he didn't really want to marry *her*. He didn't know her. He didn't know how darkness tainted her and her desire for him. She could never be his wife, his duchess. He should marry the virginal girl she had imagined for him.

"I know you would not have a happy life with me, Jamie."

"And I know you're carrying my child."

Catherine looked away. She would hurt him now. Thrust the knife in and push him away. Quickly. So it would be over. She met his eyes.

"Maybe it's not yours."

He gazed at her steadily, with no sign of insult on his face. "That's not true."

"You shouldn't be so sure of yourself."

"It has nothing to do with me. It's all to do with you."

"You don't know me."

"I know the important parts." He was serious. Not coy. Not flirtatious or insinuating. Still, Catherine felt herself flush with desire again, thinking how he knew her. She fought it down with anger.

"You know my breasts and my quim and that I sneeze and because you know these things, you think you know me?"

James looked taken aback. "I meant I have seen you mother Harry and Arabella. I saw how you handled Roger Siddons at Ffoulkes Manor and in my rooms. I have seen you face danger. You are a powerful woman, Catherine." He took her hand and looked at it. "Tiny, but powerful. And I long to have that power at my side. I have spent so long as a feckless ne'er-do-well that I need your steel."

The touch of his hand on hers. She thought of his hand on her breast, her hip. Warmth and aching and wetness flared in her nether regions. All from his hand touching hers. She pulled her hand away.

"I am weaker than you think, Your Grace."

"Just a moment ago you called me Jamie."

"I am weaker than you think, Jamie."

A small smile. "That's better."

She whispered, "If you knew my thoughts, you would know how weak I am."

"Then let me know your thoughts. When we have been alone, we have always spent our time together coupling."

She hung her head.

James crossed his legs. "I am to blame."

She raised her head. "If you are to blame, it is only because you arouse me so much that when I am with you, I can only think of touching you and having you inside me."

James uncrossed his legs and shifted uncomfortably in his seat.

Catherine spread her hands wide on her lap and clenched her thighs with her fingers as if she were holding herself down in the chair. "You asked for my thoughts. Now you regret that."

"No, no, no. I am just…well, what you said made me…I needed more room."

Catherine looked at his lap and saw the front fall of his trousers was pulled tight, outlining his own arousal.

"You see it's impossible, Jamie. There is nothing between us but lust. We cannot even sit and have a conversation without…"

"Without what?"

"Without my turning into some thoughtless, wanton woman for you."

"Catherine." He looked at his own lap. "At this time, there is only visible evidence *I* am a thoughtless wanton man for *you*."

"You think your desire is greater because it is external? If you put your hand up my skirt and between my legs, you would find I was ready. For you."

James rubbed his hand over his mouth. "I'm not going to do that."

"No. You're not. Because you have control. You can set me down in an alley in the middle of Covent Garden when I would have gladly taken you there, in public, against a wall, like a feral creature. Even though the repercussions for me would always be worse than they would be for you."

"You would not have done that."

Catherine was silent.

"You would have?"

"Jamie, you asked for my thoughts and then you deny they are my thoughts."

He was the one who was silent now. But only for a few moments.

"You know, when you refuse to marry me, you make me think I'm not good enough for you."

"Jamie—"

"No, that's wrong. You don't make me think that. I think

that because that is who I have been for so long. Not good enough. For my father and mother. And then I made myself into an infamous marquess. Remarkable only in the worst ways. But I am a duke now. I have to be good enough because I have the job. *Some are born great, some achieve greatness, and—*"

"*—some have greatness thrust upon them.*"

"Yes. I must accept I am the last, the thrust-upon. But you are the second category, Catherine. And together, we could make sure our child is the first."

She shook her head. "My wish to end this has never, ever been about your worthiness."

"You must see how I can only believe the fault is mine. Where is the obstacle to our marriage? You are carrying my child. We are both unmarried. We are both of age."

Catherine laughed ruefully. "Some of us more than others."

James did not smile.

Catherine got up from the chair and walked from one end of the room to the other and back again, her eyes on the floor.

How was she to tell him this? Her splendid Jamie. She had hoped to spare them both. But now that he knew of the baby, she knew he would never let her alone unless she told him.

The pain in her chest would swallow her whole, and she could not bring any words forth.

Yet, Edward Lovelock, who had known all her secrets and had loved her anyway and trusted her with his daughters, would have wanted her to speak the truth. To set this fine young man free. So he could go on to a better life. A better wife.

She had to find a way to speak. For Edward. For Jamie.

"I spent almost a decade with Roger Siddons. With him, I was like how I am with you. Quivering with desire, always ready, always wanting more, always hungry. Possessed, obsessed. Willing to do anything for him. I debased myself. I did things on his behalf I do not wish to speak of." She stopped pacing and closed her eyes. "But I will tell you, if you wish to know."

The room was quiet. He said nothing.

Eyes still closed, she went on, "And then he released me. I did not escape. I might have stayed in that prison for the rest of my life. How lucky I was that his attention wandered from me. Otherwise…"

She opened her eyes and looked at James. He was leaning forward, elbows on his knees, hands clasped together, gray eyes on her. He was intent. There was no censure there. Neither was there pity. He was listening. He was an open vessel, and she was pouring her poison into him.

She dropped her eyes to the floor and resumed her pacing. "I spent the next decade with Edward Lovelock. I had my best life with him. He understood me, and he loved me, and I loved him. But he did not make me wild like you do, Jamie. He soothed me. There was comfort, and there was peace."

She faced him. "I need peace. I don't want these unmanageable feelings. And I don't want to come to hate you as I came to hate Roger. I don't want to slit your throat in twenty years. I need to stop this."

James said, "I think I know what you need."

Catherine felt her temper flare again. She balled her hands into fists. "You think I haven't heard that from men all my life?"

James stood and reached out and pulled her to him. Her cheek was pressed to his lower chest. His arms wrapped around her, and she could feel his large hands pressing against her back, pressing her into him.

The suddenness of his embrace caused her groin to ache and throb again. His rough movement, his strong arms controlling her—surely evidence of the violence of his passion

—these things aroused her more than a tender touch from him might have. She could feel his heart beating in his chest, under her cheek. And below his waistline, she felt his rigid shaft pushing into her abdomen, up towards her breasts. He wanted her.

She put her own arms around his waist and flattened her hands on his back and her breasts on his abdomen. But she did not turn her face up to look at him. Right now, she could not look at him.

And then nothing. He did not move. He did not kiss her. He held her. Minutes passed. His shaft grew less rigid. She shifted slightly in his arms, and he only pulled her closer.

Some tipping point was reached.

She was lost.

But not lost in desire. Lost in grief for the girl she had been, the girl she wished she could give him now.

She felt herself dissolve. Her arms and legs grew weak. She almost sagged to the floor, but he held her up.

Tears came. She, who never cried. She had always prided herself on the genuine weeping she could produce on stage as an actress, but in life, she thought crying was pitiable and weak. She could only remember crying once in her adult life. When Edward had died.

But she had been so alone for so long. Kate against the world.

She wept and hiccoughed, and great gasps and sobs shook her body, and still James held her fast. She did not know if she cried for five minutes or for an hour. But it seemed a long time to her. Through it all, he held her and did not move.

The tears slowed, her breathing grew more even, and—she couldn't help it—she snuffled. Immediately after the snuffle, Catherine felt James take one hand from her back, and her sense of loss was so enormous she almost let out a howl.

Through her tears, she saw something white dangling in front of her face. A handkerchief.

She grasped the handkerchief, and, as she brought it to her face, she felt his warm hand return to her back and press her into him just as firmly as before.

She wiped her nose and face and waited for him to release her. It was a release that never came. He stood still and held her. There was no stroking, no petting, only his unmoving arms around her, his hands on her back, his solid front holding her up.

Finally, she was the one who broke the embrace. She stepped backwards, and he moved his arms out of her way. She looked up at him.

"You were right."

He grinned. Boyish, delighted.

She smiled back. "I did need that."

"I thought you might."

"Don't gloat."

"I'm not gloating. I'm happy. Isn't that allowed?" He took a step towards her, his arms open as if to embrace her again.

"No, no, none of that," Catherine said, backing even farther away.

"You're right," he said and sat down again and crossed his legs and looked at her. "It's just you're so beautiful right now."

She knew her eyes were swollen, her nose was red. "And none of that."

"You misunderstand me, Catherine. I'm not trying to seduce you. I'm trying to un-seduce you."

"Un-seduce me?" A little laugh escaped from her. "There is such a thing?"

"I hope there is."

"What does un-seduction consist of?"

He paused. "Friendship."

She wiped her eyes with a dry corner of his handkerchief,

which she was still clutching. "You told me you could never be friends with me."

"I was angry when I said that. Forgive me. I think there is nothing more I want right now than your friendship."

"You want it more than coupling with me?"

James ran his fingers over his short hair, his healing scar on his head. "Yes. Because I want you to know that even though we desire each other, we can still be good to each other. I can be a good husband, a good father."

Catherine wanted to tell him that of course, he could be a good husband and a good father, just not with her, but he cut her off, would not allow her to speak.

"You say I am worthy. But deep down, you don't feel it. You don't know it. I think friendship is how you might finally consent to marry me. And I know friendship can last a lifetime. Does desire? I don't know."

His words were sincere and had the ring of truth. "I don't know, either," she finally said and sat.

"Perhaps…no, you'll think I'm silly," he said.

"Tell me."

He hesitated a moment more. "Friendship might be why Orsino and Viola in *Twelfth Night* have such a great love. He comes to know her first as his friend."

"Yes," she said, "but she knows the lustful reality. That she wants to bed him."

"You don't think they were friends? She courts a woman for him."

"I'm not that unselfish. I won't be doing that for you, Jamie." Again, his possible future wife, the pure, sweet girl of the *ton*, the daughter of a marquess or an earl, came into her mind.

"The only woman I would ever ask you to court for me would be yourself, Kate. Don't you think we might be friends?"

"I don't know. What does friendship look like?"

"It looks like two rooms. Two beds."

Catherine felt a sharp ripple of disappointment course through her body. "Yes."

"Don't look so sad. I'm here. I want you. You know I want you. But let's talk of other things. Let's do other things. Ordinary things. Like we did during our days at Christmas, at Sommerleigh. Let us walk and eat and read and laugh and look at the sky. Let us try having something pure and right, as you put it."

"For how long?"

James quirked his eyebrows. "Say, to begin with, a day?"

A day. Catherine considered. "Yes."

He held out his hand. She held out hers and was careful not to let her fingers linger in his grasp.

James found the innkeeper and asked for another room and was amused by the innkeeper's sympathetic frown. He took some time alone in his new bedchamber to consider what he had just proposed to Catherine. Already he was gnawed by doubt. Would he be able to keep his hands off her? He must. He must believe this was a possible way forward for them.

All of his instincts—to cradle and caress Catherine, to kiss her pain away, to comfort her with touch—must be suppressed. Too dangerous at this moment, too likely to lead to the torrid, mindless coupling she feared. And that she thought was the sole thing they shared.

Yes, let them be friends. She did not want coddling or pity or even tenderness. She wanted companionship. He must show her he could give her that. He must show her he was more than a young cock and a full head of hair.

He ran his hand over his short hair. He did not even have his locks to offer her any longer.

He walked down the corridor and knocked on Catherine's door and asked her to come and see the Canterbury Cathedral with him. She looked askance, some guarded suspicion in her eyes.

"It's not an ambush, Mrs. Lovelock. There will not be an archbishop, a special license, and two witnesses waiting for us. It's just a sight friends might go and see if they happened to be in Canterbury."

She acquiesced. Once they were on the street, he held out his arm to her. She hesitated.

"It's to keep the other rogues and rapscallions away from you," he said.

"I thought we were going to a cathedral."

"We are. But one cannot be too cautious. And a friend can take a friend's arm."

She took his arm.

"Have you ever been to Canterbury before, Mrs. Lovelock?"

"If you don't call me Catherine, I will start calling you *Your Grace*. Loudly."

"Catherine, have you ever been to Canterbury?"

"I have not."

"I haven't either. Good. We are on equal footing."

"The Cathedral was where Thomas á Becket was murdered, wasn't it?"

"Yes, after Henry II asked, *Who will rid me of this troublesome priest?*"

"A reminder that powerful men should speak carefully, I suppose," said Catherine.

"A reminder not to vex a king."

"How differently we see things."

"Yes."

"Well, you will have to change your mind, Jamie, because I am too set in my ways."

"Gladly. I will change my mind on every subject to match yours. Except when I'm right, and you're wrong. Even in friendship, there should be friction."

She smiled at that, and her smile gave him hope.

After they came out of the Cathedral, James asked Catherine if she was hungry.

"Ravenous," she said.

Of course, James thought. She had not eaten all day, and she was eating for two. He made a note in his head: Catherine might not tell him when she was hungry.

They returned to the coaching inn. James thought they might eat in one of their rooms, but Catherine said, "At a table, in the public eye, Jamie. Please. It will help me."

They sat at a table and were brought a roasted chicken at Catherine's request and wine at James'. Catherine liked the meat of the breast of the chicken. James liked the darker meat of the leg.

"Perfect," James said. "We are like Jack Sprat and his wife. Between the two of us, we will strip the carcass clean. How can you not say we are ideally suited for each other?"

Catherine laughed and wiped her mouth. "If we liked the same joint of the chicken, you would say the same thing. *Oh, Kate, it's a good thing a chicken has two legs, because we are two! How perfect!*"

"True," James said, cutting off another piece of the breast and putting it on Catherine's plate. "That would be perfect, as well."

"My husband liked the leg of the fowl, too," Catherine said. Then she winced. "I'm sorry."

James was confused. "Why?"

"A man does not like to hear about other men from a lover's past."

"Well, we are not lovers. Not today. Today, we are friends. And friends talk about their pasts, if they like, with no fears or jealousies. And I'd like to know more about Mr. Lovelock. He has a lot to teach me. After all, you were happy with him, and he got you to marry him. Maybe you could tell me how he did it?"

She pealed a little laugh and wiped her fingers on her napkin. He looked at her, waiting. She took a sip of wine and met his gaze over the glass. She frowned and put the glass down.

"Do you really want to know?"

"Yes. Decidedly. School me."

Catherine was quiet for a long time. He thought she might cry again, and he considered moving to her side of the table and taking her in his arms. But he made himself stay in place. He willed himself to be a friend to her, to hold no expectation, to wish for no particular result.

Finally, she spoke. "When he told me about his daughters, it was with such love for them. And worry. Particularly for Harry, who was so troubled at that time by the loss of her mother. I could tell from how he spoke about them that he was a man who loved women. Who appreciated our differences but did not see them as diminishing. I was very happy to bear him a daughter, and he was very happy, too."

"Mmm. Well, I don't have any daughters. But I would be very happy to have you give me one, Catherine. And I assure you, I love women."

Catherine laughed and almost snorted. "Like most men, Jamie."

"No, no, I didn't mean it that way. I mean I have sisters. Lots of them. Seven. All younger. All unmarried. They are the dearest people in the world to me, present company excepted."

"Seven? And all unmarried. Your poor mother."

"My poor mother? She isn't going to do a thing to get them married. It's going to be up to me."

"Well, then I don't understand why you're wasting your time here. You have work to do, Your Grace."

"But I promised myself I would do my best to get married first, so I might have some useful experience to impart to my sisters. You know, how to catch a man and all that rot."

"How do you catch a man?"

"Well, first you catch his best friend and then refuse the friend. Next, you appear half-naked—"

"Jamie!"

"—in the dressing room of a modiste's shop. Then you follow a man and jump on him in an alley and kiss him in such a way as he has never been kissed before—"

"Perhaps we should alter the course of this conversation, *friend*." She laid heavy emphasis on the last word.

"Yes, friend." Too late, James realized he should have checked himself. He had turned the exchange into flirtation, and Catherine didn't want that. "Tell me more about your husband."

Her eyes shifted to a distant point over his shoulder.

"He was older than I was. Fifteen years. He was quiet. But he absorbed everything, heard everything, paid attention to everything. And when he spoke on a matter, people listened."

"He was respected."

"Yes. Before he died, I wanted him to buy a knighthood. I thought it would help our daughters. But he refused. He said, *Katie, if a man thinks more of me because of a Sir in front of my name, I will think less of that man.*"

"He called you Katie."

"Yes, he did. And Mary and Harry still call me Mama Katie."

"And Roger Siddons called you Cath."

Catherine colored. "All the folk I know from my time on the stage call me Cath."

"But you told me to call you Kate."

"Yes. I wanted you to have your own name for me, quite apart from those others."

James smiled.

"You share it with only one other person," she said.

"Oh?"

"A blacksmith's boy from the Midlands."

"Oh."

"Whom I last saw thirty years ago and who's dead in the wars these twenty-seven years. The Flanders Campaign."

"What was his name?"

"Jamie Hill." She studied his reaction.

"Good name." He drank some wine.

She looked down at the table and whispered, "I'd still like to call you Jamie."

He leaned forward. "I would like for you to, Kate. But only if the association is a happy one for you."

She looked up and met his eyes. "It is. It helps me remember a time when things were simpler. When *I* was simpler."

He felt this was good. Very good. He was entirely willing to share the names Kate and Jamie with a dead blacksmith's boy since the boy made her feel innocent. Anything that helped her see what they had could be the pure and right ideal she longed for.

He cleared his throat. "Well, a difficulty presents itself. I don't have daughters to prove to you I love women—"

"But you have sisters."

"Pshaw! A weak substitute. And no one could say I was respected. And I have not rejected my title. I am not sure how I am going to get you to marry me."

"Well, Edward married a wounded woman. I am not that anymore. Perhaps I need to be wooed differently, now."

"How?"

Catherine smiled shyly in a way he had never seen before. "I think today was a good start."

They stood in front of the door to her bedchamber. She took the key from her reticule and opened the door.

"I'm in the room down this way in case you need me," James said.

She nodded. He thought she might kiss him, but she did not. She went into the room and closed the door. He waited until he heard the key turn.

In the morning, he made a point of being outside her door when she came out, and she smiled when she saw him.

They hired a horse and a trap and went out into the surrounding countryside to picnic.

She seemed more lighthearted today than he had ever seen her. And she was less guarded than yesterday. She touched his hand gently to get his attention. She brushed a crumb stuck in a stray whisker on his chin after he had eaten a cheese sandwich.

"Not my clean-shaven Jamie today."

"That's what happens when you leave your valet in London," he grumbled.

"I'll shave you tomorrow."

"You?"

"Yes, I learned from a backstage dresser at the Theatre-Royal. You'll be in good hands."

That night again, she slipped into her own room alone, with no kiss, no sign of longing.

He had thought this chasteness between them would only last a day. Damn.

She woke early. Just before waking, James had been there, hovering on the edges of her consciousness. But he had not been touching her as in previous dreams. He had been fully dressed in a garden, grinning at her. She had a warm feeling, she wanted to see him immediately, but she did not feel an ache, a throb, a hunger that could not be denied.

She dressed and went downstairs to ask for a basin of hot water and linen and soap and all the other required items for shaving. Arms full, she went and knocked on his door. She felt calm and assured. She felt…herself in a way she hadn't for years.

"I borrowed the razor from the innkeeper, but I think it will do. Sit there, Jamie, in front of the window. Take off your shirt. It's the only one you have, and I don't want to get water and soap all over it."

He took off his shirt, and she drew in a sharp breath. The triangle of muscle that came off his shoulders and crowned the tops of his arms. The fine, golden hair on his forearms, almost matching the color of his skin, hard to see unless it glinted in the sun. The smooth skin of his chest. The beautiful smell of him.

It's a body, Kate, just like any other body. Her pulse settled.

She set to work, softening his whiskers with the hot water and soap, then turning his head this way and that, scraping his jaw, his chin, and, very carefully, his top lip, taking care around the groove between his nose and mouth. She wiped the soap from his face.

"There." She stepped back. She had done it. She had been physically close to him and his body. She had felt an appreciation but not an uncontrollable wildness.

James touched his face. "That's very good. Not quite up to Enfield's standards but very good. You can have a job as assistant valet to the Duke of Middlewich."

Catherine curtsied and affected the accent of her girlhood. "Will that be all Your Grace is needing this morning?"

He put his shirt on. "If we are going to stay in Canterbury longer, I think I will need some clothes."

"Are we planning to stay in Canterbury longer?"

"Would you like to stay?"

"I don't know what we'll do here. Surely, we might despair of finding more sights to see, but I am afraid to leave when things are going so well."

"You think things are going well?"

"Yes." She smiled. "You took your shirt off. And I kept my hands to myself. It was a good test."

"Shall I take it off again?" He went as if to lift it over his head.

"No! I mean, no, thank you. Lead me not into temptation, Your Grace."

"You have taught me a lot about women, Kate."

She wiped the razor clean. "In what sense?"

"I think my chest is as important to you as yours is to me."

"Why do you think women love to go to museums and look at the marble Greek gods there? We do not have brothels, like the men."

"You go to ogle, eh?"

"Well, not me. I am a respectable widow. With a friend who is willing to take his shirt off for me, if I ask nicely."

"Me?"

She threw a towel at him. "Yes, you. Now, let's go eat breakfast."

They went to breakfast and then to St. Augustine's Abbey. At dinner that night, Catherine discovered the innkeeper had a tall eighteen-year-old son who was roughly the same size as James. She asked to buy the son's best shirt.

"Now this shirt and cravat you are wearing can be laundered while you wear the new one," Catherine said over the dining table.

"But my trousers. And my waistcoat and coat! And my hose is dreadful."

"Do you want to go back to London? Or shall we send to London for your clothes?"

"No! You think things are going well. So do I. We'll stay. And if we send to London, it will just bring Enfield down our heads. He would arrive, full of indignation, with my trunks."

"Yes, that wouldn't do, would it? The coat and waistcoat can be sponged and pressed tomorrow, and we will have your trousers and hose laundered at the same time as the shirt. You will stay in bed tomorrow until the trousers are dry."

"Will I stay in bed alone with no clothes on, Kate?" James smiled and winked.

Catherine pretended a frown in answer. "A friend might come and sit in the same room as you and converse. Or read. Or play cards."

"Tomorrow will be the fourth day of our friendship."

"Yes."

"Do you think we might become closer friends, in time?"

Catherine turned her head and looked at him sideways. "As close as you and my son-in-law?"

"Well, I was thinking perhaps a good deal closer than that."

Catherine became serious. "I think your notion that we be friends, that we talk as friends, has been a very good one. I am finding myself capable of managing my feelings. Especially those of a carnal nature."

"You…you don't look on me as a nephew, do you?"

"Jamie, you know my problem is quite the opposite. What made you say that?"

"Something Thomas said last month. About our Christmas at Sommerleigh."

"Well, I was pretending, as were you, at Christmas. Here I am not pretending. I am *trying*."

"Good. I don't want you to pretend."

"And I don't want you to pretend, either."

"Yes, you do, Catherine. For now. And that's fine."

"What are you pretending?"

"I'm pretending I don't want to take you upstairs and rip your clothes off."

Catherine had a moment of unbridled desire when her nipples hardened under her dress, her pearl throbbed, her heart raced, she grew dizzy.

But she waited. The moment passed.

"I'm glad," she said, and laid her hand on top of his where it rested on the table. "I'm glad you want that."

"Do you want it, Kate?"

"Yes," she said and withdrew her hand. "But you were right. It's not what I need."

Her answer made James look so hangdog Catherine had to laugh. "I'll come keep you company tomorrow while you're in bed."

The next morning, after breakfast, they went to his room together. Catherine turned around and told him to strip, to put on the innkeeper's son's shirt, and to get back into the bed. He did as she said, glad to have her managing him even though undressing with her in the room made him long to manage her, her body, her desire. What had he been thinking when he had devised this fool plan?

Catherine took his clothes down to the innkeeper's wife. She was gone a long time, and he grew restless. Finally, she returned.

"I have some playing cards from the innkeeper and—what do you think, a copy of Fordyce's *Sermons to Young Women*."

James groaned.

"Or we could talk," Catherine said.

"You could come sit on the bed," James said, patting the mattress next to him.

"I'll sit in this chair." But she drew it close to the bed.

They talked this way, he in the bed and she in the chair, for hours. They spoke of their childhoods, their childhood loves. He asked her about her use of a sword and came to realize she was the boy he had seen at Antonio's last autumn. They spoke of Catherine's dreams for Arabella's happiness and James' dreams for his duchy and his sisters. James confessed his second life in service to the Crown, and she congratulated him on his acting and warned him she would not be so easy to deceive in the future.

In the future. She thought they had a future. Together. But James was wise and did not comment on her use of the word.

He asked Catherine to recite for him. She still knew all her roles from years ago, but she also knew long stretches of other speeches off by heart, as well. James applauded her version of the St. Crispin's Day speech from *Henry V*.

"Quite like Joan of Arc, you were. If she had been English, that is."

Morning turned to afternoon, and Catherine stood and stretched and yawned. "I think I'll go take a nap, Jamie. I'll have your clothes brought to you when they're dry. And since we had no luncheon, let's eat at five o'clock. Yes?"

"Yes," James grumbled and picked up the cards. "I suppose I'll play Patience if I can't convince you to nap here with me."

"We both know if I get in that bed, there would be no napping to be had."

James looked up hopefully, but she had turned and gone out the door.

His clothes were brought to him at four o'clock, and he asked for hot water, too. He washed his whole body, standing up, scrubbing himself. He thought he might shave but remembered if he did not, Catherine might shave him on the morrow. She would stand close to him while she plied the razor and would touch his face and neck.

He decided not to shave.

The trousers were not quite dry, but they were clean. His coat and waistcoat looked respectable.

At five o'clock, he went to Catherine's door and knocked.

Catherine opened the door.

James gasped. He knew that blue silk, that fine shimmery cloth. Months ago, hadn't he himself made her sheathe her breasts with such a silk?

But now that silk went from her shoulders to her toes in the shape of a dress. It had a low, square neckline. Very low. Given her breasts had enlarged with her pregnancy, it looked like her bosom might spill over the top at any moment. The inch of chemise showing was like a bit of enticing froth framing the square of the chest. And, yes, the color of the dress matched her eyes perfectly.

But James was not looking at her eyes.

"I've spent the last hour thinking I had better take it off. And then I change my mind. What do you think, Jamie? Should I wear it?"

James stepped into the room. "I think this should be the only dress you wear for the rest of your life."

"Do you like this best of any gown you have ever seen me in?"

The perfect cream and pink skin sloping into the roundness of her bosom, the dark shadow between her voluptuous breasts, the promise of what was just below the neckline of the dress. In truth, James could not remember any of Catherine's other dresses.

"I think there is only one thing I have ever seen you in that I like more."

"Let me guess, Your Grace. You prefer me in … nothing?"

James groaned. "Am I so predictable then?"

Catherine bit her lip. "But is it too daring for dinner in a coaching inn?"

James considered. "Yes. Let's have dinner in this room."

Catherine almost pouted. "We have been cooped up all day."

"Change the dress and we'll go downstairs and eat and take a stroll and we'll come back up here and you can put it on again."

"You don't want to be seen with me in this dress?"

"Right now, Kate, I don't want any other man to see you in that dress. In time, I may be able to exercise enough reason to enjoy other men admiring you but not right now."

"The innkeeper's wife helped me with the buttons since the dress was made for a lady with a lady's maid, so you'll have to unbutton me, please."

She turned around to show him the buttons. He gulped.

"There are so many. And they're so small."

She looked over her shoulder. "Only a dozen. Be careful, Jamie."

He stooped and felt very clumsy as he began with the top button. "There. Eleven to go." After several minutes, he freed the last button, and Catherine raised her arms. He drew the dress over her head, leaving her in stays, chemise, petticoat, and almost as fully dressed as she had been before.

Except the chemise and the cups of the stays were translucent and he could see the skin of her breasts and the pink of her areolas. He shifted weight from one foot to the other.

She took the dress from him and laid it carefully in her trunk. She turned to a chair where a rose-pink muslin dress waited.

"Shall I help you?"

"No, this is a dress I can do myself." She put the dress over her head. "You know I was not planning to have a lady's maid in France, so I only brought dresses I could arrange myself. Except the blue gown. I didn't want to leave that behind. I've never worn it."

James felt guilty. "Do you want to wear it? I'm sorry, I've robbed you of some pleasure. You should wear it."

"Nonsense. I don't want you fretting over some villain looking down my dress. Let's go and eat dinner."

They ate. They took a walk into the center of the city and back to the coaching inn. Catherine thought it might be the most idyllic evening of her life. The air was warm, but not too warm. There was a slight breeze. The sky was perfectly clear. There was the perfume of lilacs in the air. And she was on James' arm.

"I am glad we got out and about today."

"Yes. What should we do tomorrow, Kate?"

Catherine didn't even know what they should do in the next hour. "Today's not done yet. I want to wear my dress for you."

They returned to her room. The sky was darkening, so she closed the curtains and lit lamps. She took off the pink dress and heard James' breathing change a bit. She slid the blue silk over her head and put her back to him and waited.

She felt his tentative hands begin to button her dress.

"Start at the bottom, Jamie. That will make it easier."

"Oh, yes," he said and shifted his hands. He hummed a little as he worked with the buttons. She felt his warm breath on her neck, and she thought she could also feel his concentration, his care.

"That's done," he said.

She stepped away from him and turned.

He crossed his arms over his chest and clamped his hands under his armpits. "It's a miracle of a dress, Kate."

She felt warm under his gaze, so she curtsied and fluttered her hand in front of her face as if it were a fan. "Thank you, Your Grace."

He nodded. There was a silence. A coach drew up to the inn, and the sounds of the horses and the ostler speaking to the coachman filtered up to the room.

"Well," he said. "Good night." He turned.

Catherine had not thought much further than wanting to wear the dress for him. Why? To inflame his desire? Yes. She wanted him to look at her with lust. She wanted him to feel what she was feeling. But there was something more.

She stepped quickly in front of him and laid a hand on his chest.

"Tell me your thoughts."

He looked at the floor. "You know my thoughts."

"I don't."

"I think I'm a fool to have taken a woman who desired me and turned her into a friend."

"Shall I tell you my thoughts, Jamie?"

He groaned and kept his eyes on the floor. "Will I be able to bear them, Kate?"

"Yes, you must."

He raised his eyes to her face.

"My thoughts are…you have been very wise. You had a woman who did not trust herself with you. In truth, she may not have trusted you, either. But now, she is a good way along to trusting both parties."

"Good," he said, but his tone was mutinous.

"In fact, she may be close to being all the way there."

His brows knit together, and he grabbed both her hands.

"Do you mean it, Catherine? Don't toy with me."

She had had three—no, three and a half—days of peace

and companionship and joy with him. A short time, yes. But in those few days, he had shown her what she thought was impossible *was* possible. She could simply be with him. And be herself with him.

Yes, miraculously, be herself. Not someone's mother or wife or widow or mistress. Or Ophelia or Viola.

Just herself. Some essential Kate.

He was the ideal person. For her. For her to be herself. Which was something she had craved for almost thirty years.

He was sincere. Thoughtful. Tender. Ready to laugh with her. Ready to disagree with her. Ready to love her. Yes, he inspired a devastating lust in her, but maybe, with his help, she could hold onto herself while still lying in his arms.

He had shown himself to be a man who wanted what was best for her, not just the satisfaction of his own desires. A man who would be the most admirable sort of affectionate husband and doting father. A man who deserved all of her love. And wanted her love, as flawed as she was.

And now she knew the truth deep in her heart. She loved him. All of him.

"I mean that I think we should be lovers again."

He was on her. His mouth on hers, his hands on the small of her back, her shoulders, her neck, her face. She felt a flare of heat and an ache between her legs, and she met his lips with hers, his tongue with hers. She put her hands to his head, forgetting for a moment, and when she found no locks in her fingers, she grabbed his nape and pulled him closer.

And then he took himself away from her. Six, seven feet away. Painfully far away. He was panting, as was she.

She did not know what to say. "Thank you," she gasped, "for not ripping the dress. Will you take it off me now?"

"Hang the dress. I don't care about the dress."

She looked down. "I thought you liked the dress."

"I do." He was regaining his breath. "But I don't care about it."

"Oh."

"You must answer me, Kate Cooksey, Catherine Cooke, Mrs. Lovelock. You have not answered me."

She almost laughed. She bit her lip instead.

"You have not asked me, James Cavendish, the Most Noble Duke of Middlewich and Marquess of Daventry."

He felt himself redden. He hadn't, had he? He had told her he wanted her hand in marriage, but he hadn't *asked*.

But now he would ask. And he thought there was a very good chance she would say yes.

He felt at his waistcoat pocket. Empty. The sapphire ring he had carried from London was gone. Blast. It was in his own room. Under his pillow. He had taken it out this morning when his clothes had been laundered and sponged and he had forgotten to replace it. He needed Enfield organizing him.

He held a finger up. "A moment." He was out the door and at his own door, fumbling with the key. And to the bed and there was the ring. And back to Catherine's room, ring in his fist.

He stepped in and closed the door behind him. She was so beautiful, and it wasn't the dress. She could be in the stained muslin gown she wore to his rooms months ago, and she would still be beautiful.

The thought she might be his, forever, made his legs weak. And the knowledge she was carrying his child made him want to weep. Still, Catherine deserved a man who could get through a proposal.

He walked to her and got on one knee.

Suddenly, she seemed shy, almost girlish. She was having a hard time meeting his eyes.

"Kate," he said and took her hand with his. He opened his other hand, and the large blue sapphire shone and sparkled. "I must have you…marry me. Will you?"

"Yes," she said. "I love you, Jamie." She sneezed.

"Bless you," he said as he slid the ring onto her finger.

He made a promise to himself in that moment. No matter what, he would not rip the dress.

THIRTY-EIGHT

She cupped his face and tilted it up to hers, and their mouths met in a searing kiss. His tongue over hers, his lips claiming hers. His warm breath. She could feel he was giving her his soul, his heart, everything.

And she wanted it. And she wanted to give the same back to him.

His hands rested at her waist, barely holding her. With the passionate nature of the kiss, she wondered why he was not pulling her to him as he had moments before. Before his proposal.

He answered her unspoken question.

"I think we better get the dress off you, Kate, my love." His voice was shaky. His gray eyes were soft.

"Yes," she said and felt herself Kate, the farm girl, wanting to save her best dress. She felt young. Yes, let her be Kate with her Jamie. Starting anew. Each kiss a surprise. Each caress a mystery.

Holding her hands, James got off his knees and stood.

"Upsidaisy," she said to him.

He looked down at her, startled for a moment, and then

chortled and gave her the boyish grin she loved so much, and she laughed, too.

Even as she was still laughing, he put his hands on her bare shoulders and kissed her mouth gently, tenderly. And then ever so slowly, he moved his kisses off her lips and to her cheek and jaw and then her ear and neck, all the while gently rotating her until she had her back to him.

It had been a masterful move on his part.

Oh, Jamie.

He palmed her rounded lower abdomen from his position behind her. *Yes. Our child, Jamie.* His fingers skimmed over her waist, her bodice, touching the silk and the edge of the chemise before going to the back of her neck. Buttons undone more surely this time.

And once the dress was off and had joined her rose-pink dress over a chair, Catherine thought there now would be a tearing of clothes, an unbridled urgency. But no.

"Would you untie my cravat?" he asked. She reached up to do so, and as she did, she caressed his jaw.

"I'll shave you tomorrow," she said and had to blink several times.

"Six weeks, Kate." He grinned. "A Viking, Kate. For our honeymoon."

The promise of this aroused her as much as the devouring kiss. Not just the idea of his beard, but that they had all the time they wanted.

The cravat was undone.

"Shall I loosen your stays?"

"That would be lovely."

The stays were loosened and discarded, and she helped him off with his boots and the rest of his clothes, and he removed the delicate chemise and the petticoat and her hose and shoes.

They stood, bare to each other, and his arms were around

her, protecting her, not trapping her. They kissed again, and she could feel flames in her breasts and her cleft. His hard member was pressed between their bodies. Now, surely, he would take her, ravage her, fill her empty, aching need.

But he did not. He kissed her, and he touched her, but nothing was a grope or a grasp. And she put herself again in the mind of young Kate Cooksey, and every stroke of his hand on her skin, every brush of his whiskered lips was a revelation. And for her, the feel of him under her hands as she touched his chest and his flanks and his back and his buttocks, these were sensations wholly new as well.

When he picked her up under her arms to put her on the bed, they both said, "Upsidaisy," and burst into laughter.

And then they were in the bed together and laughing and touching and kissing. And the kisses became longer and longer, but also sweeter and sweeter, even as their hands wandered over each other's bodies and her throbbing grew. In the past, she would have felt driven to a ferocity, a wildness, to wanting only to quench her own thirst for him, to getting on top of him and putting him inside her, to taking his cock in her mouth and making him moan her name.

But now, she just wanted to be Kate with her Jamie.

There would be a time in the future for that wildness. He would want that from her, but they would have many years together. Time enough for wildness, for tenderness, for all the flavors of love except for those that spoke to cruelty and fear.

And, oh. His gentle mouth on her breast was as if no one had ever touched her breast before. And after a long time, he was on top of her, and she could feel his hard shaft between her thighs. Slowly, he went from being between her legs to being inside her. And as he filled her and kissed her, she felt a euphoria of jumbled emotions and sensations. Love combined with arousal combined with affection. It was almost too much.

As if he knew she was overwhelmed, he quickened his pace and increased the depth of his thrusts. He was making love to her and making lust with her at the same time.

She felt a seizing of her groin, and the waves of her climax broke, rolling over her and over her and she sneezed and arched herself into him and off the bed. And he was matching his strokes to her clenching, pushing into her as she tightened so she could not imagine being any fuller.

His gray eyes were on her as he was in her and even as one series of waves seemed to ebb, she would sneeze and another would begin, until she felt she might drift off the bed entirely if he were not holding her in place with his member.

"I love you, Kate."

"I love you, Jamie. Oh, Jamie."

Those eyes.

His face changed as it always did before he released. An almost questioning look, an arrest of breath, a spasm of his muscles, and the interruption of his rhythm. And as his own climax pulsed, she felt the last of her own waves recede and diminish, and the entire ocean was still. They were alone in the universe.

They were the only two.

She held him as she had never held him before. She held him. And held him. She did not let him go.

She would never let him go.

EPILOGUE

They returned to London three days later. But there was no need for more clean clothing for James since he wore no clothes whatsoever during those three days.

Catherine sent for Arabella immediately. Once her daughter arrived in London from Bath—where she had been partaking of the waters with her sister Mary and Mary's husband—Catherine took her to the morning room. They sat on the sofa, and Catherine could see she and Arabella were now the same height.

"Dearest," she said. "I am to be married."

Arabella used the flat of her palm to press out a crease in her gown. "To His Grace? The Duke of Middlewich?"

Catherine was astounded. "How did you know?"

Arabella laughed. "Oh, Mama, I saw how he looked at you at Christmas. He looked at you the same way the Earl Drake looks at Harry and how David, I mean, the Viscount Tregaron looks at Mary."

"I hope the match meets with your approval," Catherine said, trying not to betray her worry.

Arabella threw her arms around Catherine. "Anything you do would meet with my approval. You know that. And I like the duke for you."

"There is to be a baby, Arabella."

"A baby?" Arabella pulled back from Catherine.

"Yes, you will have a brother or a sister. At the end of September. It is not the usual thing, and I should explain. I tried to have this conversation with your sister Harry a year ago, before she was married—"

"You needn't explain, Mama." Arabella blushed. "Mary had quite a good talk with me last month when we were in Cornwall. I think I understand."

But Catherine wanted to be clear. She spoke of anatomy and of desire and of love. She spoke of the rules of society and how some made sense and some did not, but woe betide those who broke the rules.

"I have broken those rules, darling girl, time and time again. I have been lucky to have made my way as I did despite that."

Arabella still looked embarrassed and made a gesture with her hand that meant she wanted Catherine to stop talking.

"I see, Mama. You want me to do what you tell me to do and not do what you have done."

"In short, yes. But no matter what, I will, of course, always love you."

"And I, you."

The two women embraced, and Arabella smiled, clearly happy all talk about urges and loins and seed had ceased.

James knew Catherine would want their wedding to follow convention. They even went, with Arabella in tow, to meet the Bishop of London at St. Paul's Cathedral to ask him to read the banns. That meeting turned out to be exceedingly fortuitous as Thomas, Harry, and Harry's physician, Dr. Alasdair Andrews, happened to be meeting with the bishop at the same time. James noted how pleased Catherine was to make the acquaintance of Dr. Andrews since she had hoped to meet him at Christmas.

However, Arabella seemed even more pleased to make the acquaintance of Dr. Andrews.

James suddenly realized having banns read would mean they would not be married until July, and he decided he couldn't wait. He wanted his Kate legally bound to him, and he wanted to be sure the baby would be born after the wedding. After all, some babies did come early. A June wedding was much safer than a July wedding. He obtained a special license from the Archbishop of Canterbury, and they married four days later, in the garden of his town house in London, surrounded by the few flowers that had bloomed since James had snipped all the rest of them for his bouquet to woo Catherine.

His excited sisters and his disapproving mother were there. He had already made arrangements for his mother to move to her own house on the far end of the estate.

"She can dowager duchess all she likes from a distance," he told Catherine. "When you come to the castle, there will only be one Duchess of Middlewich there."

His sisters, for now, would stay in the castle. He had high hopes Catherine would like his sisters and *vice versa*. Their first meetings had been promising. His oldest sister Anne whispered to him that Catherine was charming and, after all, one stepdaughter had married a viscount and the other—the peculiar one—had married an earl, and perhaps Catherine could do even better for a set of utterly ordinary duke's daughters.

Arabella and Harry and Thomas and Mary and Mary's husband David Vaughan, the Viscount Tregaron, were all at the wedding, as well. Thomas seemed to rest his hand frequently on Harry's waist, which James thought was unremarkable until Catherine commented on it with surprise in her voice. James suddenly remembered his conversation with Thomas at Christmas and thought perhaps Harry had discovered a new interest outside of mathematics.

Mr. Bulverton and Isabella were not at the wedding, as they were off on their own wedding trip to the Continent. Isabella was finally going to see Paris.

When he carried her over the threshold into her bedchamber in the town house, James reminded Catherine she was dry and warm and unhurt, just as he had promised.

She whispered in his ear, "I don't know about dry."

It must be said that the white satin and silver tissue wedding dress *was* ripped in the groom's haste to find out.

In September, at the castle of the duchy of Middlewich, Catherine gave birth. It was an easy labor and an easy birth, despite James despairing ahead of time that Catherine was so small.

"Jamie, you are tall but not wide. The size of your head is quite normal. My hips are quite adequate. The baby will come out either short or long, but either way, he will fit."

"Or she."

Catherine felt sure the baby was a boy. James was certain it was a girl.

The baby was a boy. James had mixed feelings when the midwife came to tell him. He was happy, first and foremost, that the baby *had* fit and the baby and Catherine were well. And, of course, he was happy to have an heir, and he recognized this relieved Catherine of some censure she might have suffered if she had produced a girl. But he had so longed for a little daughter.

Then he went upstairs and kissed a flushed, tousled, and

tired Catherine, and he saw his son and forgot everything about the daughter he had thought of before.

"I think the blond fuzz on his head will darken to gold-brown like yours, Jamie," Catherine said as she put the baby in his arms.

"He's so little," James breathed. The baby yawned but kept his eyes closed. "What color are his eyes?"

"Blue. But many babies have blue eyes at birth. They may turn gray yet."

"You got your boy, Kate. Let me have blue eyes."

But, in truth, he would not trade this boy for anything in the world.

"What shall we name him, Jamie?"

"We have had far too many Williams, Dukes of Middle-wich, in our family. Let's name him something else."

"James, perhaps."

"I know you, Kate. You will call him Jamie. Let me have my name. But I had a thought."

"Yes, darling?"

"I'd like to name him for a man who was important to us both. A man who cared for you before my chance to love you. Our son could be Edward. You could call him Ted or Teddy, then."

Catherine put her hand on James' cheek. "It's a very sweet tribute, Jamie. But Teddy Cavendish, Marquess of Daventry." She rolled her eyes. "He sounds like a rake already."

"What was your father's name, Kate?"

"John."

"I like the name John."

"Jack Cavendish, Marquess of Daventry. They all sound like rakes!"

"Unless we name him Algernon or Percival, Kate, he will have a rakish name. What about Edmund? It's not Edward, exactly."

"I think we should call him Algernon."

The baby went without a name for a week. Then Harry and Thomas came to visit with news of their own future happiness.

"Dr. Andrews tells us the confinement will be in March," Thomas told James and Catherine.

Harry looked at the baby sleeping in his little basket. Then she looked up at the ceiling as if she were reading an answer there.

"Sebastian," she said.

Catherine and James reached for each other's hands and squeezed.

"Viola's twin brother," James said.

Sebastian he was.

MORE

REGARDING THE LOVELOCKS OF LONDON
AND FELICITY NIVEN'S NEWSLETTER

When Ardor Blooms, the free prequel novella to ***The Lovelocks of London*** series, is available exclusively to Felicity Niven's newsletter subscribers. ***When Ardor Blooms*** tells the love story of Catherine's oldest stepdaughter Mary and how she comes to meet and marry the arrogant Viscount Tregaron during her first Season. In addition to ***When Ardor Blooms***, subscribers to Felicity Niven's newsletter receive dispatches from the writing trenches, news about upcoming romance releases, and free stories.

Subscribe at www.felicityniven.com/lovelocks

The next book in ***The Lovelocks of London*** series is ***A Perilous Flirtation*** (Arabella's love story). There is a short excerpt from ***A Perilous Flirtation*** in the pages ahead. And if you haven't read the first book in the series yet, be sure to check out ***Convergence of Desire*** (Harry's love story).

AUTHOR'S AFTERWORD

Catherine Lovelock is a fictional character, but she was inspired by Harriet Mellon (1777–1837), an actress and a beauty who was painted several times by notable artists. Harriet Mellon married the widowed banker Thomas Coutts in 1815. By his first wife, he had three daughters (all of whom married lords). Upon Thomas' death, Harriet inherited her husband's entire fortune, including partial ownership of his bank, and was consequently an extremely wealthy woman and a successful socialite.

In 1827, she married a duke twenty-three years her junior. The duke was William Aubrey de Vere Beauclerk, the 9th Duke of St. Albans and a top-notch cricket player. Harriet Mellon wrote to Sir Walter Scott upon the occasion of her second marriage: *What a strange eventful life has mine been, from a poor little player child, with just food and clothes to cover me, dependent on a very precarious profession, without talent or a friend in the world—first the wife of the best, the most perfect being that ever breathed—and now the wife of a Duke!*

The Marquis DuBois de Laval—again an invention—was inspired by Victor de Fay de La Tour-Maubourg (1768–1850), who was the French Ambassador to the Court of St. James (Britain) from 1819 to 1821. He was a cavalry commander for Napoleon Bonaparte. He was shot in the knee during a battle and requested the leg be amputated on the battlefield immediately. The story was often repeated that he told his weeping valet, "What are you crying about, man? You have one less boot to polish." He did become loyal to the restored Bourbon monarchy after Napoleon's first abdication, and that was how he came to be a marquis and then an ambassador. As far as I know, de Fay stayed loyal to the crown for the rest of his life and was not involved in an attempt to free Napoleon from St. Helena's.

However, historical evidence exists to show there was real interest among Bonapartists in using a submarine to rescue Napoleon. There is a fascinating article about this conspiracy in Smithsonian Magazine (*The Secret Plot to Rescue Napoleon by Submarine*. Smithsonian Magazine. Dash, M. March 3, 2018).

The American Robert Fulton (1765–1815) was a real person. He was a painter, an inventor, an engineer, and is famous for developing the first commercial steamship. He was painting in London at the same time Catherine might have been posing for her picture painted by Roger Siddons. He did build a working submarine for Napoleon called the *Nautilus*. He was commissioned by the British government to make another submarine in 1804, but it was never built. A copy of the plans was kept at the American Consulate in London, and the plans were not published until 1920.

The siege of San Sebastian was a real event (July to September, 1813) in the Peninsular Wars. The city eventually fell to the British due to a raid on the harbor island of Santa Clara by a small force of British sailors who took the island by climbing what were thought to be unscalable cliffs. The sailors managed to get guns onto Santa Clara, and these damaged San

Sebastian's fortifications enough to allow the Marquess (later Duke) of Wellington to take the city. However, there is no evidence to support the story that the successful taking of Santa Clara was due to information obtained by a marquess from a port wine merchant. Once again, pure invention.

A Perilous Flirtation

Excerpt from Book 3 of The Lovelocks of London

Her prospects ruined by scandal.
His hopes crushed by cowardice.
A journey. A twist of fate. A reckoning.

Her desire betrayed her. Arabella Lovelock, seduced and disgraced at age eighteen by a tall, dark stranger, flees to Scotland and builds a new life for herself in a remote village.

Her wealth and beauty made him sure she was beyond his reach. Dr. Alasdair Andrews, lonely and longing for Arabella, must bring her home to her family.

A brutal snowstorm blocks their way. Forced to take shelter at a manor house in the north of England, Arabella must face the man who stole her innocence and convince the man of her dreams that she hungers for him and only him.

Sometimes your second chance is your destiny.

———

Prologue—Cornwall—May 1819

Twenty-five-year-old Mary Lovelock Vaughan, the Viscountess Tregaron, leaned over and picked up a flat stone from the shingle.

"You may have seen something shocking today at the inn," she said and tried to skip the stone across the water, but the waves were too rough.

Arabella said nothing.

"You know men and women lie down together, don't you?" Mary's voice was light in tone, but her face was serious. She continued walking down the beach, and Arabella followed her.

"Yes."

"Do you know why they do that?"

"To have children?"

"Not entirely. In fact, that is just a very small part of it. David and I haven't had any children yet, and still we lie together."

"You weren't lying down today!" Arabella burst out.

"No, he was standing. And I was kneeling, wasn't I? You weren't meant to see that, of course."

Arabella stayed silent.

"As your sister, I'd like to talk to you about what you saw, but I also don't want to force you to talk about it."

"I want…I want to talk about it." Arabella stooped and picked up a pink shell.

"You're seventeen, aren't you? I am trying to remember what I wanted then. I remember thinking kissing would be very enjoyable. And guess what, Arabella?"

"What?"

"It is." Mary smiled just a little. "And I thought I would like to press my body up a man's body and have him hold me. And that turns out to be very enjoyable, as well. And I thought I might like to do the same thing but without clothes. And that is…"

"Enjoyable too?" Arabella felt rather like squirming while talking to her half sister about this, but she also wanted to understand.

"Not enjoyable. Ecstasy."

Arabella looked up at Mary's face. Calm, willowy Mary, married to the very controlled and elegant David Vaughan, the Viscount Tregaron. Mary's dark eyes were far away now, pointed towards the sea, her mouth open slightly, her skin flushed, her dark-brown curls pushed off her face by the wind.

Then she came back to herself.

"With certain things, it is true that there is some pain the first time, but it goes away quickly. And most things have no pain, only pleasure."

"So why do the things that cause pain, at all?"

Mary laughed. "Well, as luck would have it, the painful thing is the one that produces children, and it's nothing to be frightened of, even the first time, if you are with a good man. And it is the thing that makes me feel the closest to David."

"So David is a good man?" Arabella pushed her own windswept golden tendrils off her face and looked up at the much taller Mary.

"David is the best man. For me. You will find your own best man."

They walked farther along the shore, Arabella holding her shell in her hand, running her thumb over the ridges.

"I didn't think much of the men I met last Season in London."

"No," Mary said.

"And here with you…I mean I am enjoying the trip, but I don't think I am going to have any Season at all this year. Do you know why Mama sent me away from London?"

"No, but I am sure it has nothing to do with you, only

with her. And you will have other Seasons. I hope you will be patient."

"Yes. I know that not everyone is lucky enough to meet their husband at their first ball in their first Season," Arabella teased. Mary's lips curved into the smallest of smiles, her dimples barely showing. Mary had done exactly that, of course, five years ago.

The two women walked a bit farther and then turned around to walk back.

"Do you touch yourself, Arabella?"

Arabella was glad they were walking side by side so Mary would not see her blush. Mary was wholly unembarrassed about all of this. Perhaps that was what being married did.

"Yes," Arabella finally answered.

"Good. You should. When you are married, you will know what you like, what you want. No one's feelings get hurt by acts of self-love as it is the most private of actions. It is your concern and yours alone. And you cannot get with child from it."

"What is the exact thing that gets one with child?"

"You don't know?" Mary turned to look at Arabella.

Arabella shook her head.

"You're old enough. I'm surprised Mama Katie hasn't discussed it with you. Perhaps she still has some difficulty seeing you as a woman since you are the youngest of us. She wants to keep you a girl. But I don't see you that way. You are a woman, and women your age are getting married every day and having children. After all, Queen Charlotte married at seventeen. You should know about making babies, about coupling."

Arabella suddenly felt very aware of the breeze on her chest and arms, how the tops of her legs rubbed together as she walked.

Mary went on, her voice clear and calm, "You have seen the

phallus on the statues of Greek gods in the museum, haven't you? A husband puts his phallus inside the place from which the wife's monthly courses issue. He will rub himself there and put his seed in the woman."

"That's the thing that hurts?"

"Just the first time or the first few times. When you are married to the right man, you will want it. More than that, you will hunger for it. And the man is always hungering for it."

"And only married people couple?"

"No."

"Oh."

"But you *should* be married. It's better. Not just because it avoids scandal and bastards, but because everything is better if you are having this kind of pleasure and intimacy with someone you love. I wouldn't want to do it with someone I didn't love."

"Then why do men go to brothels?"

Mary stopped walking, so Arabella stopped, too.

"It is troubling, and I can't speak for men," Mary said slowly. "They have very peculiar notions about it all. They have difficulty with delayed gratification. And they can be rather stupid."

"I see," Arabella said, not seeing at all.

They walked on, with Mary explaining why she had been kneeling and David had been standing and other variations on the pleasures a man and woman can provide to each other.

That night, in her own bed, Arabella made a vow to herself.

I am not *going to marry a stupid man.*

Chapter 1

Two months after her return to London and her mother's subsequent marriage, Arabella Lovelock had finally solved the problem of what to call her stepfather when amongst members of the family.

"Middlewich." She lifted her chin and dabbed at the beads of perspiration on her neck with her mother's handkerchief, her own having been lost on the lawn of the castle. She had just come in from playing shuttlecock with her new aunt Marianne Cavendish, one year older than she.

"I'm not calling him Papa or Father or Uncle," Arabella said. "He's none of those things. And he's only twelve years older than I am. I'm not calling him James or Jamie. That would be disrespectful. No, not because he is a duke. Now that I am almost eighteen, I intend to call Harry's husband Thomas. I already call Mary's husband David. But I am not going to call the man married to my mother, the father of my future brother or sister, by his first name. I asked the duke what the men at his club call him. They call him Middlewich. So that's what I am going to call him."

"It's a mouthful," said her mother Catherine, the very pregnant and very new Duchess of Middlewich.

Arabella shrugged. "Arabella has more syllables."

The stepfather in question, James Cavendish, the Duke of Middlewich, was just coming into the room, and he was delighted by the news. "Shall I call you Lovelock then, like we had gone to school together?"

Arabella laughed. "No, Middlewich, you must call me what Mama does. Arabella. Besides, I won't be a Lovelock forever."

She saw her mother and her stepfather exchange looks.

Really, they had to get used to seeing her not as a child, but as a woman. She would be eighteen next year, plenty old enough to get married and to change her name.

And certainly old enough to know she wanted to change it to Mrs. Alasdair Andrews.

She had waited all summer for an invitation from her sister Harry or her brother-in-law Thomas, the Earl Drake, to visit them at their country estate Sommerleigh. She had written letters to both, hinting at her desire to visit.

She thought once she was at Sommerleigh, she might feign an illness. And then Dr. Alasdair Andrews, the local physician, would have to be sent for. She would wear her prettiest nightdress. She would have her golden hair down, around her shoulders and flowing down her back, because what lady wore hair pins to bed?

He would come and lay his head on her chest to listen to her heart—oh, the thrill she would feel to see the shiny waves of his auburn hair when he bent his head down, his ear and maybe even his cheek against her bosom. Would he know, by listening to her heart, how she felt about him?

Next, his hands would touch her, all while he looked at her with his green eyes, the left eye perhaps hidden by that single lock of dark-red hair that she had seen droop down when she had met him. That lock that he had pushed back while speaking to her. And oh, those beautiful, long, strong fingers pressing against her.

Where would her ailment be? Her stomach, she thought, some pain. And he would touch her stomach through her thin nightdress. A firm but gentle touch, she thought.

And then the thought of his devastating hands, perhaps under the nightdress, made her throb in a place that was quite a bit lower than her stomach.

But the invitation to summer at Sommerleigh never came.

Her mother, newly married herself, said of Harry and Thomas, "They are on their honeymoon, I should think they will not want visitors now."

Honeymoon? What was her mother on about? Harry and Thomas had been married for over a year! Really, these married people—Mary and David, her mother and Middlewich included—were so tiresome.

She had met Alasdair only once. In June. In the study of the bishop of London in St. Paul's Cathedral. This was just after her time in Cornwall and Bath with her half sister Mary and her husband, David. Her mother had called her back to London to tell her she was marrying the Duke of Middlewich. And there was a baby on the way. In fact, the baby was coming very soon.

Arabella had accompanied Catherine and Middlewich to the cathedral to discuss their nuptial banns with the bishop. Of course, the required three weeks of banns had turned out to be much too long for the groom-to-be, and he had applied to the Archbishop of Canterbury and paid for a special license since he was, after all, a duke. Her mother and Middlewich were then able to have a lovely garden wedding a few days later, and Arabella wore her new rose-pink dress.

She had hoped the doctor might be invited to the wedding. Yes, in part so he could see how pretty she was, but mostly so she could see *him*, talk to *him*, flirt with *him*. But he was not invited. After all, he was Thomas and Harry's friend, not her mother's, not Middlewich's. She tried very hard not to sulk on the wedding day and instead be happy for her mother and Middlewich.

But how would she ever see Alasdair again? The meeting at the cathedral had been entirely accidental. To think she had almost not come with her mother and Middlewich, imagining it would be rather boring. And, in truth, because she was a little envious of her mother and her mother's obvious infatuation with Middlewich. Not that Arabella harbored feelings for Middlewich. Actually, he seemed too young for Arabella but just right for her mother. How odd was that?

No, she just was jealous of love. In general. Mary, Harry,

her mother. As always, she was last in everything. When was she going to meet him? The not-stupid man of her dreams?

And then she did.

She and Alasdair spoke together for ten minutes in total. Oh, how she cherished every single one of those minutes. She would lie in bed at night and carefully extract from her memory each exchange that had passed between them, turning them over in her mind like an old miser polishing his gold coins.

The discussion of the weather. His answers to her questions about his burr. His lovely Scottish burr. And he mentioned his home village of Bailebrae, far in the north, in Caithness County. "The lowest and flattest of the Highlands," he said. Then he asked if she liked mathematics like her sister Harry, the Countess Drake, and when she said she did not, he seemed relieved. He wanted to know more about her interests. She wanted to confess that, at the moment, she was chiefly interested in *him*. But she had not. Instead, she mentioned her love for the works of Mr. Walter Scott. Oh, the doctor had not read any of his novels or poems? But he must. Arabella could give him many recommendations.

And, yes, before they spoke together, he took her hand and bowed low over it. He was not wearing gloves, and that was when she saw his hands. Oh, how she wished she had not been wearing gloves herself. But how glad she was that she had taken extra care with her dress and hair that day. Her mother was always saying one never knew whom one might meet on an errand.

Yes, Arabella thought gleefully, one never knew. One might even meet one's future husband. And when she saw Alasdair's dimples for the first time, she knew, for certain, she had.

But the weeks of summer went by with no opportunity to travel to Sommerleigh, and she could think of no other way to meet Alasdair again. Arabella fretted and embroidered another tablecloth for her trousseau trunk as well as a christening dress and two baby bonnets for her future baby brother or sister.

Her mother's confinement was to be in September. Yes, her mother and Middlewich had only been married for three months. And yes, she understood what that meant even before her mother spoke to her about it. She was not a child. After all, Mary had schooled Arabella on that beach in Cornwall. She understood what the baby meant about her mother. Her mother had lain down with Middlewich before the wedding. In fact—Arabella made a swift calculation—her mother had lain with Middlewich during Christmastide when they had all been together with Harry and Thomas at Sommerleigh.

The law of primogeniture and the Church only cared that her mother and Middlewich married before the birth. Arabella knew of an astounding number of plump nine-pound infants who had come into the world only six months after a wedding. However, in her mother's case, it was only three months, which seemed to Arabella rather shameful. Her mother should have known better.

Arabella was sent away in September. Middlewich's seven sisters scattered to various aunts and uncles. Arabella hoped to be sent to Sommerleigh where she might see Dr. Alasdair Andrews. But, no. She was sent to Lord and Lady Dalrymple and their daughters in Derbyshire.

Chapter 2

At eighteen, Lady Juliana Dalrymple was the eldest of the five Dalrymple daughters. Arabella always said she loved the Dalrymples equally, but if she was honest with herself, in her heart of hearts, she loved the Lady Rebecca Dalrymple more than Juliana. Rebecca was six months younger than Arabella and far more impressed with her than Juliana was. Indeed,

Juliana had a smugness about her and was always intimating she knew far more than Arabella since she was older.

One evening after dinner, Juliana and Rebecca and Arabella were all together in Rebecca's bedchamber. Juliana was sitting at the dressing table, trying on every piece of Rebecca's jewelry. Arabella and Rebecca were lying on their stomachs on the bed and looking at the dresses in a copy of *Ackermann's Repository*.

"That's an old one," Juliana said.

"From this spring!" Rebecca protested.

Juliana sniffed. "When I am married, I will have new gowns made each season."

Arabella looked up from the illustrated plate that featured a pink dress with a large white band near the hem and a white hat that looked almost military in its shape.

"Are you to be married, Juliana? Are you engaged? To Sir Timothy?"

Juliana held up a pearl necklace in front of her throat. "We are engaged to be engaged."

"I have never heard of such a thing," Arabella said.

"He has not asked me, but he has asked me if he can ask me." Juliana lifted her rather fierce eyebrows.

Arabella swung herself around so she now sat on the edge of the bed, her legs dangling off.

"And has he kissed you?"

Rebecca raised her head from the periodical to hear her sister's answer.

"I told him," Juliana said primly, "we could not kiss until we were properly engaged."

Rebecca went back to the *Ackermann's* and flipped the page.

"B-but," Arabella faltered, "what…what if you don't like his kisses? What if his breath is bad? Or he is not passionate enough?"

Juliana's dark brows knitted together, and she glared at Arabella in the reflection of the mirror. "There are more reasons to get married than kissing, Miss Lovelock."

"Yes, Lady Juliana," Arabella said. "But if the kissing is not good, how could the coupling be any better?"

Arabella had shared her sister Mary's lessons regarding coupling with Juliana and Rebecca the week before. Juliana had asserted she knew everything already, but Arabella noted she had drawn near and paid as close attention to Arabella as her sister Rebecca had.

Now, Arabella felt the bed begin to shake. It was Rebecca, who rolled onto her back, laughing. An insulted Juliana turned around on the stool and faced a serious Arabella and a howling Rebecca.

"There are—" Juliana started in an imperious fashion, but she could not be heard over Rebecca's laughter. And as the seconds passed, Arabella's lips could not help quirking into a smile. Juliana lost her scowl, and she began to titter. Soon, all three girls were roaring, holding their stomachs and kicking up their feet.

A knock came, followed by the countess putting her head around the door. She was greeted by the sight of three young women, weak with laughter, tears streaming down their faces.

"Girls," she said. "You must hush." But she smiled and used a kind voice.

"Yes, Mama," gasped Juliana and Rebecca, and Arabella said, "Yes, Lady Dalrymple."

The girls quieted themselves, but as soon as the countess had closed the door behind her, there was an outburst of suppressed giggles.

"What I was going to say," Juliana said, wiping her eyes, "is there are other reasons to get married besides coupling."

"Yes," Arabella said. "Love. Which has to do with coupling."

"Children," Rebecca said. "Which also has to do with coupling."

"Money," said Juliana. "Land. Titles. Dresses. Jewels."

"Are you marrying Sir Timothy for those things?" Arabella was shocked.

"I am not marrying him yet! We are merely engaged to be engaged. But perhaps I am drawn to him for those reasons." Juliana shrugged. "We are not all heiresses like you."

"But don't you want love?" Arabella asked.

"I do," Rebecca said and slipped her hand into Arabella's and gave a quick squeeze.

Juliana bit her lip. "I don't know. It seems like love might give someone a desperate power over you."

"Yes," said Arabella and smiled. "And you over him."

Juliana narrowed her eyes. "Are you in love, Arabella?"

"I don't know." Arabella looked down at the toes of her slippers.

Juliana leaned forward, intently. "You have some secret, I can tell."

Arabella had held her thoughts of Alasdair so close for so many weeks—nay, for months now. She had never kept a secret so long. She had never had a secret so important. She longed to tell Juliana and Rebecca of her feelings.

She spoke slowly at the start. "I have met him only once. But I think," she felt herself blush, "no, I know I could be in love with him. Very easily. I want to…oh, so many things."

Now Rebecca and Juliana both joined Arabella in sitting on the edge of the bed, each one flanking her.

"You must tell us," Juliana said.

"Oh, please do, Arabella," Rebecca breathed.

"His name is Alasdair."

"I know of no Alasdair among our acquaintance in London," Juliana said. "Is he in *Debrett's*?"

"No, he is a physician and lives near Sommerleigh, my brother-in-law's estate."

"A physician?" Juliana frowned. "But your two sisters? I mean to say, one married a viscount, the other an earl, and now your mother is married to a duke. I would have thought you wouldn't settle for anything less than a baron. Won't your mother oppose your marriage to a mere physician?"

"No, she won't think it important," said Arabella stoutly. She must believe that. "My father was a cit and my mother loved him, and he loved her. And she came from farmers, you know."

The Dalrymple girls did know, of course. They also knew Catherine had been an actress before she married the banker Edward Lovelock. And she had now married a duke, seventeen years younger than she, and she was about to have his baby. The *ton* had talked of nothing else for the last two months of the Season.

"Tell us more about Alasdair, Arabella," Rebecca said.

"He is from Scotland, and he is tall and has dark-red hair and green eyes and dimples."

The description seemed inadequate to Arabella. How could she put into words the feelings that had swept over her when she had spoken with him? How she had instantly known he was all that was good and kind. How he was devastatingly handsome. And for the first time, how she had really understood why men and women wanted to lie down together, naked.

"And his hands…" Arabella was lost, thinking about those hands.

"Have you kissed him?" Juliana asked.

"I have met him only once, and our meeting was ten minutes in length, a quarter of an hour at most. In June. At St. Paul's Cathedral. So, no, I have not kissed him."

She thought of Alasdair's mouth and the dimples that bookended his smile. *But I want to kiss him so badly.*

"Do you write to him?" Rebecca asked.

"How can I?" Arabella fell backwards onto the bed. "It would be so forward. I have to find some other way to meet him again."

Juliana scoffed and got off the bed. "You have met a man for ten minutes, and you think you love him. And you want to advise me on my engagement."

"On your engagement to be engaged," Rebecca said and fell back so she was lying next to Arabella. She held Arabella's hand.

"You will see him again, Arabella, I am sure of it," Rebecca whispered.

Arabella stared up at the canopy of the bed.

She was not so sure.

Every day her memories of what he had looked like, what they had said, how she had felt, waned and became dimmer and dimmer. And he had not pursued her, had not asked her mother if he could write to her, had not come to London or to the duchy of Middlewich to pay a call. Surely, if he felt for her what she had felt for him, he would do something. He had the freedom of action she did not.

Oh, to be a man.

Arabella blinked several times and set her jaw.

No, not to be a man. To have the liberty of a man.

Acknowledgments

I am enormously grateful to everyone who has spent any time reading my writing. And that especially includes you, my readers.

In particular, I must express my thanks to Molly Gunn, Jace Anderson, Jamie Mayer, Sharon Gunn. I am so grateful to all of you for your time, your insight, your invaluable assistance in trying to give Catherine and James the story they deserve. And thank you for helping me feel like a writer.

A great deal of gratitude is also owed to my editor, Grace Bradley. Much thanks also to Dominique Englebert, Carrie Adler, Annie Reinhardt, Michael Starr, Larissa Stillman, and Comte Antoine de Lyrot—all of whom took the time to review some of my phrasing.

However, all errors are mine and mine alone. Especially the French ones.

Finally, an entirely inadequate expression of thanks to my family. I am so grateful to all of you.

ALSO BY FELICITY NIVEN

THE LOVELOCKS OF LONDON

When Ardor Blooms (prequel novella)*

Convergence of Desire (Book 1)

Clandestine Passion (Book 2)

A Perilous Flirtation (Book 3)

Harry's Christmas Present (short story)*

Love's Labor Lasts (novelette)**

THE BED ME BOOKS

Duke the Halls (prequel novella)

Bed Me, Duke (Book 1)

Bed Me, Baron (Book 2)

Bed Me, Earl (Book 3)

Jack & Helen & Phin & Caro (short story)*

Be Not Coy (short story)

Voluptuous (novella)

*available to newsletter subscribers

** part of *The Lovelocks of London: The Collection*

About the Author

Felicity Niven is a hopeful romantic. Writing Regency romance is her third career after two degrees from Harvard. And you know what they say about third things? Yep, it's a charm. She splits her time between the temperate South in the winter and the cool Great Lakes in the summer and thinks there can be no greater comforts than a pot of soup on the stove, a set of clean sheets on the bed, and a Jimmy Stewart film on a screen in the living room. She is the author of ***The Bed Me Books*** and ***The Lovelocks of London*** series.

9 781958 917039